THE BLACK TABLE

Copyright © 2025 by Paraleipsis Publishing LLC

All rights reserved.

No part of this book may be reproduced in any form or by any electronic or mechanical means, including information storage and retrieval systems, without written permission from the author, except for the use of brief quotations in a book review.

THE BLACK TABLE

Knights of Caliburn University
Book One

Jade R. Evans

ONE

GWENNA

IT'S RAINING the day I arrive at Caliburn University.

No, not raining. Misting.

Slivers of moon-white fog hover above the ground and cling to the edges of the horizon like they're trying to airbrush out reality. Just fragments of the stone halls and brick dormitories, the steeple of the chapel arising out of sheer blankness.

I love it. I'm rapturously in love with it, and especially like this: swathed in silver, glimmering at the edges, surreal.

Almost perfectly hidden.

Almost.

"Gwenna?"

The registrar's voice snaps me back to attention. I straighten in my seat, my prime directive blazing in my mind's eye: BE NORMAL. I even give her a little smile, rallying muscles I haven't used in years.

Whether I've fooled her or not is hard to tell. Our conversation thus far has been cordial at best, and the environment's not exactly warm and fuzzy: her office is dark, wood paneled, and packed with more books than feel necessary for the task of enrolling a few hundred students in classes every semester. But

I'm doing my best, and *have* been doing my best, since the cab dropped me off and I toted my one suitcase up the steps of Fisher Hall.

Now, her gaze darts from my creaky fake grin to my cardigan, to the long, long sleeves that wrap my arms almost all the way to my fingertips.

My smile falters.

Because even though it's raining—misting—it's early fall. Warm. Too warm for sweaters, especially black ones.

BE NORMAL, GWENNA.

I'm trying, I tell myself. *I'm trying so hard.*

"Well," the registrar says, with a rhetorical throat-clear. "We'll do our best to get you up to speed. Although, judging from your coursework..."

She's looking at a physical folder, a real manila one full of real printed papers. I'd have to imagine Caliburn is one of the last universities in America, if not on planet Earth, that still uses a paper filing system, but that stubbornness—or insanity—is part of the charm. I'd argue, anyway. Never mind that you're one rogue spark away from everyone's transcripts going the way of the Library of Alexandria and—

No. Danger. That way lies madness. I will not think about that.

"...three weeks late shouldn't be too difficult for you to catch up on." Back in reality, she finishes her sentence, sucking her teeth. "You'll need to take the placement exams regardless, I'm afraid. Since our subject requirements are so...singular, we can't rely on standardization from school districts—"

"That's fine," I interrupt, hopefully not too hastily. "I brought plenty of number-two pencils."

A joke, madam? No, her stony expression says. Rather not. *Fine*, I think. *Whatever.*

"We'll administer the academics this afternoon, assuming we can confirm a proctor." She gives a faint *hmm* that suggests this is an imposition, but I choose to ignore it. "Since the other incoming first-years have already taken theirs, there's not much risk for…" She coughs. "Anyway."

She hands me a typewritten schedule, which I accept with a nod—academic integrity has never been my issue—and scan it quickly. Latin, French, Calculus, a corresponding room number and building name.

Then, alone: physical fitness. Scheduled for next Monday.

My heart thuds.

"Um," I say, not sure how to phrase my question. "Is that… what is that?"

Awkwardly, I gesture at the last item on the list as the registrar squints. Part of the allure—for me, anyway—of Caliburn is its, shall we say, *limited* focus on collegiate athletics. The only team sports even *offered* here are riding, swimming, and fencing. The idea that this school, of all schools, would require gym class is as absurd as it offering to host an NCAA Game Day broadcast.

"Physical fitness," she reads, and casts me a look as though she's second-guessing my place at a school with a twelve-percent acceptance rate. "For physical education? Gym," she adds, translating. How generous.

I wince. "No, I know. I just…I didn't know that was a requirement here."

Because gym means moving, and moving means sweating, and sweating means a change of clothes.

And my clothes don't change.

BENORMALBENORMALBENORMAL—

"It is," she says simply. Eyes me up and down, like she's doing a body scan. "The swimming portion is what's most vital. I'm sure you'll pass."

Au contraire, I think. I've never been a good swimmer. I sink like my bones are made of iron. But I really, really don't want this to get worse, so I nod.

"Your dormitory assignment," she says, handing me another paper, "along with our residential code of conduct, and here's the social schedule—"

Knock, knock. The student worker from reception, a slight blonde girl with giant brown eyes, pokes her head in.

"ID card?"

The registrar waves her in, and the girl tiptoes to my side and hands me a plastic rectangle, still warm from the printer and emblazoned with the Caliburn red and black. Staring back at me is…me. Or the me of twenty minutes ago who had her picture unceremoniously snapped by what might be the only digital camera on campus, anyway: dark eyes, dark circles, dark hair thick and newly cropped to just below my chin.

Hardly a flattering portrait. But not extraordinarily so.

Normal. Almost.

"Thanks," I say.

"Sure." She disappears.

"Keys," the registrar says suddenly, and rummages around in a low drawer before producing two of them, bound together on a red cord. "Usually you'd get these on registration day, but—"

"Thank you," I mumble, taking them from her and vaguely listening as she points out which is for the main dorm door and which is for my individual room. The mist outside has turned to a drizzle, and with the sense that we're close to done, a sudden desperation to *be* done, to check the box and get started and move in and move on, has me in a near chokehold.

I grip the teeth of the keys into the flesh of my fingers and try to listen to what she's saying about social events.

"…complete listing of events, but I'm sure you'll hear soon enough which ones are *de rigeur* from your friends." She smiles, a real, innocent smile, like she sees me as someone who can and will make friends here, and soon.

How I wish.

Or, no. Not.

What I wish is to study. To read, to write. To start classes, *pass* classes, pass semesters, draft papers, flip through dictionaries, absorb every single detail I can about twelfth-century French poetry and medieval Latin orthography and live in the library until it's time to graduate. To brew endless cups of tea behind a stack of books taller than I am and three times as old, to be left alone with my thoughts and my pages and my research until the late hours of the night in a cramped cubby by a snow-drifted windowpane, to spend the rest of my life *reading*, not because it is productive or capitalistically useful but because it is luxurious, it is good, it is what I am designed for.

And then, at last, to pass the remaining decades of my life contributing to some small niche of scholarship. Something esoteric and mine, something that nearly no one else would choose but that *someone* must preserve. To spend my mortal existence putting my own small filigrees on truths written over thousands of years by thousands of hands.

God, listen to me.

BE NORMAL, GWENNA.

Except...maybe this is the Gwenna version of normal.

Maybe?

I suppose we'll find out.

With thanks given and a polite goodbye said, I stand out in the reception hallway, balancing my many new papers, and set down my suitcase to pull out my phone.

My first placement exam isn't until 1 p.m., and it's just now 10:20. Not a ton of time, but enough—maybe the perfect amount, in fact, to get the necessary chores done without dragging anything out.

With a deep breath, I tap open a new message.

To: Mom

> Registration complete. I have my dorm
> assignment too. I've got placement exams
> in the PM but I'm free until then. Where
> should I meet you?

I hit send and wait, awkwardly shuffling my weight and avoiding the gaze of the student worker girl, who's bent over an open book, her blonde hair falling like a curtain. The hallway is narrow but tall, arched and open overhead with wood panels easily fifteen feet high and hung with oil portraits. The whole effect is so Tudor-era that it's almost shocking to see an electric bulb humming in one of the wall lamps.

My chest aches with how much I love it.

My phone buzzes, yanking me back.

> Good to hear.

I stop the disappointment before it fully sets in. Of course she'll be brief, not answer my actual question. Of course. Patiently, I try again.

> So where should I meet you? Just a quick
> run to town for stuff, I figure.

This time, her answer's quick.

> Meet you?

The typing dots pop up, then disappear.
God, don't tell me she forgot. Don't tell me—
I grit my teeth. Type a response. Delete it. Hit *call* instead.
"Gwenna?"
Mom never has time for hellos.
"Who else?"
I never have time for inane questions.
"Where are you? You never told me what time your train—"
"Gwenna, I'm not sure—I'm afraid you're confused." Her

voice is almost apologetic—if you can apologize while fully blaming the other person. "We talked about this. I'm not coming with you."

"You're..." In spite of myself, my voice cracks. The blonde girl lifts her head, just slightly, and I try to speak more quietly. "You're not?"

I hate how I sound. Like a sad child abandoned at her ballet recital. Which I have been in the past, of course.

There's a pause.

"We talked about this," she repeats. "I told you, several times. I can't get away from work."

"Yes, but..." I clench my fist, my jaw, my everything. "You said you couldn't take the whole *day*. But the afternoon...you said you could take the train from the city and—"

"I assure you, I didn't." Now the lawyer's edge is there, the I-dare-you-to-depose-me certainty Laura Vale is known for. "Are you feeling all right, Gwenna?"

And there it is. What I'm sure she was waiting to deliver all along.

I crinkle my exam schedule in my hand as I try, *try* not to fall to pieces in this big, quiet, public hall.

"If you're imagining things like this, maybe this is a bad idea. Dr. Riggs said the pressure of college could—"

"I'm *fine*," I bite out. And then, because I can't resist. "I just remember what you said and what you didn't say. You said—"

"No," she interjects sharply. "You're not fine. Because what you're doing now is calling me a liar, Gwenna. Do you think that I am a liar?"

I inhale, long and careful, through my nose, and exhale through my mouth—the one actually useful thing Dr. Riggs taught me.

BE NORMAL, my mind screams at me.

Be normal, my memory screams at me. In my mother's voice.

For Christ's sake, Gwenna, do you realize what it's been like dealing with you? With all this? You're not special, you're sick. You're a sick, sick girl who lashes out for attention and leaves everyone else to sweep up the fucking ashes.

Another inhale. My visions of a cozy mother-daughter Target run, where we laugh and riff on stupid things like shower shoes and minifridges, puffs away like the fog that's now burning off the campus.

Exhale.

"I must be misremembering," I mumble. "Never mind."

My mom says something about that's what she thought and good luck on my placement exams, but I only half-hear it as I slide off my phone.

The air around me is ringing like I've just left a rock concert. The atmosphere feels at once cold and thick, hard to breathe. The student worker girl at the desk is back at her book, but I can tell she's only fake reading, her ears almost visibly pricked for whatever the weird girl on the emotional phone call is going to do next.

So I do the only thing I can think of.

I run.

———✦———

I ONLY MAKE it halfway across the quads before I need to stop and catch my breath.

Crying while running isn't easy.

Caliburn's campus is broodingly beautiful, even now with some sunlight fighting through the late-fall humidity and just-turned leaves. Flagstone paths lead to thick-buttressed buildings crowned with crenellated towers; long golden windows that arch at the top reveal glimpses of lecture halls, seminar rooms, bowed heads and gripped pencils. It smells like woodsmoke and damp forest, with a waft of strong black coffee coming from somewhere to my left—Stuart Hall, the Divinity School building, home to Holy Grounds, the coffee shop. That much I remember from the campus tour. Hard to forget, really—I'm a sucker for a pun.

I'd loved Caliburn since I learned of its existence. I tacked brochures to my bedroom walls like pin-up posters, enamored of how it was at once so austere and yet so ludicrous (because surely, it's impractical to maintain a fully Gothic architecture style when steel and fiberglass and certified green building materials exist).

And now...now I am here. Against all odds, against what my mother would argue is sound judgment.

I am here, and I am a *mess*.

I take a few, slow steps, steadying my breathing, tugging down my sleeves out of habit, scrubbing at my face even as the tears keep flowing. We must be during an instruction block, because there are only a few people scattered outside—a chatting couple on a bench, a lone figure sprinting down a path, messenger bag flying from its shoulder in the scramble for class. I have a map—somewhere, I have it, the registrar tucked it in one of these godforsaken packets—but I don't want to use it. I want to be a little bit lost right now, to find my way without instruction for once. To settle somewhere and gather my thoughts.

So my feet move of their own volition, my chunky loafers clumping one step after another as I rearrange the papers and folders in my arms lest I drop anything into the mud, and then I see it.

Caliburn Memorial Chapel.

And oh, but it's breathtaking.

A high-peaked wooden door three times as tall as I am, set inside a carved arch of stone saints and animals frozen in tableaux of good and evil—St. George and his dragon, St. Catherine and her wheel, St. Lucy with her eyes on a platter, like the architect chose only the grimmest and goriest stories to carve into granite.

Soaring above it, the steeple, gilded in the pale stream of sunlight with a rose window darkly colored in versicolored glass.

My limbs start to hum as my heart ticks up to a rabbit-quick pulse of excitement. The tears stop, the last few trickling down my cheeks as I stare up in wonder.

No. Gwenna, *no*. It's a bad idea. It's the *worst* idea, to go in there and plunge myself right into the heart of what could trigger me all the way back to a void of delusions, but it's the only idea that makes sense right now. The only thing I need: to be in the church and let its calm infuse and overcome me.

And for once, I just want to trust my own judgment.

I push through the doors like I'm claiming sanctuary.

Inside, it's cold and quiet. Arched windows let in sharp slices of light—some pure blue, some dappled with the candy colors of stained glass—and the air is so still you can see dust motes dancing and spinning like tiny sparks.

And instantly, my whole being settles.

Materially, logically, I know that the air inside this chapel—this *cathedral*, really—is no different than the hydrogen and oxygen and nitrogen swirling just outside the giant wood doors and massive stone blocks. But somewhere deeper, truer, I know, I *feel*, even if I can't prove, that there is something charged and different in here. Something vital. Something holy.

My breathing slows, easing the ache in my chest. I sink into a pew, my eyes fluttering shut, and I welcome the reprieve.

I always struggled to believe in God growing up—a less than ideal condition for a Catholic schoolgirl from a nice family, and deeply ironic considering the way the past few months of my life have transpired. I had too many questions, too many edge cases I wanted to stress-test before I committed. Yet I never struggled to be in a church—maybe because they're the closest you can get to a castle in most of North America.

I inhale. The pine-and-smoke smell of distant incense floods my senses, and my last few pathetic sniffles choke their way from my throat.

But then, just as I breathe out, I hear it.

I'm not alone.

My eyes fly open with a prey animal's instincts, and I tense my grip on my sheaf of papers, one foot planted protectively outside my suitcase. I dart a glance left, right, left, and yet *see* nothing, only hear it, *sense* it, practically, until I look right again.

A few rows up, and behind a pillar, is a corner, a dark shift in the wall revealing some sort of secondary open space: the arm of the cross-shaped church, no doubt.

I *should* leave. But I'm curious.

Silently as I can, I slip from the pew to the side aisle, taking tiptoe steps in the vastness of the stone space until I can peek around and see. It's as I thought: a chapel-within-the-chapel, outfitted with a few rows of chairs and a smaller altar: gold, carved, and set with rows and rows of red-glass tea candles before it, their little flames dancing.

And, sitting in front of it, a man.

No, not sitting, I realize.

Kneeling.

He's really and truly on his knees before the altar, head bowed, arms planted just forward on the railing and fingers clasped—praying, I suppose. And just in front of him, on the flagstones, something long and thin that flashes in even in the dim light of the chapel.

A blade. A *sword*.

And just as soon as I take it all in, he moves.

A quick flutter of the eyes and twitch of the lips and he's on his feet, lightning-quick, *too* quick, and I'm stumbling backwards over my own stupid feet until my back hits a pillar and a pair of bronze-colored eyes cut into mine.

He's tall, fearsomely tall, easily a head above my own five-nine, with broad shoulders, a strong jaw, and a serious set to his lips. Golden hair catches the winking candlelight as it falls just over his forehead, and even in the dark layers of sport coat, sweater, and button-down, he looks powerful.

Yet for all that, he doesn't menace. Doesn't encroach on me or try to intimidate. If anything, he stands back, keeps his distance, arms folded at attention behind him—which, combined with his sharp attire, gives him an almost soldierly air.

No, he just...stares.

Stares and takes me in. *Drinks* me in, practically, with a kind of scrutiny that's so intense it's almost disarming.

And before I can realize the sorry state of my being, the rumpled clothes and blotchy face and wide-eyed panic, he moves.

A hand only, slipping into his inner jacket pocket to withdraw something, which he proffers to me, a flash of white in the space between us.

I blink, computing.

When I don't move, he offers again, gesturing it toward me, stepping only as close as necessary to get within the radius of my reach.

"For your face," he explains, in a voice deep and rich as coffee at midnight.

All at once, it clicks. A handkerchief. He's offering me a *handkerchief*. Dumbfounded, I reach, take it, a smart reply frozen in my throat—*I know what a handkerchief's for*—as my fingertips close over the slip of fabric.

I draw my hand back to my chest, still flattened against the stone pillar, and try to conjure something to say.

"I...I'm..."

My gaze flits to the altar behind him, where the sword—because that's indeed what it is—now lies unobstructed from view, resting on a deep red cushion.

His eyes follow mine. Then surge back to me.

"Don't go where you're not invited."

My jaw falls slightly in surprise, but before I can get a word out, he turns on his heel, strides to the altar, and slips away through some unseen exit, sword and all.

And I stand alone, stupefied, *wordless,* in the cavern of the chapel, for God knows how many moments longer, until the tears on my face are long dry and my heart has slowed to normal.

His handkerchief still clutched in my hand.

TWO

GWENNA

FOR THE REST of the morning, I hide.

No lunch—that'd require seeing people.

No dorm—ditto.

Instead, I lay low in the library, a stone building that's as stately as the chapel but not as *dangerous*, and go down to the very deepest basement level I can find—B2, way below where most people even bother to venture. I find an alcove with a table, very much out of sight, where I can sit with my legs clasped to my chest and my forehead on my knees.

Breathe in. Breathe out. Breathe in. Breathe out.

I feel the heat of my breathing flare over my skin and think about etymology.

In Latin, the word *anima* means both *breath* and *soul*. Or, technically speaking, not *soul* precisely—not something that's immortal and outlasts your mortal body—but *life force*.

The thing that separates you from being dead.

And as long as you have that, you have something.

Don't go where you're not invited.

Duly noted. Message received.

At ten of one, I head to my assigned classroom, a cold cell of a place in Stuart Hall, dragging my suitcase along. Post-panic-attack, post-confrontation with a sword-carrying Greek God of a man, and without anything in my stomach, I'm hardly in an ideal state to take a test, but fortunately, that's been the case for most of my life, and my grades have never suffered. Possibly the only thing that hasn't. Give Gwenna a test, and she will pass it.

Latin is fairly trivial: vocabulary, grammar questions, and a sight translation from a section of Cicero's *In Catilinam* that I haven't read before, but pick up well enough. French is barely a problem. Calculus, a little less so, especially because I'm not allowed a calculator, but that's a class I intend to knock out as quickly as possible, so a lower ranking would do me a favor.

All the while, I'm keenly aware I'm being watched. The proctor they managed to find for me—presumably some TA, a hulking figure with sandy red bedhead and what appears to be a hangover—stares me down like I'm suspicious. Yet when I turn in my sheaf of papers, he barely looks me in the eye, and that's just as well, because by the time I'm out of there, I'm ready to collapse.

It's around 4 p.m. and I haven't even been to my dorm room yet. The campus isn't big, so it doesn't take me long to find my assigned hall, Broceliande—a bit of a ridiculous name, but presumably some donor who wrote a check large enough to merit a nameplate. The front door is unlocked, making my first key superfluous. I'm on the third floor, a girls-only floor, Room 326, tucked in the back. Some doors are propped open, snatches of study groups or music floating out, the occasional student slipping out to fill a water bottle or head to the library, but mostly quiet, stately, relaxing.

Even the promise of what is sure to be a thin plastic dorm mattress sounds like a relief.

I fit my key into the brass lock of 326 and turn, and find myself staring into a pair of honey-brown eyes in a confused expression.

"Well, hello there," says a husky female voice.

I blink, trying to process.

"H-hi," I stammer. Roommate, of course. College roommates. Those are things, Gwenna. BE NORMAL.

The girl staring back at me is around my age, slightly taller, with endless waves of golden blonde hair and lips held in a slight pout. She's gorgeous and not entirely happy to see me.

"Hello," she says again. "And you're..."

"Gwenna?" I say like it's a question, and feel immediately stupid. "This is my room. We're roommates." I look down at my dorm assignment, at the name I had not really bothered to register before. "You're Morgan."

She blinks, tips her head. "I know who I am. I'm just wondering..." She chews her lip and casts around the room.

So do I, for the first time.

It's bigger than I had been anticipating, with arched windows that let in plenty of light and a glimpse of the quad, a small ensuite bathroom, and a set of furniture—bed, desk—neatly tucked on either side. Except that one bed is absolutely covered in...*stuff*: clothes, books, makeup, apparatuses, and all sorts of decorative trinkets I can't even place—vases, dried flowers, long strings of beads, scarves. The other bed—Morgan's bed, presumably—is outfitted with plush purple and pink bedding. A moon-shaped lamp hangs above it, suspended from something that I can't see, and glowing almost like the actual moon itself.

She taps her chin. "There's been some confusion over rooming here at Shiz," she murmurs.

"What?" Oh God, is she a musical theater person? I don't think I'll survive that. "Were you assigned a single?"

"No." She shrugs. "I saw there was a name, but you didn't show up for three weeks, so..." She gestures airily at what I now know to be my bed, covered in her things. "I just took over. I thought I had lucked out and maybe you, I don't know, transferred or joined a cult or something. Ha."

I clutch the handle of my suitcase a little, and as if she notices, Morgan peers around me like she's expecting there to be more stuff.

"I'm sorry. I'm so rude. Morgan. Le Fay." She extends a hand with extraordinarily long fingernails painted a deep, almost blood-colored purple. "A pleasure to meet you."

"Gwenna," I say.

"I'll get...all this out of your way," she says, although not without a hint of reluctance in her voice. I want to apologize, even though it's not my fault. She did see that I was on her registration. She shouldn't have expected a room to herself.

But then again, I guess someone not showing up for three weeks does sort of imply that they're...not going to show up. And while I hate to judge based on appearances, Morgan does look like the sort of person who's used to getting her own way.

Great.

She unceremoniously arm-sweeps the pile of things into an empty laundry basket and kick-pushes it into the corner of the room.

"Deal with that later," she says, tossing her hair. "So, what are you studying?"

Same thing as everyone? I think. "First-year stuff," I say.

Morgan gives a light snort. "Sure," she says, "but eventually you want to study...?"

This is awfully interrogatory for get-to-know-your-roommate chatter. I let go of my suitcase, still standing in the doorway.

"Twelfth-century French religious writings," I say, "with an emphasis on the Cathar heresy and the religious experiences of women."

It's good to practice saying it out loud like it's something normal, and here at Caliburn, it's at least more normal than anywhere else. I have no idea what Morgan will make of it, but to my surprise, she nods approvingly.

"Fascinating," she says, and sounds like she means it. "I'm studying Renaissance demonology myself, some Italian folk magic, that sort of thing." She flicks her fingers through the air. "I imagine we'll be in a lot of classes together."

I can't tell from her tone if that's a good or a bad thing, and I really just want to lie down, which seems like a fading possibility the more we talk. I push my suitcase toward my bed, stupidly not sure if I should start unpacking or make more conversation.

But it doesn't matter, because we're interrupted.

"Morgan, I need to—"

The door swings open, and I find myself staring into the same golden-brown eyes.

"To learn to knock?" Morgan finishes for him, tilting her head.

"I did knock," he mumbles, eyes still fixed on me.

"Knocking *as you open the door* is not the same thing. It's like signaling when you're halfway into a merge on the highway." Morgan flops into her chair and eyes him. "What do you want?"

He straightens his shoulders, which almost span the entire door frame. I decide now is a great time to deal with my suitcase and conveniently not engage with him *or* her.

"Just...ah, you know," I hear him say hesitantly as I drag my suitcase to the foot of my bed. "Coming by to pick up—"

"Right, right, right," Morgan says. She puts a hand in the air to silence him and rummages around on her desk with the other one, opening a series of tiny drawers and flicking through various boxes until she locates what she's looking for—a small drawstring pouch, which she cocks back like a missile. "Think fast."

She throws it, and he snatches it from the air without even blinking.

I let out an inadvertent grunt, tugging on the handle of the suitcase and realizing the literal lift it will be to get it onto this bed. It maybe was ridiculous to try and cram my entire life in here.

But then again, *my entire life* isn't much. It's just heavy.

"Pay me whenever," she says. "You always do."

"I..." He clears his throat, visibly uncomfortable that I'm still here. "Thank you," he intones.

I focus all of my concentration on not eavesdropping, or at least not looking like I'm eavesdropping, because it's clear to me that my new roommate may be the campus weed dealer and may have some kind of situationship with this unfriendly, sword-wielding, six-foot-five golden boy who wants me anywhere but near him.

The perfect storm of a roommate match. If she snores, I'll have a full bingo card and a miserable first semester.

No. No. Not thinking like that. Everything's going to be fine.

I tug at the suitcase one more time and manage to get it halfway onto the mattress before a corner slips off the bed. It lurches for the floor, and I lurch with it, but it doesn't hit.

Not because I catch it.

Because he does.

With one arm.

Wordless, he hoists it the rest of the way to the bed and lies it perfectly flat on the mattress. Like it weighs nothing. Like it should not have been any kind of struggle, even though his arms are twice as thick as mine and his hands could fit around my waist.

"Thank you," I mutter. His response is to nod, and jerk his hand away swiftly and precisely, like he'll get an acid burn if he brushes my skin.

I get it, okay? No need to be theatrical.

"Well," Morgan says, winding a strand of hair around her finger. "I'd *love* to chat," she says in a tone that implies she'd love to do anything but, "but my new roommate here needs to get settled, so..."

"Of course." He clasps his hands at the small of his back and nods again. "Thank you."

The door clicks briskly, and his footsteps echo behind it.

I blink at my suitcase, at my roommate, at how for the last few minutes, the utter confusion of who these people are and what they're doing has successfully distracted me from thinking about myself.

Morgan continues twisting her hair, staring up at the ceiling and humming something.

"That's Kingston," she says. "And yes, he absolutely has a stick up his ass. But he won't be around much."

"Oh," I respond. I didn't ask, but okay. No mention of whatever was in the drawstring bag. Fair—she doesn't know if I'm a narc.

And…

Goddammit. And, now that she's broken the seal, I have to ask. I'm itchy with not knowing, to the point where I'm willing to make thrice as much conversation as I ordinarily would.

"And Kingston is your…"

What she says next is not what I'm expecting.

"Stepbrother."

"*Oh*." I don't mean to react or sound so surprised. I tug down the sleeves of my cardigan. "That's—I didn't—"

"Didn't what?" Her gaze whips around to me, as if she can swivel her head like an owl.

"Didn't…anything. Nothing." Like it's my fault the term is… rhetorically loaded? Besides, I was not imagining that hair flip. I may be dead inside, but I can still recognize the movements of a girl being flirty.

"Well, whatever you're not thinking, stop thinking it." Her voice is eerily cool and even as she studies her nails, then flicks her eyes back up to me. "Although, for your information, King's like a monk, anyway."

I didn't ask. But I nod.

Morgan, though, is not done. She's considering. Gears turning. When she speaks again, her words are like spiked honey: sweetness concealing the burn of arsenic.

"I certainly hope this isn't going to be the kind of situation where we need ground rules, *roomie*." She laces the final word with an expert dose of passive aggression, her pouting lips curling into a slow, measured smile. "Will it?"

Fuck. I don't want to be doing this. I want to be under my weighted blanket, listening to binaural beats and Hildegard von Bingen music and dissociating myself to sleep. I want to be brewing tea and wrapping myself in a scarf and heading to the library so I can enjoy every luscious aspect of this college and its campus, *finally*. I want to be focusing, regrouping, armoring up for the battle for normalcy that will be this semester.

But I guess the battle's started. With a sneak attack, here on home turf.

So I exhale hard. Wave the white flag.

I surrender to normalcy. *Please don't hate me. Please let me be.*

"No," I say, and I mean it.

Morgan's mouth curves, but there's no smile in her voice. "Good."

THREE

GWENNA

I SLEEP LIKE THE DEAD—MERCIFULLY—AND when I wake up, it's to a quiet room.

Warm, bathed in golden light, empty.

I'm *alone*.

The sheer uncut relief of being unperceived is druggingly good, such a welcome rush that I almost pull my blankets back over my head and bask in it like a cat in a patch of sun.

Then I remember my mission. And, I notice the white strip of a folded letter slid under the door.

Slowly, I swing my feet to the floor and pick it up, my heart pounding with…not excitement, not anxiety, but *something* as I slice it open hard and fast enough to draw blood on my index finger.

GWENNA VALE
LATIN 302 — EMRYS
FRENCH 203 — BOULANGER
CALCULUS 101 — NEWMAN

Well. There it is. Typewritten notice of my placement exam

results. Calculus can screw itself, but the rest I'm pleased with, and as I sink back down on the mattress, skimming my schedule, I even allow myself a smile.

I'm going to class today.

And soon, I realize. It's Friday, which means I have—I check the schedule—just French today, at 10:00 a.m. in Lecture Hall 3, which gives me just under an hour to get dressed and into place. I'll have missed both sittings of breakfast, but so long as I can procure coffee at some point, I'll live.

Slowly, I stand again. Outside, lime-green and fire-orange leaves alike fringe the windowpane, with just a glimpse of blue sky and cottony clouds beyond—cold, though, judging by the hissing and clanking of the massive iron radiator. To my left, Morgan's side of the room is haphazardly tidied—duvet roughly thrown back over the mattress, her strange little trinkets in disarray on the desk while leaving the center clear, a sort of manmade fairy circle—but she has done me the courtesy of leaving a note on the little framed chalkboard beside her desk.

Class. Back c. 3:30.

Friendly, I think sarcastically. Then I chide myself for being such a bitch: clear is kind and kind is clear, as Mom likes to say, and about *that*, at least, she's right. I drag a fingertip along the edge of Morgan's desk, just for the thrill of it, and for a moment, I consider fishing around in her billions of tiny drawers to see what earthly delights she has in store to traffic to people like Kingston, but I quickly think better of it. As valuable as it could be to have *kompromat* on Morgan and her potential drug-dealing side hustle, I also don't want to risk getting flung even further onto her bad side.

For all I know, she's got poison in there, and I doubt she'd hesitate to use it.

Besides, knowing that Morgan has vacated the premises for the duration means I can shower without worrying about…

I don't let myself finish the thought as I rush to peel out of the heavy sweatshirt that served as my nightgown and dart into the bathroom. The mirror is big, framed, and shows every corner of the white-tiled space, but I studiously avoid making eye contact as I strip out of my underwear and yank at the shower knobs for a blistering torrent of water that drags a hiss out of me when it hits my skin.

Hot water hurts, but hot water makes steam, and steam hides my body, my skin, from view.

Quickly, blessedly quickly, the stall pumps so full of steam that I'm practically in a cloud, and can't make out anything except for my hands occasionally emerging to squirt out soap and shampoo from the provided bottles. After a slapdash scrub and a balletic leap to avoid the mirror once again, I wrap myself in one of the picnic-blanket sized towels folded to the side of the sink, give the top several firm rolls to secure it under my armpits, and shove my toothbrush in my mouth so I can go reread my schedule.

I look over the letter at the sink—textbook purchases, where to find the syllabi, et cetera—and am just about to spit out a glob of spearmint foam when I see what's at the end of it.

Physical fitness test to be conducted at Field House at 8:00 a.m. Monday 9/18.

My stomach plunges.

But what I read next has me actually choke.

Student is required to present promptly with proper bathing attire; failure to appear will be grounds for immediate academic probation.

I barely even notice my hand shaking, the clatter of my toothbrush falling to the shell-fluted sink. A ringing sound hums and zings in my ears, the floor going skewed under my feet. I try to stay cognizant, not to let the panic grip me, but then the towel slackens from my grip.

No.

I clutch at my covering, scramble clumsily for the soggy

terrycloth as it crumples to my feet, but I'm too late. My security blanket peels away from me and leaves *it* exposed.

Instantly, my hands clench onto the counter for balance. I thrust my gaze up, not wanting to see myself, any inch of myself, arms or legs or the pale center of me, but it's too late. I'm too weak. The mirror pulls me to it like a magnet, and *it* is there.

All of it.

The mottled pink shine of taut burn scars spidering up to my elbows.

And the silvery-white lines—cut, *carved*, now healed—above my heart: one across, one down.

Fuck, I think. *Fuck.*

Proper bathing attire.

Grounds for immediate academic probation.

This will never work.

I want to scream.

I want to smash the mirror until my palms are ragged and bloody.

I want to hide.

NO, GWENNA.

No. I won't do any of that. I *don't* do any of that.

I don't do any of Dr. Riggs's breathing exercises or cognitive reframing techniques either.

Instead, shaking, I step back, stumble to the floor and sit, legs folded, fully naked, and give in to the voice in my head.

All shall be well, and all shall be well, and all manner of thing shall be well.

All shall be well, and all shall be well, and all manner of thing shall be well.

All shall be well, and all shall be well, and all manner of thing shall be well.

It's not a prayer, not exactly—technically, it's from the writings of an obscure medieval female mystic called Julian of Norwich.

But it does make me feel better.

I exhale.

Monday. A lifetime away, practically. One thing at a time.

Slowly, I raise my head just enough to look myself in the mirror.

I can do this. I *will* do this.

Somehow, I will figure it out.

For now, I have to go to class.

On unsteady legs, I rise back up, blood rushing to my head, and succumb to the breathing exercises as I dress as quickly as humanly possible, tugging the first clean clothes from the top of my suitcase, pulling the sleeves of another black sweater as far as they will stretch and sheathing my legs in the blackest opaque tights I own.

And as I do, something flutters to the ground, gentle as a butterfly.

A handkerchief.

Kingston's handkerchief.

Frowning, I stoop to retrieve it. I didn't even realize I still had the thing, and I certainly don't want to keep it.

Then again, I realize, I don't want to engage with him again, either. Certainly not now that I know he's the stepbrother of the roommate who, at best, begrudges my very existence.

I look down to where I've been absentmindedly rubbing the hem and see a line of dark thread beneath my fingertips. Two simple rows of stitches: one across, one down.

A cross?

My heart stutters.

Or a sword, Gwenna. Think about it.

I stuff the thing in my pocket and leave for class.

SEMINAR ROOM three is at once cramped but high-ceilinged, and as soon as I walk in, I'm hit with a dilemma: where to sit. This isn't St. Catherine's Preparatory anymore, where we're assigned by last name, but it's also not a cafeteria full of students who've known me since the fifth grade and have already decided they're not going to let me sit with them. I'm unmoored, unknown, and, I realize as the door clicks shut behind me, the last person here.

The professor is a stylish, middle-aged woman with the deep-dyed crimson hair only actual French women seem to possess. She weaves me in with a smile that is accommodating, if not fully friendly.

"*Ah, la voilà,*" she says. "*La nouvelle. S'il te plaît.*" She indicates the classroom, a large square table with a small handful of students gathered around it.

I nod. "Merci." I sigh and do a quick calculation: two girls next to each other, one with long, dark straight hair, pouting lips, and tan skin like she's just gotten back from Saint-Tropez, the other I recognize as the student worker from the administration building yesterday, blonde hair and skin the color of skim milk with some freckles and a ski-jump nose. They both give me studiously blank expressions and then turn back to their books.

Besides that, there are two painfully scrawny guys with glasses, and one guy who seems to be twenty going on forty-five with a thick ponytail and an actual briefcase. He gives me a kind of "Hello, milady" look that gives me a full-body reaction.

No thank you. None of that.

I've been standing still too long, so I choose the move of least resistance and sit at the end of the table.

"*D'accord—on commence,*" says the professor, her French as fluid and chill as a mountain stream. "If you could take out the poem assigned for reading, the Hugo. You'll discuss in groups to prepare for the writing of your *explications de texte*. And I," she adds ominously, "will form the groups."

With quick flicks of her fingers, she separates us off, a move I suspect she has done only to break up the blonde girl and her brunette friend.

To my great fortune, the brunette is assigned to me.

I pick up my bag and slide to the seat next to her.

"*Enchantée*," she says, in a cardboard accent. I pull my sweater sleeves down out of habit.

"*Moi aussi*," I reply, hastily pulling everything and everything out of my bag, stopping just short of dumping all the contents out entirely before rooting around for my book of poetry and a pen. I wait for her to make the first move, given that, you know, she's been taking this class for three weeks and knows *what poem was actually assigned*, but nothing.

"*Donne-moi un moment pour lire le text?*" I say to her—give me a sec to catch up, basically. Still, no attention. Instead, she sighs, glances at the clock, glances at the thin gold watch draped around her wrist, drums her fingers on her chin. She glances at her friend, who looks equally uncomfortable after being paired off with the ponytail guy, then stares at the door like she's waiting for a package delivery or something.

Nothing to me.

Okay, have it your way. I flip open the book and, with a furtive look at everyone else, find the poem we're assigned and turn to it: Victor Hugo, *La tombe dit à la rose*.

At least it's short. I start the first lines.

La tombe dit à la rose :
The tomb said to the rose
- Des pleurs dont l'aube t'arrose
The tears with which dawn waters you —
Que fais-tu, fleur des amours ?
what do you do, flower of love?

I wrinkle my nose. Sentimental as hell, symbolism about as sophisticated as an eighth-grader's. But I keep reading.

La rose dit à la tombe...
The rose said to the tomb...

I scan the rest of it, trying to get the gist enough to have an intelligent conversation about it, barely even noticing when the door opens and shuts.

"Sorry," comes a smooth male voice. "I mean, *désolé*."

My conversation partner shifts beside me, and I take advantage of the distraction to speed-read the rest of the lines.

Que fais-tu de ce qui tombe
What do you do with that which falls
Dans ton gouffre ouvert toujours ?
*In your...*whatever a *gouffre* is, a mouth, maybe? *that's always open*

The professor murmurs something and clucks her tongue, telling whoever it is he'll need to join a group.

La rose dit : Tombeau sombre,
The rose said: Somber tomb,

I hear footsteps and the sound of him setting down his bag.

"We're an odd number now," the professor is explaining in spitfire French, "so I suppose you'll have to be ménage à trois." She murmurs a little French laugh.

De ces pleurs je fais dans l'ombre
Of these tears I make in shadow

It's not until a shadow falls across the page of my book that I realize she's put him with us.

Un parfum d'ambre et de miel.
A perfume of amber and honey.

He sits down, and I look up.

This is no scrawny nerd or ponytail geek.

A shock of black hair that's mussed in all directions, either from styling or from bedhead, hard to tell. Eyes the kind of lucid blue-green that forcibly puts me in mind of Caribbean beaches and air that smells like coconut and salt. And a pair of lips arching so smoothly, so perfect and proportional, they could have been carved on a classical statue.

But when he smiles, it's all flesh and blood.

"You're new," he manages.

I blink at him, scoop some hair behind my ear.

"And *you're* late!" My partner, at last, comes to life, and the tone of her voice has completely changed: airy, angelic, breathy. And then I realize. She has the hots for him. Beyond obvious, and I suppose—objectively, aesthetically—I can see why.

The latecomer nods. "Bonjour, Elena."

I chew the end of my pencil, spit it out. Try to focus.

"Hi," Elena says, then tips her head like she's just remembered me. "This is…"

"Gwenna," I answer.

Another nod. His Adam's apple bobs as he swallows. "Gwenna," he repeats. Then he extends a hand. "Lanzelin Dell'Acqua. Lanz."

I take it and shake, mildly taken aback by the formality. Not to mention the *name*. Who's named something like that? My mind whirrs through my languages, phonemes, roots, and I don't realize I'm frowning until his expression matches mine.

"*Ca va?*" he asks. You okay?

I give my head a little shake. Be normal.

"*Oui*," I answer. But then…I can't resist. "*C'est…italien, ton nom de famille?*"

He smiles, and it's such a boyish look of genuine delight that I almost—*almost*—smile back.

"*Si.*" He puts a hand to his chest. "A little Italian, a bit French. And some—"

"German," I venture. "Swiss."

His smile broadens. "*Immer ja.*"

The barest hint of a frown shimmers over Elena's forehead. *I come in peace*, I mentally telegraph to her. *I'm not here to horn in on him. Or anyone.* My mind flashes to my dorm room—to Morgan and Kingston. Why does everyone keep assuming the worst of me?

"We should really be reading," Elena says, pointed but still sweet.

"Elena!" barks the professor. "*En français, s'il te plaît!*"

"*Desolée, madame.*" Elena shrinks a little, but not without a glare at me—which, to my mind, is unfair. I'm not the one *not* speaking French *in French 203.*

Lanz, evidently, doesn't care much either.

"What are we reading?" he whispers in English, lowering his voice with a glance to the professor.

Elena gives a little laugh. "One of the poems." She offers up her own open book to indicate the page, leaning into him as she does. I catch a whiff of her perfume and get the sense that she prepared extensively for this class, and I don't mean doing the homework.

"Okay," he says. "*Merci.*" His accent, compared to hers, is fluid, natural, although tinged with something non-native—whatever that pan-European heritage is, coming into play. I half-wonder how someone as cosmopolitan as this guy ends up at a tiny, unranked American college, but I also don't much care.

"And what are we doing, exactly?" He switches to French deftly, and this time the question is directed at me. I look up.

"We're supposed to be discussing the text for writing an *explication,*" I reply. "And then a—"

"*Attention!*" calls the professor. "*A la discussion, s'il vous plaît.*"

So much for that. At least I managed to read the poem. And it's starkly simple enough that I'm sure I can bullshit an answer if I'm called upon.

"Very well. Claire," the professor calls on the blonde girl. "What sort of text do we have here?"

"A poem," answers Claire primly in prep-school French. "Which comprises a dialogue between a rose and a tomb?"

She phrases it like a question, even though it's the most undebatable part of the entire exercise. I twirl my pencil in the air and look out the broad arched window to the campus beyond—Grove Quad, if I'm not mistaken, looking vibrantly green in the burgeoning morning light. I think longingly of the coffee I intend to pick up from Holy Grounds as soon as this class as over, maybe find a bench to sit on with my books—

"And...Mr. Late-to-the-Party," the professor says, leaning on her desk and nodding indulgently at Lanz. "What themes do we see presented here?"

I force my attention back to the discussion, to the person who's been called on, and that's when I notice he's been staring.

At me.

"Ah...it..." Lanz stammers, looking down at his book and flipping pages back and forth, even though the poem itself only takes up two paragraphs. "I'm sorry, one moment—"

I'm not the only one who notices, either. Elena, sitting between the two of us, shoots me a look as rigid and cold as marble.

Heat prickles up the back of my neck and scalp in spite of myself. I did nothing, I want to say. I simply *came to class*. I do not know you, or him, from Adam, *mademoiselle*.

The professor snaps her elegant fingers. "Too slow. Your partner, Madamemoiselle Elena?"

Elena goes stick-straight in her seat. "Um..." She glances down at the book, at Lanz, at her friend Claire, as if any of them has the answer written on their face.

"*L'amour*," she manages at last. *Love*.

The professor raises an eyebrow. "*L'amour*?" she repeats.

Elena looks lost. "Um...*oui*," he says. "It's about a rose, so—"

"The poem is titled *The* tomb *says to the rose*," the professor interjects. "Or did you not even read that far?"

I snort.

But my amusement is short-lived, because the professor wheels on me next.

"Ah, our little novelty. Mademoiselle Gwenna, you think you've unlocked the theme properly, then? Enlighten us." She folds her arms, her long fingers settling elegantly on the draping sleeve of her blouse. "If *anyone* in your little threesome was paying attention."

In fact, I was, I think. "*J'avancerais plutôt que ce poème traite du thème de la mort—ou, plus précisément, de la relation entre le changement, la transmutation et la mort éventuelle de toutes choses dans le monde, qu'elles soient volontaires ou non.*"

As I answer, the professor curls a smile, but it's not her attention I feel. It's Elena's.

Whether or not she's understood anything I just said.

I conclude, suck in a breath, and turn to her.

"Death," I say, in English. "Not love."

A beat of silence. Then the professor claps—with delight, it seems.

"*Formidable*," she declares. "*Brillamment argumenté.*"

I duck my head, loathing the attention even as the tiniest flicker of pride lights in my chest. Elena, for her part, looks like she's swallowed an entire lemon studded with thumbtacks...and she's aiming the look right at me.

Sorry, I try to thought-beam to her. *But maybe read the poem if you don't want to get embarrassed—*

"Show off," she mutters, glancing from me to Lanz.

And that just makes things worse.

Because Lanz is also staring. At me.

The professor must notice, too, because she wheels on him. "Something to add? You'd like to contribute to the commentary on theme of the poem, then?"

He sits up straighter. Big blue eyes at attention. Clears his throat.

"*Non, mais…*" He begins, averting his gaze to the floor. Then back up.

And my God, but those eyes are hard to look away from.

"*Mais ici…l'amour, la mort. Ce ne sont pas la meme chose?*"

But here…love, death. Aren't those the same thing?

Silence.

Even I have to admit, it's sort of a good point. No, a legitimately good one. But accidental, surely—a broken clock that's right twice a day.

"*Touché,*" the professor says, after a moment. "But we shall conclude there for the day. A draft of your *explications* due to me at Monday's class. *Bon week-end à tous.*"

The room hums back to life, people packing up and shouldering bags, and I scoop my things together as swiftly as humanly possible—but not swiftly enough, because as I do, the professor draws to our corner of the table.

"You might do well with a tutor, Mademoiselle Shalott." She purses her lips, looks from Elena to me. "Or at least start by reading the text, hm?"

I can feel, literally feel, the waves of hot wrath emanating from her to my left. I don't dare look up until the latest possible moment, until I'm certain Lanz is almost gone from the room.

But not quite. Because I glimpse him as he slips through the classroom door, him and the long, black carrying case slung over his back. Like you'd use for…a lacrosse stick, maybe? Except it's the wrong season. A rifle? God, I hope not.

Elena, my erstwhile group partner, sees my staring and huffs. I muster every ounce of strength I can to tamp down my bitchy impulses and go for a joke.

"I hope that's not a gun in there," I joke.

Elena laughs, in genuine disbelief—at me, not with me. "Sorry, what?"

"In that..." I trail off. Never mind. Never fucking mind, whatever I've said is so stupid I want to self-immolate.

"It's a sword," she says, like I'm four years old. "For fencing?" She exchanges a look with Claire, her blonde friend who's sidled up to her and whose expression in response reads something like *told you the new girl was weird.*

My stomach sinks.

"Lanz is on the fencing team," Claire supplies. "Didn't you know?"

What is this, Caliburn University Quizzo? I clench my fists under the table. "No. Why would I know that?"

Elena snorts again. "Because of *that.*"

She looks down at the table, and when I follow her gaze, I see it there, nestled among my notes and textbook:

The handkerchief. Rumpled, but unmistakably marked with its tiny sword.

"I..."

I have no good explanation for why I have that on me. Even for *myself,* I don't have a good explanation.

But it doesn't matter. Elena's seen it and drawn her own conclusions—and whatever those conclusions are, they are not making me look good.

She and Claire hustle off, whispering together about Friday night plans they clearly don't want me to overhear. But I do catch one thing:

Camlann House.

FOUR

LANZ

CAMLANN HOUSE IS in a fucking state.

The door swings open to a foyer cluttered with gear and clothes, stacks of mail and papers overflowing the letterboxes, muddy boots cast in unmatched pairs and dirt ground into the Oriental runner.

But then again, nothing compared to the state of my head.

"Jesus Christ," I mutter.

"Not here, I'm afraid," comes a voice from the parlor. "But I can take a message."

"Shove it, Kai."

I drop my case by the door and kick off my own shoes in whatever direction as Kai cackles. I ignore him and flop onto one of the parlor couches, head on the armrest, hand covering my eyes. Even the oil portraits look disdainful.

"So Freudian," Kai remarks from the other corner of the room. "Do you need me to analyze your psyche?"

I pull my hand away and stare at him. If things are a mess, then Kai is undoubtedly the cause.

"Does King know about this?" I say, sweeping an arm around to indicate the general…everything of it all.

Kai doesn't look up from the paper he's grading. "What Kingston doesn't know won't hurt him."

You have no idea, I think.

But just thinking *that* makes my head swim even worse.

I can't stop thinking about her.

I sink back into the couch and let the calm of the parlor wash over me, pressing one hand to my sternum as I feel the jittering of my pulse slowly, slowly start to quiet.

Does she know?

No. There's no way. I mean, she doesn't even know *me*, or didn't, until about an hour ago.

The odds of her just *knowing* that I'm under a stupid, generations-old family curse…

But she did ask about your name, part of my mind reasons. *Maybe she* does *know*.

Or maybe she was just curious because it's a weird-ass name, another part retorts. *You're not the center of the universe*, Lanzelin.

"He's downstairs, by the way," Kai goes on, answering my next question. "Drilling."

"Mm." I return my hand to my face, rub my temples. That's no surprise. If Kingston's not eating, sleeping, or in class, he's drilling. Or conditioning. Doubly so after what happened on Wednesday.

Open exhibition, a bunch of teams from our league. Scrimmage against St. Ignaty's Seminary.

Kingston lost.

"Did he remember it was just a practice match?" I ask rhetorically, still not opening my eyes.

Kai snorts. "He wants that Moroslav bastard skewered. I'd do it in two parries if he'd just fucking *let* me."

I open one eye. "Moroslav fights saber?"

Kai slams his book on the table. "*I* fight foil."

Right. Not a single day can pass without Kai bitching about

not being team captain, not fencing foil, whatever else is eating at him. It's pathetic, if I'm honest, and Kai seems to realize this, too, because he backs off, a faux-sympathetic expression on his brow.

"What's wrong with *you*, Pretty Boy? Tummy ache?"

I rub my stomach self-consciously. I don't *not* feel nauseous, but I'm not about to admit that to Kai. "No."

"Tough class?"

I shake my head. "Just French."

That's another thing, I realize. Love and death? Sure, it's an eerie echo of the exact meaning of the curse that I've known about since I was old enough to understand what death *was*. But then again, what poems *aren't* about love and death, especially French ones? A coincidence—one with extremely high odds.

But if it was just a coincidence, then why do I feel...like this?

"Oh ho ho." A wicked smile curls over Kai's lips, and he catches his teeth in his lip ring. "Struggling with your vows?"

"What?" It takes me a minute to even process who he's talking about.

"Girl trouble," Kai says. "That brunette with the tight ass barking up your tree again?"

"Oh, Elena?" I flutter my eyes shut. Shake my head. "No." Not even close. "I mean, yes." She certainly is *attentive*. It's like she doesn't remember that I'm even *on* the damn fencing team, the way she's trying to hang all over me. "But...no."

Irksome or not, Elena Shalott is not even top five in the Lanz problem leaderboard right now.

And I'm not about to tell Kai, of all people, what's top-ranking.

My whole body feels warm, flushed. Aching.

It's not just horniness, either. I almost wish it were; that'd be easier to deal with. It's something else. Something more...feral, almost. My protective instincts, my inner golden retriever clawing to get out, a pull so compelling it feels borderline pheromonal.

And that's the heart of the whole problem. I am, in fact, doomed.

The Dell'Acqua curse.

Love shall claim him once, then again;
Death shall come with a heart split in twain.

Doomed to fall in love, easily and over and over, and then die with a broken heart. That's me. That's all the men in my family, apparently—if you believe in those sorts of things, and I sure as hell do.

Because I've seen what they can do.

Magic is real. Good, bad, everywhere in between. It was just my bad luck to be born into a family with the deadly kind ready to wipe out every one of its male descendants whenever he falls for the right—or wrong—girl.

And until then, there's nothing I can do about it but ride the wave.

Except…

Except if that's her, if that is *the girl*, well…

I saw her for all of, what, forty minutes, and I feel like this? How am I supposed to survive a semester?

Forget riding the waves. She's a freaking tsunami.

"*Fuck.*"

I hear the sound of a book slamming shut, a few footsteps, and open my eyes to the tip of Kai's foil.

"Jesus," I croak. He took the safety button off; this is pure, sharp metal, inches from my flesh.

"As I said before," Kai says, grinning. "He's not here. Just me." He nudges the foil a millimeter closer. "Spar with me."

I pull back, climbing up the arm of the couch so the tip's out of range.

"Not right now."

"Seriously? Come on." Kai jabs the foil, and I duck—as best I can, still on the couch.

"No, Kai!" I yell. "Go...fight with your brother if you're so horny to spar."

Kai licks his lips. Both of us know him and Kingston sparring is a recipe for disaster, especially with King in whatever sour mood he's in post scrimmage.

Still, Kai withdraws.

"Pussy," he mutters.

I wince as he sheaths his weapon and flings it down by the fireplace, grumbling about being bored out of his skull, and I'm just about to close my eyes and rub my pounding temples when I hear my name.

"Lanz."

I look up. It's Callahan, wild-eyed and staring.

"I need to talk to you," he says.

His voice is that low and gravelly sound that strums a chord buried deep inside me.

Which I try not to let show. Just swallow hard and nod. "Sure."

"God, you are all so fucking *morose*," Kai complains. He slams his book shut and shoves it into his bag. "I'm going to grade these somewhere less *tomblike*," he announces. "Come by Holy Grounds if you change your mind about sparring, pretty boy." He glares at Cal. "You too, Virgin Mary."

The front door bangs shut after him, leaving me and Callahan and the mess of a place that is Camlann House.

We stay like that a beat, silent, both listening for the departing thuds of Kai's footsteps, waiting to see if Kingston emerges from downstairs. When he doesn't, Cal jerks his head to the door, and I follow, flexing my hands as I go.

For a fencer, Cal's big and broad—his past as a swimmer more than evident—and I always feel slight walking next to him. King and I are both tall, but more on the lean side, classical fencer build. Kai's more muscle than anything, but Callahan's six-six still has a few inches on even him.

I studiously avoid the Knights of Caliburn crest carved on the first landing of the stairs as we take the right-hand split, and we stop at the first door on the second-story landing: Cal's room.

Inside, it's tidy—especially compared to downstairs—but not just in the militarily-regimented way that Kingston does his hospital corners or the psychopathic way Kai racks up his blades. It's…cozy, I guess, and that's what I've always liked about it. Mixed in the with the same things we all have at Camlann—deep red bedspread, wooden cross on the wall, armchair and corner desk and window seat—Cal's arranged little pieces of thoughtfulness: old maps tacked on the wall, postcards from Italy and Lake Geneva, an amberglass diffuser wafting the light scent of sandalwood.

The door closes behind us. And when it does, Cal seizes me by the shoulders, slams me against it, and claims my mouth with his.

God. It's good, the taste of him, the warmth, and I moan against his lips as my fingers find their way to his hair, pulling him into me with desperate force.

This, I realize, this is what I need right now, body and soul.

But too soon, Cal pries himself away.

"I think he knows," he says. "King."

My heart stutters in my chest. "What?" I give my head a shake. "Why?"

Even as I ask, I am begging, pleading for it not to be true. Not now. Not this. Every inch of me, and especially the eight inches now straining hard in my boxer briefs, just wants to be lost in him, taken over. Thinking about Kingston at all is literally deflating.

Especially if he knows.

Cal licks his lips, rubs his fingers together—the thumb and

index, where he wears his rings. "He went to chapel yesterday. Did you know that?"

"Oh," I say, feeling the smallest burst of relief in my chest. "Well, that's just King's way of—"

"*And* to see Morgan."

Oh. I draw in a deep breath through my nose, trying to calm my electric nerves. "What'd she give him?"

Cal shakes his head. *No idea.*

Fuck.

"That doesn't mean anything," I say, after a moment. "Or, no. It does." I snap my fingers. "The scrimmage. Moroslav's in his head. That's probably it. That's all."

"That's all?" Cal repeats, incredulous. And I know what he means.

Caliburn is undefeated so far this year.

So is St. Ignaty's.

But Caliburn always wins. Always.

"King'll get back on track," I say, and hope I'm telling the truth. "He always does."

"Mm." Cal considers. Rubs his chin. His warm eyes find mine and the concern in them, the angst, leaves me feeling ready to either melt or burn up in shame.

What are we doing, I think, not for the first time.

This whole thing started as a…loophole. A technicality of hermeneutics, a selective but valid interpretation of the vows.

No blade drawn in anger,

no blood spilled in vain.

No knight lost to passion,

no honor profaned.

The traditional read is a vow of celibacy, obviously. No women, period. Keep your focus. Retain your energy. Don't get lost to passion. For me, and my stupid family curse? Win-win. I couldn't be tangled up with women. Couldn't risk it.

But that's the problem with an oath written centuries ago. Back when women were the only *speakable* option.

It leaves a hell of a loophole.

You can't be lost to passion if your passion's right there *with* you, right? That doesn't count. Not if it's another one of us. Not if it's another knight.

I didn't think so, anyway.

Neither did Callahan.

Callahan, the only one of us to take the vows as an actual virgin, the quiet, hulking giant, the one with lips that taste like blackberries and salt and whose fingers can do things to make your head spin.

The first time was an accident, unpremeditated, a late night and a dip into the wine cellar that led to a brush of fingers and ended with a bite mark on my neck placed just where my lamé collar would cover it.

After that, it became a habit. A secret, but not one either of us could give up.

Assuming, of course, we don't get caught.

"Well, if you're sure…" Cal takes a step back towards me, grips the frame of the door with one hand so I'm half-pinned under him. His eyes lock on mine, golden and pure, searching.

"You're sure?"

"Yes," I say.

Sure *enough,* anyway.

Sure that I'm trembling being this close to him now and not touching him.

And that must be enough, because by way of response, Cal ducks his head to my neck, the nip of teeth followed by a sucking, bruising kiss. The twinge of pain makes me stiffen, and Cal draws back.

"You all right?" he rumbles. His golden eyes are bronzed over with desire, a lock of sandy hair fallen over his forehead.

And for a moment, I want to tell him.

About her.

The girl in class.

The one who...knew me.

Even if she didn't know me.

But just as quickly, I know I can't. I know this is something I have to lock deeply, firmly inside me, and let it eat away at my soul until there is nothing left of me.

Because that is who I am, and that is what I do.

I nod—"perfect"—and clutch for him.

We kiss, and kiss, and kiss, harder and harder and firmer, until Cal is pushing me to his armchair and tugging up the hem of my sweater. I work at my belt buckle, frustration and need prickling all over me as his lips feather against my chest until *finally* the damn thing is gone and I feel the sweet press of his hand around me. One long, slow stroke, and then another, and already my hips are bucking and tensing with the need for release. I grit my teeth, fighting for control as Cal rips away from a kiss to sweep his tongue over the callused skin of his palm, and shudder as he returns it, slick but gentle, to my cock.

"Why do you make me *wait* like this?" I grumble hoarsely.

Cal's eyes flash. "Because you like it."

He slides to his knees, and—

God, but he's right.

The undeniable truth about me is that I am an A-plus yearner. I can pine for *years*—decades, if I had to, although at twenty years old I haven't had the runway to test that out yet.

Coming to Caliburn, to Camlann House, should have changed that, should have cut off the neural pathways or whatever and redirected my energy to where it's best used. Our practice. Our honor. Our brotherhood.

I haven't been perfect at our vows. Obviously.

The hot flat of his tongue runs over my length, and I shudder.

"Please," I whisper.

And this time, he obliges.

God forgive me.

It's Cal's hair that I grip with my fingers. Cal's lips sending me over the edge and Cal's mouth that I flood with heat.

But it's her face that burns in my mind.

FIVE

GWENNA

DINNER. Finally.

All I have to do is eat this, pass a few more hours, and go to sleep, and I'll have completed my first day at Caliburn.

Successfully.

Or mostly.

Never mind the roommate who seems to resent my existence. Or the French class where I seem to have made *another* enemy by daring to speak with the blue-eyed class hottie I have zero interest in.

Or the guy who told me point-blank to watch myself. *While holding a sword.*

I grip the handles of my tray and look for a place to sit.

The dining hall at Caliburn may not look like a high-school cafeteria, but as I proceed with my dinner tray and look for a seat, it sure feels like one.

None of the linoleum floors, fluorescent lights, and chipped-edge tables of St. Catherine's. This is plush carpet, glowing lantern lights suspended from a cathedral ceiling, and long wooden tables that could've been borrowed from Henry VIII's personal collection. Even the tray feels more elevated than the scarred gray plastic I'm used to, with actual handles to hold onto and a neatly folded napkin—cloth!—in a matching Caliburn red.

I have no appetite, but after having nothing but coffee all day and procrastinating dinner until the last half-hour of the second sitting, I know I should force something down. And the Friday menu—locally-caught whitefish in a beurre blanc sauce with thyme-honey carrots—does smell terrific, and I say this as someone with the deep-seated aversion to fish Fridays that only Catholic schoolgirls can appreciate. It's a weekend, at least, which means no formal second sitting—those are every other Wednesday, not that I ever intend to pay the extra for high dinner service, let alone find a *gown* to wear—but still fairly crowded, which isn't helping my seating dilemma.

And, unlike at St. Catherine's, I don't think taking this tray to the girls' room to eat is a possibility.

The weight of my bag starts to dig into my shoulder. Every second I stay and stare is another second I'm making it weird, but there's too much information pouring at me all at once—the social calculus of who knows who, who'd welcome a stranger, whether it'd be better simply to eat by myself except for the fact that there are no lone seats available. As my eyes flick around the room, I catch a glimpse of a familiar face—Morgan, my beloved roommate—but if she's seen me, she's studiously pretending not to have, frowning at a book she has propped up against an empty glass.

"'Scuse me." Someone sidles past me from the serving line, waving to friends. "Hey, cut that shit out!"

That's it. I take four decisive strides and plunk my tray down at the first of three empty seats—next to, I realize, another recognizable face.

"Bonsoir, mademoiselle." The ponytail guy—Brett? Brent?—from this morning gives me a little imaginary doff of the hat. He seems…harmless enough, if a little dorky. I suppose that's the sort of cohort I'll have to get used to in a medieval studies track. Might as well bite the bullet and learn to adapt. "Brett. From class."

"Hello," I say, hoping the English will be enough to clue him in that I'm not in the mood for conversation. I shake out my napkin and cut a bite of my fish that I chew absentmindedly as I look around the room. Every panel in the wall's hung with an oil portrait of some dean or another—all men, all white, no surprises there—with the style of dress getting gradually more up-to-date a decade at the time. We must be at the bleeding edge, here, because the nearest portrait shows a golden-haired man in a modern three-piece suit who's broad-shouldered, imposing, and much less portly than his compatriots.

I chew and read the brass plaque.

Luther Victorinus Pendragon
President, Caliburn Board of Trustees & Dean Ex Officio, 2008—

"Ah, yes, the illustrious board president." Ponytail Brett, says, straightens his glasses as he follows my gaze. "Quite wealthy, from what I've heard."

"Hm."

"You know him?"

What? No. I shake my head. "Just...an ironic name, is all."

Ponytail Brett frowns. "Luther?"

I set down my fork. "As in, Martin? The Protestant Reformation?" I gesture at the fish on my plate. "Are we not a nominally Catholic university?"

We. It's not until I say it that I realize I've already, subconsciously, attached myself to this place.

And I like that.

If it'll have me. If I can stay.

"Oh. Ha!" Ponytail Brett laughs a little too loudly. *Calm down, buddy, it wasn't* that *good of a joke.* "I never thought of that, but you're right! Especially since he's the one who funded so many of the rare book archives—"

"You've seen them?" I interrupt. Maybe too forcefully, because Ponytail Brett looks startled.

"Oh," he says. "I mean...no, not yet. Except the ones they rotate out on display. I don't think first years are allowed to handle the books at all, usually. But—you're history?"

"Medieval studies," I say.

He brightens and nods. "Even better. There's this seminar—Latin, with Dr. Emrys—where you get to read directly from the archives. In facsimile, obviously, and it's competitive to get in, but—"

"Dr. Emrys?" I shuffle around my bag, pull out my schedule.

LATIN 302 — EMRYS

Ponytail Brett's eyes go wide. "Whoa, really?" He casts a bashful look at me. "You must be, like...a genius."

"Oh, I...don't know." I stir my beurre blanc self-consciously, gaze drifting to Morgan, who's furiously flipping pages through her book. I wouldn't have her as the study-at-dinner type—or study much at *all* type—but then again, you don't get to Caliburn without at least a *little* academic inclination.

"Rumor has it there's an original copy of Magna Carta in the archives," Ponytail Brett goes on.

I snort. Not likely. Ponytail Brett shrinks a little.

"Okay, yeah, maybe not," he admits.

Because there are only four of those on Earth, I think. Then I chastise myself. Do I *need* to be such a bitch? Ponytail Brett is the only person on this campus who's been anything more than chilly to me. And he at least knew enough not to call it *the* Magna Carta.

"Could be a reissue," I venture. "Later thirteenth century, or early fourteenth."

"Yeah!" He sighs, leaning into his hand. "I'd kill to see that up close."

Me too, I think, and I'm about to say as much when there's a *clunk* of someone setting down a tray beside me. I look up, and see...

Elena.

"Oh," she says, pursing her lips. "Um." She glances over her shoulder, to Claire, who's waiting an arm's length away, and bugs her eyes at Elena in response.

I hold still, expecting some apology or flimsy excuse for why she doesn't want to sit next to me, but none comes. She just lifts her tray and leaves, turning her back like she never even saw me. So abrupt it's genuinely a little shocking, and freezes me in place to watch them depart. And as I stare, I inadvertently lock eyes with someone *else* who seems to be staring at them.

Morgan.

She sees me, blinks, gives the *barest* flicker of her lips that is either a smile or a nervous tic, and slams her book shut.

God, I'm really crushing it, socially.

I set down my fork, what's left of my appetite evaporated, and mumble some farewell to Brett as I take my bag and get up, walking slowly enough so that I'm not dogging Morgan's steps on the way out.

She exits to the right, following the path that goes to Broceliande and her—our—room, so I instinctively head left.

That puts me on the path to the Divinity School, and that means coffee. And with coffee, I can stay up until, presumably, Morgan either goes to sleep or goes...to do whatever she does on Friday nights.

Impulsively, I pull out my phone to check for communication: nothing. No texts, no missed calls. I should be relieved, but all I can feel is suspicion. Like my mom is waiting for me to make the first move, secretly testing whether I'll reach out like a normal, happy little college girl or if she'll have to force me into contact.

Just the thought of it makes me so pissed that I decide to text her out of spite.

> Great first day of classes! Going to hang with some new friends tonight. Miss you.

I pause, consider.

Then delete the last two words, and hit send.

AFTER THE CHAPEL and the library, Holy Grounds might just be my favorite place on campus.

It's dark and crowded and cluttered and full of life, even on a Friday evening—a perfect place to hide in plain sight. The armchairs are mismatched and overstuffed, the coffee machines are ancient, dented things, and the decor is a combination of art museum posters, zine-line linocuts, and prayer cards from various shrines around the world.

"People bring them back from vacation," says the barista, a guy who's so thoroughly bald he doesn't even have eyebrows, catching my stare. "If you ever visit a saint, bring one back. Good karma."

I blink. "Um, sure."

He nods, and taps a a sign in front of the register. "Got an answer? No one's gotten it yet. Fabulous prizes are on the line."

I look down, to where TRIVIA QUESTION OF THE DAY is chalked on a small board.

What book of the Bible is included in the Catholic Vulgate, Dead Sea Scrolls, and Septuagint, but NOT the Masoretic texts or Protestant Bible?

Dear God. Obscure much? Even for a coffee shop located in a divinity school, that's a deep cut.

"Any guesses?" He hums the *Jeopardy* theme song, and points a little lower on the chalkboard. "There's even a hint."

So there is: *Hint: It contains the verse "It is good to guard the secret of a king, but glorious to reveal the works of God."*

Wait. I might actually know this. I screw up my face in concentration, rack my brain, to the term paper I wrote for Theology in junior year...

"Tobit," I say. "The book of Tobit. Is that right?"

"Hell yeah!" The barista offers me a high five, which I awkwardly return. "Congratulations. You've won our fabulous prize."

He hands it to me: a cake pop. On a stick. Decorated like...a unicorn.

"Wow," I say. "Um...thanks. I guess I'll..." I have no interest in eating this, but it seems rude to refuse. "...take it to go."

He grins. "You got it."

Coffee procured and cake pop in a tiny brown bag, I find an armchair and I sip my drink as slowly as possible. With nothing else handy, I read my French poetry anthology to kill time, until people have gradually trickled out and the staff is starting to sweep up.

Finally, at 10 p.m., I give in and head back.

Broceliande is mostly quiet, with just the occasional snatch of music and light seeping out from a closed door, a random peal of laughter and chatter as I scale the staircases, one, two, three. When I reach 326, though, the room seems dark, and I twist my key, eagerly anticipating my faceplant into my bed and the bliss of being alone.

But I'm *not* alone.

"Christ!"

Morgan's sitting at her desk, the overhead lights off and just a makeup mirror illuminating the space. She's dressed entirely differently than I've seen her before: a glittering, one-shouldered black top with a sleeve that billows to her wrist and a miniskirt that's dark and viscous-looking as an oil slick. Not a quiet night in, I suppose.

She presses a hand to her chest. "God, you scared me."

"Sorry," I say. *Just...living here*, I think. *As I've been assigned.* I shrug my bag onto the bed and slowly settle next to it, gritting my teeth against the frustration of *not* being alone.

A flick of an apologetic smile and Morgan resumes her mascara-swiping. I preoccupy myself with taking everything out of my bag: textbooks, notebook, scarf, the paper bag with the stupid little cake pop. With that accomplished, there's nothing really for me to do but study my hands and avoid staring at Morgan.

"I'm sorry," she says. "I couldn't help but notice. Do you have beef with Elena Shalott?"

I blink, give my head a little shake.

"What?" I frown. "I mean...no. I don't even know her."

"But she doesn't like *you*," Morgan presses. She's turned around in her seat now, makeup abandoned, her eyes trained on me like she's working something out.

"I...guess not," I say. "We had French together this morning." I consider, for a half-second, going into more depth, the group discussion and Lanz and her glaringly obvious crush on the guy, but I think better of it. Veering too near to gossip that I don't want to get myself entangled in. The whole point of college is to focus on school, not popularity contests. I don't need that here.

"Hmm." Morgan presses her lips together. "Interesting." But she nods, like she's approving of the state of things.

The back of my neck prickles. "How so?"

"Oh, just..." She gives a dismissive wave. "Kind of an...enemy of my enemy thing, let's just say." She tips her head, and flicks her gaze just briefly over my sad little collection of bag contents, before going back to her mirror.

An impulse takes over me. My hand grabs the folded paper bag, holds it out to her. "Do you want this?"

Morgan turns, and seeing my offer, wrinkles her nose, suspicious. "What…is it?"

God, I'm an absolute genius at making friends, I think. "A… cake pop," I say. "Unicorn." I fish it out of the bag and demonstrate. "I got the trivia question right at the coffee shop and they insisted I take the prize. I told them I didn't want it, but…" My gaze drifts to all her mystical, magical trinkets. "I figured maybe you would?"

I don't fucking know. This is all so stupid. I should've just chucked the damn thing in the trash.

But Morgan unwrinkles her nose. She reaches for it, holding the paper stick between impressively lacquered fingertips, and studies it.

"Aww. It's cute." And then, she unceremoniously takes a bite, cleaving the thing's head in two. Something syrupy and red drips from the center, and Morgan claps a hand to her mouth.

"Oh my God," she says. "They put blood in it? That's…"

"Hopefully fake," I say, without thinking.

And suddenly we're both laughing. Morgan even coughs a little, struggling to swallow.

"It's good, kinda," she says, frowning. "Pomegranate flavored, or something? Hm." She polishes off the rest of the poor thing, brushes crumbs from her lips. But this time, she doesn't go back to her makeup mirror.

"I'm going to the cap tonight," she says. "Are you?"

I stare at her. "The what?"

"Cap," she repeats. "Caliburn Academic Parlour?"

I'm still not following. She's not dressed for anything academic.

"A party," she explains, at last in plain English. "They're scheduled every week, ish. A cap or a gap—general assembly of persons. Those are more lowkey. Board games and shit. Caps are, like…party parties." She pauses. "Do you…want to go?" She asks it half-hesitantly, drumming those long nails on her desk, and I can't tell if she's just asking to be nice.

"And no, I'm not just asking to be nice."

"Jesus," I say sharply. Can she read minds?

But Morgan looks genuinely nonplussed, and I inwardly slap myself on the wrist. BE NORMAL, GWENNA.

Okay, well, what would a normal person do?

As if on cue, my phone buzzes beside me on the bed.

> From: Mom
> I'm so glad to hear it. Send me photos when you can. Love you.

Fucking hell.

"Earth to Gwenna?" comes Morgan's voice. "Party?"

"Sure," I hear myself say. "I…love parties. I mean caps."

Who, actually, *am* I right now?

My fingers tense in the bedspread, almost involuntary, and I force them to relax.

I'm Gwenna. Normal Gwenna. Happy Gwenna. Enjoying-her-time-and-not-struggling-at-all Gwenna.

Gwenna who goes to parties.

Right?

Morgan laughs. No, *cackles*, almost. "You're a very bad liar, did you know that? But I'll believe you." She shakes her endless wavy hair out and surveys me up and down. "Do you have anything… else to wear?" she asks, biting her lip.

"If I say yes, would you believe me?" I return.

"No." She gets up and clasps me by the wrist. "Come here."

SIX

KAI

THERE'S ONLY three things I want to do at any given time: fence, fuck, or fight.

Even more so when it's a Friday night.

And given that the latter two are fully off-limits according to my precious vow, I've spent the past two hours drilling up and down the piste until my muscles ache and the entire salle ripples with body heat.

Clang.

I let the saber clatter onto the floor right beneath the sign that says KINDLY DO NOT DROP WEAPONS—fuck you and your blade integrity—and sink onto the bench.

It's not enough. Physically exhausted, mentally wired. Me in a fucking nutshell.

I fumble for my cigarettes, strike a match on the sole of my Ballestras, and suck in a drag.

I blow a cloud out into the salle. It's absolutely deluxe, this place: three practice pistes to spar on, a side room full of pristine weight machines and dumbbells, and an entire arsenal of kit: Negrini jackets, tailored to size and imported from Verona; weapons with razor-sharp aluminum and custom, 3D-printed handgrips; Hungarian-made masks in our trademark Caliburn red.

Fencing, the sport of kings. The gentlemanly art. A prince's duty and a scoundrel's gambit.

I hate how much I love it.

And I'm sure that if little twelve-year-old Kai, in the cinderblock recreation centers of his youth, could see this place, all polished wood and nameplated lockers and pristine gear, he'd probably hate it too.

He'd certainly hate me.

But that was before Luther Pendragon came into my life and turned me into the swordsmanship machine I am today. *And we're ever so grateful, Daddy Pen. Another ruffian youth saved from a life on the streets. God bless you, sir.*

I take another long pull on the cigarette and tip an imaginary hat to my foster father.

"King sees you doing that in here and he'll have an aneurysm."

Pretty Boy—Lanz—fixes my cigarette with his moony little stare of disapproval. Damn, I didn't even hear him come in, and these floors are built with spring in them that makes every step audible. Talented motherfucker with the footwork, I'll give him that.

I puff out a smoke ring and lean back, propping an ankle on the opposite knee. "Ooh, you promise?"

Lanz's jaw twitches. Delicate flower, so anxious over rule-breaking. I snort and take another drag. The only rules I'll stick to are the ones carved in literal stone over the mantel of this place, and even then I'll bend them to the breaking point.

But sticklery bullshit about tidiness, appearances, keep our hair combed and shoes polished like the All-American good boys we're supposed to be?

I catch my lip ring in my teeth. *No fucking thank you.*

I breathe out the smoke through my nostrils. Lanz pulls out an epee from his wall rack and inspects the guard.

"No practice for you today?" I ask, innocent enough.

Lanz shakes his head, jamming an Allen wrench into a tiny screw to tighten it. "Rest day."

Suuure, I think, and lean forward. "Good news. It's nighttime now." Grinding out my smoke in the palm of a crumpled glove, I catch the grip of my saber on my toes, kick it up into the air, and snatch it to levy at Lanz. "En garde."

He keeps his eyes trained on his weapon. "No thanks."

God, he's boring. All of them are, to be honest. I'm not a team player except when it comes to the literal sport. And even then, I have my compunctions.

I drop my saber with a clatter. Lanz eyes the KINDLY DO NOT DROP WEAPONS sign and lets out the tiniest sigh.

"Big plans for the evening, then?" I stretch back out and put my hands behind my head, watching him. If I can't fight him, I can at least be a pain in his ass.

Lanz shakes his head. "No. I mean, there's a cap tonight, but—"

My ears perk up like a bloodhound in a burial ground. "Say what now?"

Caliburn's of *course* too good to have normal college ragers, so instead, we have caps. I'm not a joiner—Camlann House being the notable exception. And generally, if you ask me, all the forced merriment—the balls, the formal dinners, the symposia and teas—is just a way to waste tuition dollars and maintain elitist bullshit.

But this gets my attention.

Because on a night like tonight, when my blood feels too hot in my body and I'm ready to crack some skulls?

Any party's a good party. Even a Caliburn party.

His shoulders tense up like he regrets saying anything. I'll bet he does. "There's a cap tonight," he says. "At the Porter's Club. But I, uh...I don't think I'm going."

I sit up straight. Alight. Interested. Piqued. "Oh, I think you should. *We* should." I jump to my feet, strip off my lamé so I'm just barechested in my fencing trousers, and point at him.

This time, Lanz actually looks at me. "Why?"

I pause. He has a point. Why? Why, given that the prerogative of any college party—get laid—is off-limits for us?

My instincts and impulsiveness are a snowball cascading down the hill. A spark on bone-dry tinder. Now that I know about this, I need to have it. That's just how my mind works, and I have no way of explaining that to anyone.

I can only shrug.

"Because it's there."

I duck into the lockers, take a swig of my emergency Mezcal, and hit the shower, ice cold.

I close my eyes as the water flows over me, shoulders and back and limbs, aware of every inch of my body.

Fact is, I'm human. Male. Robust, red-blooded, heterosexual. And as such, I love girls. Women. Ladies. Love their bodies, their faces, their long hair and soft skin and the way they smell. Fuck, even thinking the words is stirring up my cock a little, and that's in the middle of a literal cold shower.

It's not like I want to tempt fate or challenge myself to resist. A party's not supposed to be some forty days in the desert thing to test my mettle.

And I'm not scheming to figure out how close I can get to the line without crossing, either—seeking out literal backdoors like some kind of repressed Evangelical trying to get his dick wet without a blight on his conscience. Not that I haven't had the opportunity, since there's more than a few lovely coeds who've dropped anvil-sized hints they'd like to *improve their grades* in the Early Modern Art History seminar that I TA. As much as it pains me, I resist entirely: no furtive handjobs, no above-the-clothes action, not even so much as a sweet little kiss goodnight.

No, for me, the restraint, the choke of the leash before anything gets interesting, is part of the fun. I get off on my own blue balls. Sick fuck that I am.

And when fencing won't do the trick to keep the demons in my brain at bay, that's where I go.

Straight into the crucible.

Which, tonight, means a party.

I emerge a few minutes later, toweling my hair in my street clothes, to find that Callahan has joined Lanz in the salle, whatever conversation they were having dying instantly as soon as I walk in.

"Oh, don't stop on my account." I chuck the towel onto a bench and give my head a shake, smoothing the sides of my hair with my palms. "What's good? You down for a cap tonight, big guy?"

Callahan says nothing. Man of few words. Just looks at Lanz.

I crack my knuckles and bite back a groan. "I can't get *either* of you fuckers to go to this thing? Come on."

"You're a TA," Lanz mutters. "Should *you* even be going?"

Next to him, Callahan grunts from behind his book.

"What?" Lanz cries.

"It's not explicitly *dis*allowed in the code of conduct," Callahan rumbles.

I grin. "My man," I cry, and rub my hands together. "Come on. We're burning daylight. The night is young, and the girls are only getting drunker—"

But neither of them is looking at me anymore. Staring right past me to the door.

I don't need to look to know who's there.

"Friday plans?"

I square my shoulders, tense and untense my arms, and slowly turn my gaze to him.

Kingston. He's the closest to casual he gets, wearing a navy T-shirt and dark gray joggers and his usual judgmental expression. Arms folded, but at attention.

Prick. I have half a mind to rip my saber up from the floor and—

"There's a cap tonight," Lanz answers for me. *Thanks for that, Judas Iscariot Dell'Acqua,* I think. *You under some kind of truth-telling spell? Jesus.*

"And you're going?" Kingston asks. Not Lanz. Me.

I suck in a breath and call on my last shred of self-restraint. "If it please the court," I say mildly. The adrenaline's already streaming into my veins, the need to be moving, *going* somewhere. And heaven have mercy on whoever stands in my way.

Especially if it's Kingston.

He wrinkles his brow. "I don't think that's a good idea."

"Of course you don't," I mutter. Then, louder, as cheerful and casual as I can. "Good thing it's not up for referendum, then."

Kingston's jaw twitches.

Hit him where it hurts, it seems.

"It's a free country," Lanz observes, to no one in particular.

"*Not in here,*" Kingston barks. "This isn't a democracy." He shoots a look at me. "Weekends are for practice or rest."

"I practiced," I say. "Just now. Smell my fuckin' lamé if you don't believe me." I grab my leather jacket from its peg, shrug into it. "I'm good."

"You skipped yesterday."

Seriously? "I had to proctor a placement exam," I point out.

"At one p.m." Kingston's eyes rise meaningfully to the clock. "What about the other twenty-one hours of the day?"

"Jesus *Christ,*" I mutter. "Your micromanaging bullshit is

exhausting, you know that? Shit, I need a rest from *that*." I take a pronounced step forward. "Now, *if* you'll excuse me."

But he doesn't. Of course he doesn't. Kingston steps directly into my way.

I clench my jaw hard enough to crack a tooth, tighten every fiber of my body.

We're really doing this? Picking me to pieces just for the hell of it?

Or no, not just for the hell of it, I realize.

Because one of us didn't lose on Wednesday.

Me.

"What's that supposed to mean?" Kingston asks, sharp and direct yet somehow annoyingly cool.

"I dunno," I say, doing my best to match him in kind—cool, calm, and collected. "I'm just saying…" I hold my palms in the air innocently. "Maybe if you kept your eyes on your own piste, *bro*, you wouldn't lose to Moroslav."

His parry is quick. "This has nothing to do with that," he all but snaps.

Touched a nerve, I mentally singsong. "Oh, doesn't it?" I say. "Because it sure as hell looks like you're punishing me for *your* failure. And that doesn't strike me as especially leaderly behavior, *captain*."

He works his jaw. "Discipline isn't punishment. It's a precondition for success."

"Save it, Foucault." I shrug my jacket up my arms. "I'm leaving, and you can deal. Why don't you go nod off on your magic beans or whatever your witchy step-slut packed up for you and leave the rest of us to actually live our lives?"

That's it.

Wire tripped.

Kingston lunges for me.

I duck, but he doesn't even move to strike. Just gets his perfect face right up in mine.

"Speak like that again," he grits out between locked teeth, "and Father will hear about it."

Oh, fuck you.

I haul back and ram my fist into his eye socket.

The blow knocks him backwards, stumbling and clutching at his face. But other than that, nothing. Barely even a grunt on impact.

I shake out my knuckles, grinning and breathing hard, the rush of lashing out mingling with the pain of the hit like a drug in my veins.

"Don't worry," I pant. "I'll do my hail Marys. It's a venal sin, right? Curable."

Kingston just stares. Stares with a bruise blooming under his cheekbone and a trickle of blood coming out of the corner of his perfect little mouth. Refuses, *refuses* to give me the satisfaction.

"Put ice on that." He nods at me. "That's your sword hand."

Oh, fuck *you*.

I lunge for him again.

"Fuck y—"

But this time, someone grabs me—Callahan, giant bastard, throwing an arm around my neck.

"You think you've convinced me? Now I'm *definitely* going," I yell. "I want to be as far away from you and your miserable, pathetic, *chickenshit* idea of what we're actually doing here *as possible.*"

Kingston glowers. Touches two fingertips to his eye socket. And disappears back upstairs.

I rip myself away from Callahan and follow suit.

Outside, it's chilly. Good; I need the fresh air. I'm a few solid strides away from Camlann House when footsteps catch up to me.

Lanz and Callahan, nipping at my heels like little fucking puppies.

"Relax," I say, without looking at either of them. "Mommy and Daddy fight sometimes."

"Not like this, though." Lanz. I whirl on him.

"You wanna throw down, too? I'll snap you in half, pencil dick."

"Stop," bellows Callahan. "Both of you. Just..."

Lanz backs up a step, palms in the air. "We just wanted to make sure you were okay."

I square my shoulders. "I'll be fine." I always fucking am. "Just let me have some goddamn fun and I'll behave." I press my palms together in fake supplication. "Cross my heart and hope to die."

I look from Lanz to Callahan, only half-joking in my plea. Not like I need their permission, but the last thing I want to do is drive them further into Kingston's fealty. Rule number one of being an absolute prick: don't make more enemies than necessary, and don't make your enemies more *friends* than necessary.

"Okay," Lanz says at last. "But I think we should go with you."

Oh, *now* they want to tag along? I shake my head. "I'm good."

Callahan cracks his knuckles. "It wasn't a question."

SEVEN

GWENNA

TWO MINUTES into the party and I think I'd rather be anywhere than here.

Morgan outfitted me in a long, purple blouse with sleeves that cover my arms and even the tops of my hands (which I changed into in the bathroom, and she didn't seem to think was odd) along with a pair of pants that are dark, shiny, and almost squeak when I walk—leather, or faux. I didn't go so far as to put on a full face of makeup, but accepted her offer of some dark red lip stain and even ran a comb through my hair.

Gwenna, party-ready.

Porter's is the campus bar, but that title makes it sound sticky and damp when the opposite is true. It's in the basement of the dining hall building, almost cavern-like, and now filled with bodies and soft colorful lighting and the pulsing music of a DJ stand and surround-sound speakers. Beneath the arched openings to the bar, a bartender pours beers on tap and serves bottled cocktails offered on a hand-chalked menu—botanical gin and tonics, smoked old-fashioneds, hardly college jungle juice—and a table offering snacks that no one seems to be touching on various layered stands stands waiting to the right.

As soon as we walk in, Morgan seems to be vibing—nodding her head to the music, swaying her hips, and casting her eyes around the room. I get the sense that she's eager to mingle, and probably desperate to be with anyone but me, her charity-chase instincts having run out somewhere on the walk across campus, so I mumble something about getting a drink and I take my leave of her with a big-pasted on smile. She hums something in parting that I can't quite hear and weaves her way to the center of the dance floor, the lights above us drifting green to blue to purple and back, cutting through the fog of an unseen smoke machine.

Well, here we go. What would a normal person do?

I clench my hand around my phone in my pocket. A post, obviously. A cute, "look at my fabulous life" selfie that shows me happy, healthy, letting my hair down but not *too* much. A quippy caption that's just a tad humble-braggy. *college life,* all lower case, followed by a string of...cloud emoji or whatever happy people use. And...boom. Picture perfect, literally. And then I can get out of here.

Problem is, Porter's is dark as a cavern. Because it...basically is. And the last thing I want to do is attract attention with a photo flash.

I shoulder my way through dark bodies and the relative light of the bar, digging out my phone and sliding open the camera as I do. I hold it aloft, the front camera straining to reflect anything but grainy darkness back at me. I'm experimenting with distance and angle, trying to get more light on my face without straight-up staring into the bar like a lunatic, when—

"Cheese," says a deep voice.

Someone grabs my shoulder and leans in, pressing the side of their head to mine and staring up at my phone. I jump back, startled.

"What the fuck?"

The phone jostles from my hand and tumbles to the floor—but doesn't hit.

Because he catches it.

Whoever he is.

I blink, dumbfounded, as this…person straightens and holds out my phone to me. Tall. Messy hair. Leather jacket. A goddamn *lip ring*. And a grin.

"Careful," he says, leaning in through the noise, smelling like citrus and smoke. "Don't want to break anything."

I snatch the phone away and glare at him, embarrassment flaming my cheeks. It's bad enough that I'm all but obligated to be here, do this, play pretend, and now this…whoever he is has to barge in.

No, not whoever. The puzzle pieces click.

"You're the proctor," I say—aloud, by accident. Shit. I want this interaction concluded and here I am prolonging the damn thing.

He blinks, running a hand through his hair and studying me. I don't like it. Too close. Instinctively, I pull my sleeves down further.

"I am," he says slowly. "Which makes you…" He squints. "Gwenna."

I give the briefest, tiniest nod. I don't like the sound of my name in his voice.

Then, all at once—those reflexes—he sticks out a hand. "Kai. A pleasure." Again, the grin flashes. "So, are we taking a selfie, or…"

"No," I say firmly. I clench my phone in my fingers. This was a stupid idea. I could have easily faked a photo without actually *going* to the cap. And now I'm all but pinned against the bar with the press of bodies and pulse of karaoke backing tracks crowding in on all sides.

Kai stuffs his hands in his pockets. "Suit yourself. Buy you a drink?"

Without waiting for an answer, he signals for the bartender. Goddammit.

"Whatever the lady wants," he says, nodding in my direction. "On me."

The bartender, an older gentleman with a mustache and waistcoat who looks like he should be riding a giant old-fashioned bicycle, just raises an eyebrow. "Porter's is included in your meal plan." He looks at me. "Yours too. What'll it be?"

"Ah..." There are too many things happening at once. A pull of tension tightens behind my eyes. "I..."

"Is he bothering you?"

I whirl around to see...him. The guy from French class.

Lanz.

God, it's a regular who's who of people I've had run ins with so far on campus, I think. I can't tell, genuinely, whether I'm glad to see him or annoyed. Maybe neither.

"Relax, pretty boy," says Kai, the slightest edge to his voice. "I'm just chatting with her." He puts his palms in the air. "See? Room for the holy spirit."

Lanz darts a glance at me.

"I'm fine," I say.

The bartender coughs.

"I was just getting Gwenna here a drink," Kai says, nodding. He points to his chest. "Paloma. Easy on the grapefruit." Then points to me.

"Does she even want a drink?" rumbles a third voice.

Oh, great, gang's all here. This one—appearing from nowhere at Lanz's shoulder—is new. Broad and tall and strong looking in a way that even Lanz and Kai can't compete with. Handsome, too, although his expression is also decidedly blank.

I half-wonder what these guys are even doing here if they

don't seem to be interested in the, well, partying aspects of the party, but my curiosity is cut short when the bartender hands over a frosted glass, accented with a spring of dusty purple blossoms. To me.

"Lavender gin and tonic," he says, and gives me a wink. "I think you'll like it."

"Thank you," I say dumbly, and accept it. I don't *not* drink, but it's also—how would Dr. Riggs put it?—not recommended for someone in my condition.

But Dr. Riggs isn't here. And I am—for the foreseeable future, it seems.

As the caterwauling strains of a funk duet strike up behind us, I take a sip—it's not bad. Herbal, but astringent from the gin, with the sweetness of tonic to balance it all out—and, worst of all, barely any burn of alcohol. The kind of girly drink that'll put you under the table without you even realizing.

The four of us just…stand there.

"Oh," Lanz says, suddenly remembering his companion. "This is Callahan. Cal, this is—"

"*This*," Kai interrupts, "is Gwenna. Hotshot polyglot and Caliburn's newest student."

"She can introduce herself," Lanz retorts.

I suck another sip of my drink—better with every sip—and roll my eyes. I can defend myself too, but whatever.

Callahan—Cal—nods. "Polyglot?"

"High marks in French and Latin," Kai confirms, accepting his cocktail from the bartender. "Thank you, my good man." He gulps half of it. "Not that I peeked at the results, or anything."

Weird, but okay. I take another sip of my drink, and I'm suddenly, acutely aware that people are looking at us.

Not just people passing by and trying to get to the bar.

People in a general two-foot radius.

No, not at us. At them.

"You all right?" Lanz asks. Asks *me*. I all but jump.

"Yes," I say. "No. I mean...do you guys owe everyone money, or something?"

Kai guffaws. Callahan's jaw works. Lanz's cheeks tinge pink.

"No, no, it's just, ah—"

"We don't go out much," Callahan rumbles. He rubs his hands together, fiddling with two rings on his right hand, thumb and forefinger.

Kai nods. "Seems like our appearance at a cap is something of...a novelty." He sips his second. "Since we so *rarely* leave the confines of Camlann House."

The sensation of being watched, *observed*, is getting to me. Prickling up my neck with animal anxiety, the instinct to flee. I dart a glance around the room, taking in everyone taking *them* in. Callahan follows with a deep stare, more like he's sizing everyone up as a threat than seeing who's out there.

"So you guys are...roommates?" I ask, in spite of myself.

"Teammates," Callahan corrects.

"Fencing," Lanz says.

Oh, right. "Swords."

Lanz laughs a little. It's not a bad laugh, lighting up those blue eyes of his. He's had his hands in his pockets this whole time, I realize. Like he's keeping himself on lock.

And I'm not the only one who notices. Because now I can see two eyes in particular burning a hole in my skin. Elena and Claire, both decked out in glittery party gear and both staring absolute daggers at me.

I don't like where this is going. Not at all. The familiar prickle of anxiety at the back of my neck is swiftly turning into a full-body burn of panic.

And just as I feel a pang of gratitude for the wall of *male* that's keeping me from sight—

"We should be going," Callahan says.

"Right." Lanz nods. "We're sorry to have bothered you. Aren't we, Kai?"

Kai cuts a look at Lanz that says he's anything but. But he nods and takes a step back.

Something lurches in my chest.

Don't go.

I don't know where that comes from. A foolish little yelp of impulse, my mental framework going haywire. Like the panic of being seen can be blotted out, shielded, by three broad-shouldered boys.

And yet—

"Wait," I rasp. "Wait, you…"

No. *Get a grip, Gwenna.* I give my head a swift shake. What the hell was I even planning to say, exactly? Going to beg them to form a protective circle around me? Because they're not the solution. Or even the problem.

I just need to…get out of here.

Escape, calm down, and figure out some Plan B for proving how carefree and well-adjusted I am.

This whole thing was a mistake.

I clutch my drink a little tighter.

"Thanks for the…" I trail off, realizing I don't know what, if anything, I have to thank them for. "I'm going to…"

But they've already disappeared.

"Gwenna!"

Blonde hair, a tart little smile. It's Claire.

"I'm so surprised to see you here," she says, in a tone of voice that suggests this isn't precisely a compliment. She swings her hair over her shoulder, revealing collarbones dusted with shimmer above a bronze-colored tube-top. "The caps are pretty… lively early in the year."

"Yeah," I agree. "You can say that again."

We're on the edge of the dance floor, not mixed into the crowd but just beside it, and the pumping of the music and writhing of the dancers makes it feel as claustrophobic as an iron maiden.

Next to her, Elena sips her drink, shifts her weight toward me, smile tilting just a little too slow, like her center of gravity isn't quite cooperating. Her drink sloshes over the rim as she takes a step closer.

"So you're Little Miss Thing," she whisper-shouts in my ear. "What's your *deal*?"

I blink. "I'm...sorry?"

"You come out of *nowhere*, show up weirdly, like...late," Elena says, glancing at Claire, "you show off in French—"

My chest clenches. *I wasn't showing off.*

I hate that. Hate that so much. Any time I show enthusiasm, get into what I'm doing, it's always *Gwenna, stop showing off.*

Like that's why I'm doing it. For attention.

Is it so hard to believe that maybe I just *like* it?

That I'm *good at it?*

Elena's still talking. "...and somehow you're in with the *fencing* team?" The incredulity in her voice has strayed from gossipy-casual to genuinely harsh.

I grip my glass harder. "I'm not *in with them*," I say as evenly as I can. "And I wasn't showing off."

"*Sure*," Elena drawls. "You're just carrying around that little handkerchief for no reason. No reason whatsoever."

"I..." There's no easy explanation for why I have it. *I'm* not even sure why I have it.

"They don't date, you know," Claire interjects. "They're sworn not to. For...focus and stuff."

"Okay?" I say. "I don't want to date them."

Elena laughs. "Oh, really? Then why were they all over you just now?"

Is she serious? "*All over me?* Come on." I laugh, trying to break the tension. But it backfires. Hard.

"Don't fucking *laugh* at me," Elena says, voice shrill enough to draw a few stares. "Who the fuck do you think you are?"

I shrink, instinctively, from the sudden attention. "Nobody," I say. "No one. I just—"

"Hey, knock it off."

I whirl around to see who's speaking.

It's him. The pierced guy from earlier, with the tattoos—Kai. Leaning against the bar, eyeing us.

Elena is *not* pleased at being interrupted. But her voice is sweet as ever. "Excuse me?"

"I said knock it off," he repeats, cool and calm. "Take it down a notch, eh? And maybe lay off the G&Ts."

"You're one to talk." This, from—to my surprise—Morgan, who's at the bar just a few people away. "Cool it, Kai."

"Cram it, succubus," Kai fires back at her.

Elena's face goes instantly blank, placid as a sunny day. "I'm sorry," she says, "but this is a private conversation. Do you mind?"

Before Kai can object, Claire expertly sidesteps, boxing him out. Morgan, wherever she was, appears to have disappeared, too.

Then Elena turns back to me.

"Listen," I say hastily, spreading my hands wide. Maybe I can reason with her. Girl to girl. "I get it, okay? You like Lanz. Fine. Cool. I am…*so* not interested. Like, truly, I promise you. No issues here."

It's the wrong thing to say. Elena's face contorts. "Who said I liked him?" she hisses, face pink. "Stop spreading rumors about me."

"I…what?"

"I'd never try to get them to break the rules. And risk our winning streak? How could you *say* that?"

She sets her jaw, narrows her eyes at me.

And smacks the drink from my hand.

"Oops," she says flatly, not even pretending to look sorry. "My bad."

A thousand pieces of glass scatter across the floor, earning yelps and *omigods* from the crowd.

Now everyone's looking.

"Maybe *you* should lay off the drinks, sweetie," Elena says from above, breath hot in my ear. "Maybe—"

"Maybe *you* should step the fuck off."

This time, Kai doesn't let Claire block his path. He practically shoulder-checks her out of the way, sweeping a gaze up and down my whole body. "You okay?"

I can't move. Can't even nod.

"Oh my God," Claire murmurs, a hand to her mouth. "Oh my God, oh my God."

Elena, for her part, takes a moment—lips parted in shock—before she snaps back to standing. It's astonishing—from quivering emotion to calm and collected in just two dabs of the eyes.

"I'm sorry," she says. "Things just got a little—"

"Save it," Kai barks. In a single, swift motion, he kneels and returns, something clear and glimmering now in his hand.

It takes a moment to register. *A piece of glass.*

"Oh my God!" Now Claire leaps backwards, drawing a chuckle from Kai, who jabs the glass after her.

"Yeah? I know how to use it, too." He pivots to Elena, cocks his head. "You wanna go?"

"Kai. *Stop.*" Lanz barges in from Kai's other side, grabbing his wrist with surprising ease. "Just stop."

"What?" Kai says, trying and failing to shrug him off. "I'm just coming to the aid of a *damsel* in *distress*."

His words are loose, sloppy. Behind him, Callahan looms, thick arms crossed, as Lanz's grip flexes with the effort to keep Kai's hand immobile. And all around us, the crowd is getting louder and louder, murmurs into the occasional shout, the heat of more and more eyes burning into my skin.

"Let me go," Kai says, yanking away from Lanz again. "Let me—"

"*Drop it.*"

That voice.

Clear as glass, cold as ice.

Kingston.

He cuts through the crowd effortlessly, people simply *parting* for him to cross, mouths falling open and eyes goggling in astonishment, and I catch snatches of words:

Is that...

...but he never...

...can't believe, holy shit...

Claire lets out a frightened *meep* sound. Elena cowers, but not without a glance at Lanz. Lanz, for his part, is impassive—blue eyes trained on the middle distance—as is Callahan just behind him. Kai is sneering, flings the chunk of glass to the ground with a faint *tink tink* sound.

But Kingston...

Kingston is looking at me.

Standing at attention, arms crossed, his golden eyes steady, focused.

And I have never, ever wished to be invisible more than right now.

"Are you all right?" he asks.

I shake my head. Noncommittal. *Can't speak.* I swallow the rasp in my throat and try again.

"Fine," I say. "I'm fine."

"Liar," someone mutters. It's Morgan, threading her way to the front from the same direction Kingston just came from.

But Kingston seems satisfied with my answer.

He breaks his gaze away. Sweeps a look around the room.

Something—disgust? Disappointment?—curls in his top lip. The most emotion I've ever seen from him.

He straightens his posture.

"Get out," he cries. "Everyone. Party's over. Go home."

Murmurs of disappointment, even a light groan of protest, but everyone obeys, and frighteningly quickly. Claire rushes to Elena's side, handing her a purse and staring fury at me as they leave through the main double doors, and the tides of humanity sweep out person by person, no one's eyes ever leaving me.

Finally, finally, it's empty. Just silence. I look for them—for Kai, Lanz and Callahan, Kingston—but they're already shadows in the doorframe.

And I…

I'm…

My blouse is still dripping, my heart is still pounding, and my fingers are sticky with whatever's left of my cocktail.

I'm a disaster.

"Come on," someone whispers, a perfumed arm draping over my shoulders. It's Morgan. "Let's get you out of here, roomie."

EIGHT

KINGSTON

I SIT at the table alone.

It is, by design, a meeting place. A center, literal and figurative, of our order. Our team. Our brotherhood. The deepest and oldest chamber in all of Camlann House, sunk a full story below the ground,

But right now, it is my sanctuary.

I press my hands into the ebony wood surface and close my eyes. Try to call up guidance, ask forgiveness, seek penance to do.

It isn't working. Hasn't been. Not for days.

The chapel—I was interrupted.

Morgan's tonic—a cheap replacement for real discipline. Effective, but short-lived. And not anything I want to be dependent on.

Practice—always.

But the fact remains.

He's in my head. Moroslav. And I don't like it.

I inhale, exhale. Tense, relax.

A buzz against my thigh. My phone. I ignore it.

Two seconds later, another buzz. Harder—unnaturally so. Almost hard enough to hurt.

I pull it out and see the contact: Morgan.

Of course. I swipe it unlocked.

"Jesus, King, pick up on the first right next time or else I'll make the damn thing explode."

"Good evening, Morgan." I have to hold back to wince as I put the phone to my ear; whatever power she channeled to make it vibrate like that has the case hot and crackling with energy. "You need—"

"Get to the cap," she says, breathless. "Now. There's a fight starting, and—"

"Kai?" I feel my fingers tense.

Morgan gives a brief *ha*. "Yes and no. It's more—"

What does she mean? "Not the other two?" That's not like Lanz, and certainly not like Cal.

"No, no. It's—Christ, would you let me finish?" Morgan rushes on. "It's a girl thing, I think. But Kai's getting aggro."

I let out a long, steadying breath. "We don't start fights."

"I *know*," Morgan says, "and I'm not *asking* you to start one. I'm asking you to *end* it. Isn't that something you *have* to do?"

I don't say anything. She knows the answer.

"That's what I thought," she finishes. "Porter's. Get down here. *Now.*"

A sharp *crack* and a flash of blue light sends the phone from my fingers and thudding onto the table.

I pause only a moment, then stand. Not allowing myself to feel the reluctance.

She's right. This is my duty.

It's all of ours.

MINUTES LATER, outside Porter's. I roll my shoulders, release tension. Unneeded wear on the muscles.

I start walking. Footsteps at my side: Lanz.

"You all right?"

I nod, eyes front.

I don't like interfering like that.

No, correction: I don't like *having* to interfere like that.

I don't like that this kind of confrontation is happening on campus. My campus—our campus.

Not when what we need is peace. Concentration. Absolute focus.

Lanz drops away, and the four of us make the walk back to Camlann in silence, nothing but our footsteps on the gravel.

I certainly have nothing to say.

The house is dark when we step back in. A dramatic sigh from my left—Kai. My jaw clenches against my will.

"Well, now what?" he says, throwing himself on a couch.

"Everyone to bed." I answer without looking at him. Because as soon as I lock him in my sights, I can't be held responsible for my actions.

Instead, I head for the staircase to the salle.

Kai snorts and mutters something I don't allow myself to hear.

"What about you?" Callahan asks me.

"I'll sleep later."

I flick on the lights, the walls white against the stark black of the window glass looking out on the night, and unrack my blade. Take to the strip.

En garde. Parry 4. Riposte. Recover. Again.

No opponent. No mask, even. Only myself.

Minutes pass, or hours. The balls of my feet ache and my calves are taut with fatigue, shoulder and forearm burning.

Still, I persist.

Because now, especially now, there is something inside me, a burgeoning sense of dread I can't shake, not with prayer or magic or drill after drill after drill.

That girl is going to be a problem.

NINE

GWENNA

I DON'T REMEMBER FALLING asleep. But when I wake up, Morgan is staring at me.

"There she is," she says. "Good morning."

I don't respond, just slowly, very slowly, push myself up to sitting, careful to keep the arms of my sweatshirt taut at my wrists.

"Um," I croak. "Hi."

"*Hi,*" Morgan repeats emphatically. She blinks. "Do you... want to explain what happened last night?"

I rub the side of my forehead.

A fight. Two mean girls. Four boys, coming to my rescue...sort of? Including Morgan's stepbrother, which *what the fuck*—

"I could ask you the same thing," I say.

She purses her lips, crosses her arms, sits back in her bed. She's got on purple silk shorty pajamas, a matching set. "I asked you first."

Fair enough. I blow out a breath, scratch the back of my head. Hard to think before coffee. "Um...Elena hates me, I guess." I shrug. "I really don't know."

"Why?"

"I mean..." I chew the inside of my cheek. "I think she likes that guy Lanz? On the team?"

Something flickers in Morgan's honey-colored eyes. Intrigue. Agreement.

So I go on.

"But I guess she doesn't want anyone to know. Or...something." I lift my hands and drop them against my bedspread in defeat. "Isn't this the kind of shit we're supposed to leave in high school?" I wonder aloud.

"You would think," Morgan says drily. She studies her nails. Nods. "That tracks."

Tracks? With what? I think. But Morgan doesn't elaborate.

"I don't much care for Elena," she says airily. "She's been going all moony over him since the start of the semester. Like she doesn't know all of the fencing squad is uninterested with a capital U."

I shiver, thinking about *that* part of last night.

And now that it's reentered my brain, I can't not think about it.

"Yeah," I say hoarsely. "About that."

"Hm?" Morgan looks up.

"The...all of them?" I say. I don't even know how to describe it. "Showing up like that?"

"Oh," Morgan says, as if she'd somehow forgotten about it. "*That.* Yeah. It's part of their whole code. *Very* chivalrous. They always have to come to the defense of a woman in need. Isn't that cute?"

I blink. "Code?"

She nods. "That, and the no dating thing. And a few other rules. Personally, I think they take it all a bit seriously, but..." She scrunches up her mouth. "They have their reasons, I suppose."

Elena's face flashes into my memory.

And risk our winning streak? How could you say that?

"Must be working," I say.

Morgan frowns. "Working?" she repeats. And for the first time all morning, there's a little edge to her voice.

I'm not sure where I stepped in it, but I clarify quickly. "Like, they always win their fencing...matches? Right? So it must be working."

"Ah." Morgan relaxes. "That they do," she murmurs. "That they do."

A beat of silence passes.

"Well, thanks for...defending me," I say suddenly. "And for lending me the clothes," I add. "I appreciate it."

Morgan smiles beneficently. "Of course. What are roommates for?"

I'm...not sure, I think. *But maybe this.*

"You looked great, by the way," she adds, pushing her way off the bed and up to her wardrobe. "If you're ever lacking appropriate attire, just holler."

Something about the way she says it pings a memory in my mind.

And dread fills my stomach.

I sink back into the bed, staring at the ceiling.

Morgan notices, and almost jumps when she sees me lying prone. "What's wrong? Are you diabetic or something? Do you need orange juice?"

I frown. That's random. "No, I..." I blink hard. "I just remember I have my swim test tomorrow."

"Ah," Morgan says. "Okay." I can tell by her tone that she doesn't see the issue. And—fair point. I can't blame her. "So you'll go to your swim test. It's a pain in the ass, don't get me wrong, but...you can swim, right?"

I nod. "Yeah, but...I don't even have a swimsuit."

That's not the problem. That's not even close to the problem. But I'm not about to share more about what is.

"Why do we even have to have a swim test?" I mutter.

Morgan turns back to her wardrobe.

"One of those campus legend things, I think," she says, picking out hanger after hanger. "The founder had a daughter who drowned, tragically young and beautiful, blah, blah, blah, and so one of their conditions for funding the university was that every student had to know how to swim."

A beat of silence passes. Then Morgan unceremoniously dumps the heap of clothing in her arms onto the bed.

"Here. Take your pick."

My eyes widen at the array of options before me. Swimsuits. All of them bright, many of them embellished, and none of them especially modest.

"Oh," I say. "Um…" I scratch the back of my neck.

"You hate them," she says. "You think I have terrible taste."

"No," I say quickly, although to be honest, it's not the *least* tacky collection of swimwear I've ever seen. One of them, at least, has a high neckline, a sort of turtleneck situation…and very low-cut bottoms.

Morgan folds her hands on top of the bathing suits. "Then?"

I breathe out. What's the most reasonable way to phrase this? The least…suspicious?

"I just…don't like showing that much of my body," I say. "Is all."

I fold my arms over my chest, almost on instinct.

Morgan, to my surprise, nods. "I respect that," she says, and I actually believe her. She shoves the bright tangle of nylon and hangers to the side. "Here. I'll do you one better."

TEN

CALLAHAN

THE WATER IS SO cold and calm I almost hate to disturb it.

Splash.

Almost, but not quite.

I plunge under, breath trailing from my lips in bubbles, hands knifing in front to pull my body to surface, and breathe.

Lake swimming isn't like pool swimming. No burn of chlorine or squeaking echoes of a massive gymnasium, *thweets* of whistles or coaches yelling *come on, O'Brian, push it!* Just water, poured out wherever the rain put it, speckled with pine needles and faintly swirling with silt.

I shake my head to clear the water from my eyes and inhale again, treading water. It's early; the sky above is steel gray and the water looks almost leaden beneath it, the only color the deep green of the forest that rings the far edge. Another thing I like—no concrete lip to cling on, no slick tiles to push off of, only a slow sweep of sand up to shore.

I dive back under.

Swimming used to be everything. Was going to give me everything, or so I'd been told since I hit my growth spurt late in elementary and the coaches from Catholic Memorial started eyeing me up as I swam laps at the Boys & Girls Club off Morrissey Boulevard. An education. A scholarship—to Caliburn University, no less. A way out of Neponset and into real life. Something to make nice Meggie and Sean O'Brian proud of their only son.

Now, it's occasional. A visit to who I used to be. A memory. Just like my parents.

I kick in earnest, slicing my arms and turning my shoulders through the churn of icy water—no temperature control here—and suck in air through my bluing lips. I don't know if the cold is the point, or the quiet, but either way, I need it. Need this, even after everything.

Somewhere to my left, down in the depths of Camlann House, the other three are doing their morning conditioning, but I get dispensation for my own version—Kingston's insistence. The mental benefits just as important as the physical, he says, and mentally, I need to swim. Even if I can't do it competitively. I wonder what they get up to in there, idly try to picture it—weights, cardio sprints, stretching—and before I know it my mind has focused in on just one of them in my mind's eye. Flushed skin, bright eyes, lips parted with effort—

God.

I'd known I liked boys before Lanz. Six years at Catholic Memorial, torturous hours at swim practice and the locker room looking at their lean forms, their broad shoulders, the rare and furtive glance of more, all had me burning up on the inside. But I couldn't do anything. Couldn't risk it. Didn't want to, if I'm being honest: didn't take risks by nature. Still don't. I made it all very clear. When the girls from Fontbonne came up to me at a mixer or a field day, everyone knew that Callahan O'Brian was saving himself for marriage.

Then everything fell apart. I couldn't swim. Couldn't earn my keep. Started to sink. And he was the one to pull me out.

A burn in my lungs—I'm straining—and I gasp to the surface, panting hard. I catch my breath, feel the acid ebb out of my muscles, and for a moment, I float.

The lake at Caliburn is more than just an ordinary lake. Especially for them—for us. For the fencing team.

But for me, Callahan, all it needs to be is ordinary. Cold, calm. Holding me up.

Then I hear someone else.

I pivot upright, pushing water to spin myself in the direction of the sound, and there I see it: a line of buoys on the far side of the lake, the shore closest to the Field House and farthest from Camlann. A single lane, for a single swimmer. I frown: no one ever swims in the lake, not this early. An occasional drunken dip after a cap, yes. An early-morning swim? No. Unless you're me.

Through the wisps of fog, I see two figures emerge: both female, one in a red one-piece and ponytail and the other in an honest-to-God wetsuit, ankles to knees.

Immediately, almost instinctively, I recognize her.

The girl from last night. The one we...defended. The first time I, at least, had ever had to uphold that part of our code.

And I recognize the other one, too.

Elena. Swim team captain—late roster add for the women's team, apparently took Caliburn's scholarship as a backup. But this isn't practice.

What is she doing?

My breathing, just leveled out, picks back up again.

I'm done—I should be done, the others will be done inside and getting showered and eating before team meeting—but I can't swim back to shore.

Not yet.

Call it protective. Call it *over*protective. Call it compensating for the people I couldn't save.

But I can't just leave her here.

ELEVEN

GWENNA

THE LAKE LOOKS as cold and miserable as I feel.

It's the color of iron, but smooth, unlike the churned-up clouds of the sky overhead. I shiver, despite the coverage of the wetsuit that, improbably, Morgan not only owns, but let me borrow. It covers my scars, and apparently adds buoyancy to boot, which will help, because I sink like a stone.

Too late, I realize I should have brought a swim cap, or at least a hair tie. It'll be ridiculous trying to thrash my way through the water with my hair loose, but I don't have time to go back now. I already had to reroute when I got to the field house and saw the notice on the door: SWIM TEST STUDENTS PLEASE PROCEED TO SOUTHWEST SHORE. I'm lucky I'm even close to on time.

On the surface, a row of orange buoys bob up and down like cereal marshmallows in milk, and I idly wonder what the actual test is. Out and back, laps, treading water. I rub my upper arms.

In front of me, there's a small plaque sunk into the face of a rock—a name and a few lines of Latin in simple brass.

Vivian Thorne

Loved much, lost too soon.

Custodiat hunc locum amoenum in eterna.

May she watch over this lovely place for eternity.

It's a nice sentiment, until I remember the rumors that someone drowned in this lake. Was it her? And they put a memorial up *right by the lake*? That's downright macabre.

"And...there you are."

The voice behind me is cold and sharp as broken glass.

I turn and my stomach drops.

Pacing out from the field house, clad in a red one-piece, is Elena. Her brown hair is scooped back into a perfect ponytail, and her beautifully shaped brows are drawn.

Oh no, I think. *She's taking the test with me? But she's been here for weeks. She should have—*

She lifts her arm to reveal a clipboard, a stopwatch, and my stomach plunges further.

No, I think. *Of course she's not* taking *the test. She's* proctoring *it.*

"Welcome to your physical fitness test," she says, the barest hint of heat creeping into her words.

I look around us. Are we being watched? Monitored? *Who proctors the proctors?* I think idly, a bit of dark humor as I stare out into the choppy surface of the lake.

My stomach tightens.

I don't want to do this.

Even more than I didn't want to do it before.

I should say something. I have to say something.

"Elena, about the other night," I start. "I—"

"*Save it.*" The words are all but barked out. Elena looks up at me, eyes fierce, but then her expression softens. "I mean..." She clears her throat. "Just...don't worry about it, Gwenna. I was... overreacting. Had too much to drink." She smiles, tips her head. "And I certainly didn't realize you had the whole fencing team behind you."

Neither did I, I think. I wait for her to say something more, but she doesn't. I'm halfway to forming some words myself when she jumps back in.

"Before we begin, I have to ask you some questions." Elena clicks her pen. "You are...Gwenna?" She says my name like it tastes bad.

I nod. "Yes." Although how I wish I wasn't.

Suddenly, I wonder if this is even worth it. The swim test. The semester. Proving myself at all.

I could give up. I could go home.

I could let them win.

"Question two," Elena interrupts my train of thoughts. "Can you swim?"

"Y-Yes," I stammer.

Instantly, she looks up.

"Yes?" she says. "Or no?"

"Um—"

"It's a simple question," she practically snaps. "Can you, or can't you?"

"I can..." I don't know how to finish the sentence. I've never swum a lap for a race, or even just for exercise, but I've been in bodies of water and survived. "I can not drown," I say at last.

Elena sets her jaw. But her eyes brighten.

"Interesting," she says, tapping her clipboard with the pen.

"Interesting?" I echo.

"I'm only supposed to administer this if you confirm that you can swim. Otherwise, it's too dangerous." A little smile creeps over her lips. "I'm sure you'll do fine. I'm a certified lifeguard, after all. I would never let someone innocent drown."

I choose to ignore the adjective. But a slow panic is feeding into my skin, taking over me from the bottom up, from where my sneakers are uneven on the sand to the crown of my head being ruffled by the lakeside wind.

Like her sweetness is all an act.

Like I'm about to make a mistake.

"The test is," Elena goes on, "swim to the furthest buoy and back, and do it under the time limit."

"Time limit?" I repeat. "Which is?"

"Fifteen minutes," she says, almost laughing. "You think you can manage it?"

"Yes," I say, this time with more confidence than I feel.

Fifteen minutes is an eternity, I tell myself. And the buoys are...I squint. I've never been a good judge of distance based on eyesight alone. Fifty yards? Maybe a hundred? Walking it would be no problem. Running it, even. Swimming the greenish water of the lake that's lapping at the sand...that, I'm less certain about.

"Oh, and you'll need to..." She eyes me up and down. "You can't wear a wetsuit."

"What?" My stomach sinks. "Why not?"

"They help you float," Elena says simply. "That'd be cheating." She tips her head. "You do have a normal swimsuit under there, don't you?"

I do. But.

"Your time starts," Elena says, unceremoniously, and holds up a stopwatch. "Now."

She clicks the button with a thumb, then frowns down at her stopwatch in confusion. "Oh, would you look at that?" she says, and holds out the tiny screen. "Seems I already started it. You've only got ten minutes left."

I clench my fists. Shift my weight from foot to foot.

No, I decide. I don't trust her. I *shouldn't* trust her. With her here, this isn't even a swim test anymore. It's a setup, a trial of more than my ability to swim, and one that I know for certain that Elena wants me to fail—no matter how giggly she is about it.

"Tick tock," she says, waggling her stopwatch. "You're down to nine and a half minutes."

My muscles stiffen involuntarily. Fifteen was brisk but generous. Under ten will be a push.

But what choice do I have?

I reach for the long-tailed zipper at the back of my neck and slowly pull it down, peeling the wetsuit from my body.

I can feel her staring, know she is, even without looking, because who wouldn't?

My body's a testament to everything that's wrong with me.

And now she sees it.

Just get it over with.

Toeing out of my sneakers, I step to the edge of the water. It's cold, bracingly so, but I have no choice. There's no going back.

I go in up to my ankles, take a deep, deep breath, and spring forward.

It's not an elegant dive, more of a belly flop with my hands out forward, but it's something. A plunge, head first, a sign that I'm going to try.

The water eats me. Cold as an acid burn, Morgan's swimsuit pasted to my skin, and I gasp as I emerge, hair streaming behind me. Before me, the buoys bob in an obedient line, a garish orange against the steel gray, and I suck in another breath, resolute.

Be normal, I tell myself.

I surge forward with my right arm, then my left, face just kissing the edge of the water as I do the freestyle. My middle school swim lessons feel like a lifetime ago, from the lifetime of a different person, and in a way they were.

But I've remembered enough to move forward. I've remembered enough to keep going. To not drown.

And that's what I'm going to show Elena. To show everyone.

I slice forward—right, left, right, *breathe*; right, left, right, *breathe*—and chance a look ahead when I emerge.

I've barely gone anywhere. Surpassed maybe one and a half of the buoys, and there's another half dozen or more to go. My muscles lock—from nerves or from the cold, I can't tell.

But I refuse to stop moving.

I thrust my chest forward again, pulling with my arms, pushing at the water, wasting energy, I know, judging by the froth I'm stirring up. Right, left, right. I open my eyes again, and this time it truly feels like I've gone nowhere, except for the fact that the sandy bottom has dropped away.

In its place, a void has opened beneath me. Like I'm floating on top of an abyss.

The cold tightens around me. My chest constricts around my organs like my ribcage is a closing bear trap. And maybe it's my imagination, but I swear I can feel a pulse of pain in the two scarred slashes just above my heart.

No, I think. *No.* I'm not going to fail. I'm not going to give her or anyone else the satisfaction.

But I'm sinking, sagging, and I can feel it. My hips are dragging. My feet are stumbling against waves and currents rather than kicking at the surface and powering me forward. And all the while, I hear nothing, nothing but the muffled scattering of drops and the frantic panting of my own breathing. Nothing from Elena, no time markers, no words of encouragement, obviously, and no indication that she'll save me if it comes to that.

And it might be coming to that.

It's too cold, I think. Too cold to swim in. Too, too cold. How quickly does hypothermia set in?

Left, right, left, right—

I'm seesawing now from side to side, not keeping myself flat like I know I should, but I'm fighting my instincts. My body wants to contract, to shiver. To warm up the blood flow in those organs.

And I can't. Not if I want to move forward. I can't indulge a moment of care for myself. I have to push, I have to—

I slip under.

For a second, it's so calm. Still. A weightless, breathless silence. Nothing to see. Nothing to hear. Nothing but the sensation of my hair fanning out around me like a spectral mermaid.

No.

The word flashes in my mind's eye like a firework, like a sudden vision.

No, I can't. I can't give that to Elena, to my mother, to the rest of them.

No. No. No.

I may not be brave, but I am angry. And that will have to be enough.

The chill presses in on me as I claw upward. I pinwheel my arms above me, ineptly pushing and scratching my way to the surface, to the light I can just barely barely make out, even with my eyes open and gritty with the silt of the lake.

And when I open my eyes, I see it.

A shimmer just beyond the silt and dark.

Pale hair undulating like streamers, face still and luminous in the water, her eyes open and trained on me. Glimmering—*glowing.*

A human. A woman, in a flowing dress of unearthly greenish white, her eyes black voids, her face placid.

Vivian.

I don't know how I know it's her. Lack of oxygen, a panic response, another mental break. Who knows, who cares.

It's her. I know it's her.

Shining. Protecting. Beautiful and unreal and probably *not* real.

But she's not going to let me drown.

Except then I blink, and she's gone.

The water is just water, not glowing. And just as quickly as my resolve had appeared, another thought takes its place.

Too late.

I waited too long. I sank too deep. I'm not going to be able to make it on my own.

I pushed too far, and this is the consequence.

Yet just as I'm thinking it, something firm and warm wraps around my waist...

...and then I'm rising, pulled irresistibly upward like I weigh nothing. Soaring and surging upward until—

Crash. I, *we*, break the surface of the lake. My burning throat and lungs gulp for air as my panicked vision swims in search of focus.

"I've got you," a male voice says. "Don't panic. Don't flail."

It's not Elena. It's—

But before I can see the face of my rescuer, he's pulling me to shore, left arm wrapped around my waist, right arm cutting forward, almost effortlessly, in time with his legs, moving faster as a duo than I could have managed by myself. The return trip seems to take half the time, like we're just gliding over the surface, skimming smooth as a sailboat, until my knees are hitting soft sand and I can crawl forward.

Coughing, gasping, I fall out of his grasp, and that's when I look back and see it's the boy from Saturday night. Or one of them. The tallest one, the biggest and most silent.

Callahan.

What the hell was he doing out at the lake at this hour?

Pine needles and dirt cling to my fingers, push into my knees as my breath catches and sticks and water burns out of my throat until finally, finally I'm breathing regular again.

"You shouldn't be out here," Callahan says.

He hasn't stood, just sits on his knees in the lapping edge of the water, looking at me with concern. He's wearing skin-tight, knee-length swim trunks...and that's it. Yet he doesn't seem cold at all.

I splutter. "You're one to talk," I manage.

He doesn't react, and I feel an immediate pang of shame. He just rescued me, maybe saved my life, and this is how I act?

I swallow, which hurts.

"I'm so sorry. That's not what I meant. I just—"

"I come out here for conditioning," he explains. "Before we practice in the morning. It's..." he trails off. "My own form of discipline."

He gives me a probing look, searching for signs of damage, and I notice for the first time how handsome he is. An arresting thought to have at a moment like this, but it's hard *not* to notice, especially when he's wearing barely anything and water is clinging to the ends of his long, thick eyelashes.

"What did you think you were doing?" he said, his tone softer than it should be, less accusatory.

I shake my head, checking for water in my ears, and as I do, look around the shore. There's no one.

I'm alone.

"I was...she..." I sweep my wet hair out of my eyes. "God damn it. My swim test," I say. "That girl Elena was here to proctor it for me."

Callahan's jaw tightens.

"The swim tests are done in the pool," he says.

What?

"But I saw a sign—"

"She's swim team captain," he mutters. "She should know better."

I fold my arms against a sudden, chill breeze.

"I think she *does* know better," I mutter. To myself or to him, I'm not sure.

Because I get it. Get the joke.

Funny prank. Let the new girl drown. Let her join Vivian in the depths of the...

I shiver.

Whatever I saw in there, I don't want to think about. Don't want to be real.

Because it isn't. None of it's real.

Not what I saw here.

Not what I saw in the church back home.

Not real. Not real. Not real.

All the while, Callahan says nothing. Just narrows his eyes, almost imperceptibly, firms his mouth to a line.

"You're shivering," he says, and I realize I am. Shaking, practically. I hug myself tighter, push myself to standing, and he scrambles up after me, offering an arm that feels steady and strong as a bough of oak.

"Thank you for—" I shake my head. "I guess rescuing me."

Callahan nods and withdraws his hand swiftly once it's clear I've found my balance, like he doesn't want to risk touching me too long. But it's different than the way Kingston did it. No edge of disgust that I may or may not be imagining. Just simple, precise duty.

"You should look after yourself around here," he says. "Please take better care, all right?"

I'm astonished. No one's ever said anything like that to me.

Take care, in a way that sounds genuine. Shuddering with cold, as water drips down my back, I nod.

TWELVE

KAI

WROUGHT IRON, stone, and silence.

The ceilings arch overhead, banners hanging dark like reminders of everything we're supposed to uphold. We sit—Kingston, Lanz, and me—lined up at the Black Table like obedient soldiers.

I hate it. Like we're in a fucking cathedral instead of the second basement level of Camlann House.

But that's the point. The quiet, the secrecy, the ceremonial bullshit. The empty ivory throne that's ceremonially unoccupied, the round table. Supposed to be egalitarian—no one at the head, no one at the foot. A cute little circle.

But somehow, Kingston always manages to take things over.

"Next meet," he declares. "Coming soon." His hair's still damp from the shower, golden strands clinging to his temples. We were up at 5 a.m. for conditioning, and for once I woke up raring to go, like I was pre-caffeinated and had done a bump to boot.

Maybe it's the lingering effects of Saturday—of something actually interesting happening for once. Sure, it's mostly a hazy blur for me, and it all got cut short when Morgan bitched and moaned to Kingston and sounded the alarm, but still.

A change of pace. A fight I neither started nor found myself at the center of.

And call me a whore for drama—among other things—but my interest is piqued.

That girl Gwenna could be trouble.

And I *like* trouble.

"Sainte-Odile is watching," Kingston goes on. "So we need to—"

"Watching? What, in their crystal ball?" I cross an ankle over my knee and lean back, earning me a dagger-sharp stare from Kingston. *Bro, keep it up and I'll put my boots right on the fucking table.* "I just mean," I clarify, "what meet footage of us could they possibly have gotten? We don't film." I toss a side eye at Lanz. "Unless Pretty Boy here has an OnlyFans where he's selling us out."

Lanz flushes pink. Sweet summer child. But Kingston, humorless bastard, shuts it down like he always does.

"An assistant coach at the scrimmage," he says. "Watched and took notes."

Just that, but it lands like a bell toll.

Sainte-Odile's fine. School out of Quebec, same old-style fencing as us. Good enough to trip us up if we're sloppy, but usually that's not a problem.

Usually.

I grip my knee until it aches while King and Cal get into details about Sainte-Odile's lineup, but my mind keeps drifting. Back to Saturday.

You'd think, with us being avowedly celibate and all, that we wouldn't be the subject of relationship drama on campus. But you'd think wrong. A place like Caliburn tends to attract the, let's say, *nerdier* variety of male students—not exactly physical specimens—which leaves our poor, lustful coeds with no one to pine after but the athletes—us, basically. Because what's sexier than forbidden fruit? Hell, I'd bet folding money that more than a few mattress springs in Broceliande Hall have been worn out from some desperately horny girls squinting their eyes shut and rubbing one out to fantasies of yours truly.

So the fact that Elena Shalott's been creaming her panties for Lanz since orientation day isn't exactly groundbreaking.

But an honest-to-God catfight? That's a real novelty.

Especially when one of the kittens seemed *totally* uninterested in the prize. I don't know who this Gwenna Vale is—besides some kind of Latin genius, judging by her placement test results—but what I do know, I like.

That, to me, is a girl worth keeping an eye on.

"Where's Cal?" Lanz frowns, and it's only then that I notice Callahan isn't here yet. I look left and right, exaggerating my search.

"Getting his land legs back?" I shrug. "I don't fucking know."

How someone goes from a championship swimmer to a championship fencer in the course of a little less than a year is beyond me. That takes at least equal parts discipline and raw talent, and personally, I've only got one of those. When Callahan turned up as essentially a walk-on to our squad, I was skeptical to say the least. But I have to hand it to the big guy: he's got the goods.

Kingston does his little disapproving schoolmarm frown. "It's not like him to be late. Did he—"

The door bursts open. And there he is. Callahan.

"So good of you to join us," I say. *Someone* has to break the tension, and Kingston's sanctimonious silence pisses me off more than anything. "We were just discussing how Sainte-Odile is going to kick our ass. Want to weigh in?"

Cal ignores me. "She almost drowned."

"What?" Kingston says, irritation in his tone. "Who?"

"The new girl," Cal says. "Gwenna."

Even the sound of her name has my already-pumping blood going faster. I can't help it.

"In the lake," Cal goes on. "I was out swimming and—"

"The hell was she doing out in the lake?" I ask. Is this girl nuts? The water's probably fifty degrees max, and you've gotta have polar bear DNA like Callahan O'Brian to survive that, let alone opt for it.

Or...

...or does she know?

I feel Kingston's glare before I see it. Because he's wondering the same thing.

"Did she see anything?"

"Seriously?" This, from Lanz. "Cal comes in and says someone almost drowns in the lake, and the first thing you ask is whether she *saw anything?*"

Kingston glowers. "We never know when the Lady might awaken. And if this girl was out there on her own, she might know to look for—"

"No, no," Callahan says, shaking his head. "It wasn't like that. It was some kind of setup. Her swim test. Elena Shalott was proctoring her test. Tricked her into going to the lake."

Whoa. Juicy. My eyebrows go up. But Kingston isn't having it.

"That's not our problem." His voice could split stone. "Any of our problem."

A pointed glance in my direction. I press a hand to my chest, eyebrows high. *Me, your honor?*

Kingston ignores it. Callahan, meanwhile, protests.

"But—"

"Can we focus, please?" Kingston all but roars. "Need I remind you why we are all here?" he goes on, voice iron. His eyes flick down to the center of the table, to the hidden Caliburn crest designed into the wood itself.

"We have a mission," he goes on. "We have a charge. A

commitment to excellence in the pursuit of the greater good." His stare pins Cal in place. "I understand you're the newest, Callahan, but getting involved in this kind of—"

"No," Cal chokes. "I'm fine. I'm sorry, Kingston."

He drops into the seat next to me, face pale, knuckles white. On his other side, Lanz, too, looks worried. Way more worried than anyone should be. And Cal glances his way, just once, quick and desperate, like he needs reassurance only Lanz can give.

Well, fair enough. Because he sure as hell isn't getting it from me.

"Yes," I mutter, flipping open my pocket knife to clean under my nails. "Heaven forbid we perform under pressure. Let's all build ourselves a little hermetic tube so we never make contact with the outside world. Just study hard, play with our swords, and figure out where X marks the spot so we can find—"

Kingston narrows his eyes at me.

"*Quiet*," he barks.

To my surprise, I shut up.

It sounds ridiculous when I put it that way, I know. But to be fair, it sounds ridiculous even when I *don't* put it that way. It sure as hell did to me, anyway: *seek the Holy Grail?*

Fucking *excuse me?*

But damned if I haven't seen shit since then that's convinced me. Convinced me enough to sign on, body, mind, and soul.

A loyal knight. Just like all of us.

Kingston starts droning strategy again, voice flat, eyes sharp. Cal stares straight ahead. Lanz fidgets like he always does: 10% man, 90% nervous energy.

That's the real problem with this table. It's supposed to be this sacred thing that brings us all together, unites us in brotherhood and service, proves us all to be equals no matter what and blah blah fucking blah.

In reality? It's all tilting one way. Ever since the Lady of the Lake made her decision.

Ever since she picked Kingston.

He's supposed to be leading this. Leading us.

But this death grip of his, this hero complex and hardass attitude…

It's ripping us apart.

Finally, when what feels like two hours have passed and I'm hungry enough to gnaw off my own arm, Kingston declares we're done.

"Kai. Wait."

Except, apparently, me.

I skid to an exaggerated stop, just a few feet from the door and just a few steps away from whatever's waiting for us in the dining room, which smells absolutely fucking delicious.

So this had better be important.

"Yes?" I say. All innocence. *Until proven guilty*, I think.

At the table, Kingston sits with his back straight, arms folded, like the anal-retentive CEO he'd probably have ended up becoming if his destiny wasn't all wrapped up in this wild fucking goose chase for a magical cup.

"Father knows," he says. "About this weekend."

"Oh?"

I only half-remember what happened. But I remember enough to remember that I was probably a dick—a justified dick, but not like that matters.

I fold my arms.

"So you ratted me out," I clarify. "Is what you're saying."

"I informed him that you'd had an incident," Kingston says. Pitch-perfect bureaucratese. Jesus Christ, he really could be one of those psychopath billionaires. Christian Bale could play him. Or that cannibal guy from the Facebook movie. "As in keeping with the code we follow."

"Oh, well, *then*," I say, soaking my words in sarcasm. "What'll it be this time? The iron maiden, or the rack?"

Kingston doesn't laugh. Doesn't even fucking *twitch*.

"Repercussions aren't up to me," he says. "If the Consistory feels that the violation was severe enough, then the code says—"

"The code says, the code says," I singsong. "You know what we used to say, on the *mean streets* of Chicago?" I all but snarl. "Snitches get stitches. That was our *code*. Is that what you want, *bro?*"

Sudden as a lightning strike, Kingston gets to his feet.

"I *want*, Kai," he bites out, "for you to get your goddamn *act* together. Take this seriously. For once." He hardens his eyes on me. "Do you even understand how *critical* this whole thing is? Do you—"

"Maybe. Maybe not," I interrupt. "What difference does it make?" I shrug, resisting every urge to haul off and deck him again. Twice in three days is *probably* too much. "I'm just hired muscle. Work me 'til I'm useless, then cut me loose." I plant my palms on the table, lean over so we're eye to eye. "And if you don't know how to do that, just ask your fucking father."

THIRTEEN

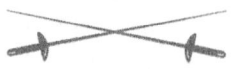

GWENNA

THE DAY DOESN'T GET BETTER from there. I hustle back to our room and take a scalding hot shower, but Morgan's already gone for her three-hour seminar, so I brave the dining hall alone. Not that I'm even that hungry.

Someone "accidentally" spills an entire glass of water across my tray, leaving my waffle and bacon soggy. When I'm rushing off to calculus, someone holds the door, only to let it slam in my face and almost stub the toe of my boot.

And as I'm walking through the building after class, I hear two girls whispering to each other, a few feet away.

I am, fully and entirely, *persona non grata*.

I don't give them the satisfaction of a reaction and just hide my face, walking briskly to the only place that I think will be safe, the alcove at the very back of the library on the B2 level. It's where I spent my first day and where I'm starting to suspect I'll spend a lot of days, crammed where there's no sunlight and very few people, surrounded by compact, movable shelves that don't even work with a touch button, but instead a series of hand cranks. Inside them are all kinds of dull, thick, undigitized records. The sort of minutiae that you'd have to be dedicated or a PhD student to get into. And further beyond that, the archives.

Point being, nobody comes here. Not when there's a beautiful collegiate gothic aesthetic main study room, not to mention countless corridors with armchairs and study rooms.

But maybe that's for the best.

I crunch on the apple I swiped on my way out of breakfast and sit with my heels on the seat of the chair, compact and folded over.

They want to bully me? Play pranks? Fine. Sticks and stones. Name calling doesn't bother me. What is this, preschool?

I chew the apple, tasting like dust in my mouth, as a single tear trickles down my cheek.

Be normal, I think. *Be happy. You belong here as much as anyone else. You belong here more than anywhere else.*

When I get up at last with just ten minutes to get to Latin, my scarf hooks on the edge of the chair, pulls itself from my throat as I stand up. It looks comfortable there, the deep red against the polished wood of the arms.

Impulsively, I decide to leave it there. A test, maybe, to see, who, if anyone, comes down here. If I return and it's gone or moved, I'll know.

If not, I've got a place to hide. And that, more than anything, is valuable.

———+———

LATIN 302 IS at the very top of the Classics building, and I fail to account for just how long it takes to scale the stairs. There's no listed textbook, so I'm coming with just a notebook and pens and the half-digested apple in my stomach and a fierce curiosity for what this Dr. Emrys is all about. *This truly is the heart of what*

Caliburn University means, I think, thudding up step after step in the echoing stairwell.

This is what we're meant to be learning and studying: the oldest, the most obscure, the trickiest, the least useful, in a lot of senses.

This is, and this must be—

"Gwenna."

My boots skid to a squeaking stop as I get to the threshold. The room is smaller than I had expected, with just two windows and a cramped series of two-person tables pushed in front of a battered teacher's desk at the front. A handful of stares fall on me. Five people. That's all there is in this class. And one of them is, yes, the professor.

"You are Gwenna?"

Oh. I pant out a breath or two from the effort of scaling up the steps as much as the shock of seeing him here.

Kingston.

I never would have had him pegged as a Latin student, let alone one this advanced. Maybe that's dickish of me to say, but... in my experience, the guys who get really into the study of dead and ancient languages look a lot more like Ponytail Brett and a lot less like GQ models.

"Very well," says the professor. "I'm Dr. Emrys, and I'm glad you finally made it."

He smiles, an avuncular smile. Kindly, but no nonsense. "Please, if you would," he gestures at the only empty seat in the room, the one next to Kingston.

Great, I think. I grip my bag strap harder and slide into place.

"Your timing is fortuitous," Dr. Emrys goes on, "as we've just finished the, shall we say, warm-up portion of our semester. As the rest of these illustrious students know, I don't teach based on mere translation or memorization. I am here to recruit you to the legions of scholars who have studied these texts for thousands of years. To crack open some of their mysteries and telegraph their meaning to the world."

Okay, I think, *a little intense*. But then again, classics professors tend to have a flair for the theatrical. And this man, well… theatrical might be too strong a word, but he's certainly quirky. He's dressed in classic college professor garb, tweed jacket, rumpled sweater, the whole bit, but all in a shade of dusky purple, like he's cosplaying Professor Plum from the board game Clue. His hair, shockingly white, as is his beard. I'd say he looks like Santa Claus, except he's much too thin. And while there's a twinkle in his eyes, I wouldn't say he's coming off particularly jolly.

Instinctively, I sit straighter in my seat, pull out a notebook, and set a pen on top of it. To my left, Kingston moves his own note supplies an inch further away. I set my jaw. He could just be being polite, or he could be avoiding me like I have leprosy, like everyone else on this campus seems to be, except his stepsister.

"As you all may know," Dr. Emrys goes on, "These codices, manuscripts, and books are not only valuable for their looks and for their rarity, but for the knowledge that is contained within them. These days, we see scraped sheepskin bound in leather, written upon with boiled ink from a quill clutched long ago in a freezing scriptorium, and think of it as some kind of bespoke treasure, which, to be sure, it *was* a luxury. A flock of sheep in every book." A few murmurs of laughter from the class, not from Kingston or from me. "But in their essence, books were created then for the same reason they are now: to record, to transmit, to explain, to make permanent and articulate the mysterious truths of nature, and the vagaries of human thought. We stand on the shoulders of giants. Don't we, Gwenna?"

I startle a bit. "Um. Yes. Bernard of Chartres?"

There's a flicker in his gaze, like I've passed a first test. "That is," he says, "indeed, who coined that phrase."

He turns to the desk, and to a sheaf of paper.

"Now. The primary work of this semester is transliteration. Not *translation,* or not *only* that. Trans*liter*ation: copying the way so many monks and learned men of yore copied before. It's one thing to translate black and white text from a typeset book in the Harvard Classical Library, all cleaned up and prettified for you. It's another entirely to deal with the messy realities of the primary document: poor handwriting, damaged leaves, muddiness all around. But for you, who are in this class, you are here because this is a pursuit you intend to continue for the rest of your scholarly careers, and indeed your lives."

At that I slide a glance at Kingston. I really don't see him as go-to-grad-school-and-get-an-obscure-PhD material, but what do I know?

"This is the grunt work that you must now be familiar with, in sum," says Dr. Emrys. "And now…we practice." He steps around to our tables, handing out a facsimile of a manuscript page, a photocopy or something similar, but clearly the source material is vellum, crackling with age and the barest sheen of animal fat that can never be tanned out of a manuscript page, scratched up and down with minuscule, the handwriting I know of but have never really *read*. I can make out an occasional et or ut, but at a glance, it all looks like tiny lines, little hash marks like a prisoner would keep on the wall of his cell to mark the days.

It's dense, impossible.

"Why so small, you may ask?" Dr. Emrys goes on. "For good reason. Which is…" he turns this time to Kingston.

"Scarcity," Kingston says simply. "Books were rare. More words on a page was economical."

"Indeed, indeed," says Dr. Emrys, nodding approval. "Not a particularly future-proof solution, but the men, and I'm sorry to say they were mostly men, of the 9th, 10th, 11th, 12th centuries, did not have the college students of the 21st in mind when they put these collections together. So!" He rubs his hands together. "Dive in, in partners, and we'll see who can make the best of it."

"What do you want us to do?" says a girl's voice from the back.

"Copy out. Transliterate," Dr. Emrys says. "It's a text you'll find familiar once you figure it out."

I look at it and can't believe this is the truth. It feels like a magic eye painting, something I need to stare at from varying distances until it all slides into place. "We've got about 35 minutes left in class, so I'll give you an even half hour. First pair to complete transliteration and translation wins..." He frowns as if he hadn't thought this far. "I'm not sure. Something enticing. Perhaps you'll name your prize—if any of you finishes, that is. And...*pergite!*"

Notebooks are flipped open, pens uncapped. Everyone hunches in over the paper. Everyone, of course, except Kingston, who sits with a ramrod straight back and simply inclines his head.

Wordlessly, he glances between the page and his blank sheet of notebook paper. Printing out with careful precision some options for the first line. Mostly gibberish, from what I can tell. The requisite Latin endings for words, *um*s and *us*es, but not coming together into any words I'm familiar with.

He pauses, looks at me, staring.

"Do you need help?" he asks, voice low.

I blush, in spite of myself. "No," I say fiercely. *Although we're supposed to be working as a team*, I think, *but I suppose that only applies to you if there's a sword involved. Otherwise it's every man for himself.*

Instead, I chew the end of my pen, wishing I had something more substantial to eat, and study it.

My approach is more haphazard than Kingston's. He's writing

straight across, copying out every word line for line. I write down columns, options for each word, and for where they could divide.

It's fiendishly hard to tell. There's no spaces between words, nothing at all but guesswork, so I draw slashes for various places they could fall in my transliteration, like solving a jigsaw puzzle in reverse. My handwriting has always been terrible, and all I have is a crappy ballpoint on a drugstore notebook while Kingston, of course, has creamy perfect bound pages and what looks like an actual Montblanc fountain pen. Well, fine. I don't need expensive stationery to do this well. I've translated Latin in classrooms with black mold and water-wrinkled textbooks. Hell, I took the AP exam at the local public school that was later found out to have a radon leak. This, by comparison, is luxury.

No, not even by comparison, I think. I indulge myself in a pause and look around. *This is* it, I think. Bookcases crammed with the full Loeb Classical Library of Cicero and Vergil and Ovid, fading posters of the Colosseum, of Mont-Saint-Michel, of the Bayeux Tapestry, the clanking radiator that's not doing much to keep the room warm, the quiet murmuring, the eccentric professor, the smell of paper and distant woodsmoke.

It's my dream. It's what I wanted. And I'm here.

I will not let anyone take this from me, I vow. Not Elena, not Kingston, not even myself.

A rumble yanks me out of my daydream, a rumble I realize with horror is coming from my own stomach. I press my forearm against the front of my sweater, trying to muffle it, but that does nothing, of course. Kingston moves, but barely, like I startled him, but he's instinctively too polite to acknowledge the audible bodily functions of anyone next to him, especially, I suppose, a girl.

I bite my lip and swallow my spit, as if that maybe is enough for my stomach to digest and stay quiet. I scratch more along the words, darting back. *If the sentence ends here, which it would because that's the verb, then that would mean…no, that doesn't make any sense.*

I scribble out an entire column of words and start again. Meanwhile, Kingston is writing elegantly, no scratch-outs, only lines neatly arranged like soldiers on the battlefield. I keep going, and again, a stomach rumble. Fainter this time, but still noticeable.

Behind me, someone snickers. I'm sure it's hilarious, I think. If everyone on campus weren't determined to make my mealtimes so difficult, maybe I wouldn't be starving by the time my afternoon class rolled around.

This time, Kingston does move, and I flinch, ready for him to say something cutting, or to scooch further away from me, but he doesn't. Instead, he dips down to his own leather bag and slips a hand inside retrieving something crinkly that he sets on the table between us.

It's a plastic sleeve of almonds. Roasted. Unsalted. Unopened.

"Ah, the humble almond." Dr. Emrys appears in front of our table. "Feeling a bit peckish, Mr. Pendragon?" He smiles. "Did it occur to you to ask for permission to eat in this class? I don't like making a habit of it, even around facsimiles."

"They're not mine," Kingston says. "They're hers."

Hers, I think. Like he can't even say my name. And what is he trying to do? Pin this whole thing on me so that I get in trouble again for something completely trivial?

"In many medieval depictions of Jesus Christ," Dr. Emrys says, hefting the package aloft, "the almond plays a critical role. Do you know what that is?"

Kingston shakes his head, even looks at me as if I'm supposed to know. I shake my head too.

"The risen savior is depicted within an oblong shaped aura of light," Dr. Emrys goes on, "not a halo per se, but a whole body encasement with two pointed ends—like a narrow football, I suppose, although American football wouldn't be invented for centuries." He opens the package, tips a nut into his hand, and holds it between his thumb and forefinger, pointy sides, up and down. "You see? A mandorla, they call it. Italian for…"

"Almond," I finish.

Dr. Emrys smiles broader. "Precisely." He hands me the package. "No crumbs, Ms. Vale. And you're not to make a habit of this."

Stunned, not sure what to do, I just nod and accept the package from him like it had been mine all along. I look at Kingston, wondering if I should thank him, but he has gone back to his work, eyes focused once more. I sit there dumbly, not knowing what to do. I don't have any reason to think he's being nice, but I don't feel like I should trust him either. Then again, the package was sealed. They're Blue Diamond brand, nothing weird that I haven't heard of. And if he's trying to pull some shit…

My stomach growls again. *Stupid human body*, I think. I pour a small handful into my palm and crunch them away.

It's not much, but it's enough. And maybe it's the infinitesimal rise in my blood sugar, or maybe it's just the fact that Kingston did something wordless and arguably kind for me, despite giving me a literal cold shoulder sitting next to him. But when I look back at our manuscript facsimile, I see it.

"It's…" I whisper. I glance at Kingston, still trained on his notebook. "Kingston," I say, realizing too late how strange it sounds to say his name aloud.

He snaps to look at me, almost eerily quickly, and…those eyes. There's something about them. Not the color so much as the focus, the intensity. It's not cruel or judgmental, just…singular.

Like once I've commanded his attention, he'll take in nothing else until he's satisfied I've said my piece.

I don't like people seeing me like that.

Generally.

But I don't mind this.

I swallow, the almond dust clinging to my throat. "It's macaronic," I whisper. "Look." I trace my pen over the letters without writing on the facsimile: a cluster of letters, and then a little bit of ways, another. "It's Latin *and* Greek. The whole thing's a trick question."

Kingston looks away from me, stares at the paper. Stares so hard I think he might be avoiding engaging with me until I realize he's reading, without even having to transcribe it.

And then, at the corner of his mouth, the barest twitch of muscle. Satisfaction. Agreement.

"Of course it is," he murmurs. And darts a look at the front of the room.

I lean forward, the excitement of discovery bubbling in my veins. Because it's so *clever.* "Here." I pull back my paper, scribble out my nonsense Latin, and redo the letters I've identified as Greek.

Kingston reaches over and adds the Latin from his own paper, transferring it to mine, his broad hand so close to mine and yet not touching, his muscle movements controlled even at that fine level.

And soon, we've filled it. A few wonky places, a few uncertainties, but it's...

"In the beginning was the Word," I read, "and the Word was with God, and the Word *was* God."

I wait for Kingston to smile. To *react*, in any way, at all, to be even the least bit pleased that he—we—cracked the little code of it all.

But all he does is raise his hand.

"Professor?" he says. "We've finished."

I don't know why, but I'm...disappointed.

Dr. Emrys comes over, eyebrows raised with interest. "Have you now?" He inclines his head, looks down at the paper, traces with his finger, nods. "Very clever," he says. "Very, very clever." But he looks not at Kingston, but at me. "I don't suppose those were some magic almonds, were they, Ms. Vale?" His lips are quirked up, but the tone of his voice makes it sound like he's almost serious.

I shake my head. "Just good old-fashioned scholarship," I respond.

Dr. Emrys's narrow face breaks into a broad smile. "That's what I like to hear," he says, giving our table a little tap. "Well done, Ms. Vale. And your accomplice," he adds, nodding at Kingston. He gives his hands a single clap. "All right, then. We do have a winner in our little competition here." He smiles at our table as heads rise slightly and pens lower. "Our very own Heloise D'Argenteuil here has cracked the code."

"What code?" someone else says.

"This isn't anything. It's just letters."

"Ah, yes, but..." Dr. Emrys looks to me.

So, too, does Kingston. And the intensity of that stare, that focus, almost robs me of speech.

"It's...macaronic," I manage. "I mean. It's written in Latin and Greek. Two languages. And once you figure that out, you can see that it's—"

"The Gospel of John," Kingston finishes for me. Everyone falls silent. Everyone *stares* at me, and not with jealousy.

"A valuable lesson here," Dr. Emrys says, folding his hands at the small of his back as he wanders around the classroom. "You go in with a preconception of what you'll be reading, you come out with only with what you expect to find. But we mustn't think like that. We must be open to all possibilities and broaden our knowledge, constant in our quest and pure in our spirit." He taps the side of his nose, and throws a sidelong glance at Kingston.

"That's all for today, I'm afraid," he says. "Next time we start a conversation in earnest." The class comes to life, the rest of the students packing up and leaving. I sit there looking at Kingston and my joint efforts—a mess, really and mostly due to me. My stomach hurts less, though, and that much I suppose I can credit him for. I look up, turn to say thank you, but he's already gone.

The only record he was ever here just some neat calligraphy letters on a page.

FOURTEEN

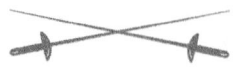

KINGSTON

AFTER CLASS, I don't waste time.

My destination is a quick walk across campus, the opposite direction of Camlann House, but equidistant from the Classics building. When I get there, it's quiet, dark, yet somehow not calm.

The receptionist nods as I stride in, not bothering to ask me for an ID or anything to prove who I am. She knows who I am—so does everybody—and she knows exactly why I'm coming here. I wouldn't be surprised if even *she's* heard about what happened this weekend.

I get to the paneled wood door at the back of the hallway and pause, rock back on my heels, breathe out. I want to use my key, unlock the door, storm in, be self-righteous, indignant. But it's unbecoming. The very fact that that's what I *want* rather than what I *think I should do* is an indication that it's wrong.

He won't listen if I come in like that, anyway. It's never worked for Kai. It certainly wouldn't work for me.

So I swallow my pride and knock on the door.

"Come in," comes my father's voice.

I do.

It's too big a room for an office, almost the size of an auditorium, vaulted ceilings, shadows cutting in from three-story windows, a platform that could hold a throne instead of a desk, low bookshelves, a few armchairs for casual meetings with deans, professors, visiting scholars, antiquities dealers, whoever's coming by, and the requisite array of brown liquor in decanters.

And in the midst of it all, my father. Luther Pendragon.

Behind me, the door shuts with a mechanical finality. I straighten my posture, keep my weight in both feet, my head lifted, my eyes trained forward, almost as if I'm ready to step en garde, but not.

My father is sitting, his reading glasses perched on his face, a few papers in his hands. The lenses glint in the light, obscuring his good eye from view and making it impossible to tell where he's looking, except for the feeling he's burning into me.

"I want out of Dr. Emrys's class," I say, quick, to the point, before I lose my nerve. "I'm done."

My father says nothing, shuffles the papers, places them face down so I can't read what's written, and removes the glasses.

"I beg your pardon," he says.

"Out of the class," I say again. "It's…" I pause, hesitate, just a half second, a half second too long, even though I know what I'm going to say, have been reciting it in my head the whole walk across campus. "It's a distraction. It's too taxing. It's, I think, why I—"

"No." His response is just as swift, a parry that clatters my words to the ground. "It's out of the question."

He purses his lips, slowly stands from behind the desk.

"Frankly, I'm astonished you even thought you could propose such a thing, Kingston."

Luther Pendragon is formidable. Though I'm taller than him now, it doesn't feel like it, and his six-foot-three form commands the entire room. In the tailored suit, the polished cufflinks, the

Italian silk tie, he looks the part. He lives the part. He *is* it, embodies it.

The silken patch that covers his right eye only seems to intensify his stare, as if the left has doubled in strength in the absence of its partner.

"Truly unbelievable," he says, coming slowly around from the back of the desk. "All of you. First Kai at the cap this weekend—"

"That was—"

"Don't interrupt me," he says.

I lower my head a fraction of an inch. Obey.

"I've already informed Kai of my disappointment. Extensively."

It wasn't Kai's fault. Not exactly. I know that, and I could speak to that, but he won't let me speak.

He wants it to be Kai's fault. He wants me not to contradict that.

And I'm helpless to disobey.

"That kind of upset cannot happen on the Caliburn campus," my father goes on. "Is that clear?"

No, I think. He doesn't want it to be Kai's fault. Kai is only the whipping boy.

It's my fault. Ultimately, and always.

"Disorder. Drunkenness. Damage," he goes on. "It brings scrutiny we do not need."

I know this. He knows I do.

Yet he continues.

"And you," he goes on. "Your focus waning. Your faith wavering. And you blame it on your schoolwork?"

I say nothing.

"Shameful, Kingston, that's what that is. Shameful."

I say nothing.

"You lost in a scrimmage to St. Ignaty. Did you think I wouldn't hear of that?"

I can only stare at the ground. I can't look anywhere else. I am tense, head to foot, waiting, waiting for the blow. And when my eyes close, I hold them shut a fraction of a second longer than usual.

Bracing.

But there is no strike, of blade or of fist.

There is just her face. Concentrating. Focused.

No.

My eyes fly open.

"Answer me," my father roars, and I realize he's been speaking to me. "What good comes of you quitting, Kingston? What good, to anyone?"

"Not...quitting. Not permanently," I mumble, freshly ashamed at how weak my voice sounds. "Only for the season, the semester. I'll come back to it when—"

"You will not," my father interrupts. He glances back at his desk. "I've just finished the logistics. A new tranche of documents coming into the library. French, German, Italian, all over the place. All at Emrys's asking. All for *your* benefit."

I clench my teeth hard. So hard I can taste blood at the back of my mouth.

Because I know he's right. I know it shouldn't be too much. It's part of what we do. The purity of purpose, the excellence with the blade, the quest for the ultimate knowledge.

Swordsmanship. Scholarship. Self-mastery.

It all comes together. It all has to.

And yet...

"It'll still be there," I say, voice a little stronger now. "Still be there once we've completed the season and..."

"But will he take you in the class?" My father cuts in. "Do you know what I've done to appease that doddering old fool? The lengths I've gone to, the strings I've pulled, the sheer amount of money I've spent..."

There's a heat to his words now, the flicker of power waning slightly.

"You know the kind of scrutiny we're under. This sort of... unorthodox arrangement with him is already testing the limits."

It's more than that. And we both know it.

Because what he doesn't say, would never say out loud, is that it's heresy.

To the rest of the world, the White Brothers of Saint Vincent are a harmless, secluded sect of monks in the south of France. They mask their faces, pray ceaselessly, keep bees and keep away from the world.

To us, they are judge, jury, and executioner. The Consistory.

Founded in 1098 by the heretic antipope Clement III of Ravenna, who saw in the emerging chivalric tradition a chance to leverage the secular in pursuit of the sacred. Charged since then as keepers of the grail protocol. Fervent, exacting, zealous.

A mage like Dr. Myrddin Emrys is not someone to be tangled with in their kind of holy pursuit.

Unless, of course, it succeeds.

In that case, of course, all sins are forgiven.

But only if.

"I do," I murmur.

"Do you?" my father says, rubbing his brow. "Because you do nothing, *nothing*, it seems, but keep me in a bind. I'm at Emrys's beck and call to source these manuscripts. Smugglers. Kingpins. Ungodly amounts of money. All so he'll deign to allow you to *interpret*, and only so long as you're the worthiest of all scholars, *which you must be.*"

My chest tightens, the back of my neck going stiff.

I know I must. I know that I must stay in Dr. Emrys's good graces and be an exemplary scholar. I know I must stay pure of heart and spirit and body. And I know I must never lose to another swordsman.

Something my father could never quite manage. The dark, silken void of the eye patch is testament to that.

"What if I'm not?"

Now my father goes cold. "What if you're not *what?*"

"What if I'm *not* the worthiest of all scholars?" I say. "What if someone else is?"

"What," he says, the word pointed and dark, "do you mean by that?"

I stand straighter.

"There's this new student in Emrys's class who's..."

Unstable. Unpredictable. Brilliant. Challenging.

Christ in heaven. It had to be the same person. The center of all the student unrest and the standout pupil in the most competitive class.

I clench my fists, my abdominals, my shoulders to my calves.

"What makes you think," my father says slowly, "that you have any right to be less than the top? Do you not know what is at stake?"

Of course. Of course I know. I have never not known.

This is the quest of all quests. The burden that outlives the bearer. The last true charge of the broken church.

"It...doesn't work like that," I say, weakly. "You know how Emrys is. He's..." I cast around for the right word. "...*mercurial*. I think he's taking a liking to—"

"And that's why you want to quit?" my father interrupts. "Simply because now there's a challenge? A challenger?"

No, I think. *That's not it.* It's that, it's that...maybe for the first time there's someone else who can do this crazy thing, who could figure out where it's been hiding all these years. Who can think like Emrys, in riddles and puzzles, in contradictions as well as facts and records.

"Listen to me," my father says through clenched teeth. "Look at me."

I don't want to, but I do. He clasps one shoulder in a broad hand, his one good eye boring into me.

"This is about more than you," he says, slowly and carefully. "This is about all of us, about everyone, the good of humankind. This could change, could fix…"

He doesn't have to say anymore. I push his hand from my shoulder.

"I understand," I say. Too sharply, I realize.

"*Do you?*" he says again. "If this new student is as good as you say, you think Emrys is taking some sort of shine to him, then you dog his steps. You keep tabs on him. You don't let him uncover a single thing without you looking over his shoulder."

Him. His.

Too late, I realize I didn't mention *who* this student is.

Who *she* is.

"Is that clear?" my father asks. "Do you understand? Do you truly understand?"

I don't answer. I look anywhere but him, around, at the massive expanse of this office, if it can even be called that, the platform and the massive desk, the pebbled glass of the windows, the way the light seems to warp around my father's silhouette.

For a moment, I consider telling him.

Revealing the truth.

If this star student is a woman, there's no way he'd encourage me to stay this close.

But as long as he doesn't know…

"I have no arguments against it," I say at last.

The truth—a version of it. I've learned this is the only way to address Luther Pendragon—litigious logic the only language he speaks.

"That's right," my father affirms. "You don't."

There's nothing more to say. Both of us know it. I give the barest nod and turn, heat seething under the surface of my chest, anger, constriction, all of it unproductive, all of it needing to be banished and worked out of me through prayer or exercise or study.

Yet when I get to the door, it doesn't open. Won't open.

I stay there, waiting, at attention, as I hear my father make his way to his desk, settle in, and carefully press the locking mechanism.

With a sigh and a click, it opens again.

Freedom.

"I'll be looking forward to you fencing Sainte-Odile," my father's voice says from behind me.

Or the closest to freedom I'll ever know.

Once more, I have nothing to say.

So I leave. Nothing but echoes behind me, and no time to waste. Practice comes soon, and the captain of the team cannot be late.

I pick up the pace as I take my leave of the building, the chill wind like a whip at my skin.

I tug my coat collar up, its protection minimal, and try to turn my attentions to the next matter at hand: footwork drills and equipment maintenance. Practice spars and strategizing.

But I can't master my own thoughts. Can't look away from the stark truth of what faces me now. My father may not have said it in so many words, but he never has to. I took his meaning all the same.

Gwenna Vale is no longer simply a problem.

She's my problem.

FIFTEEN

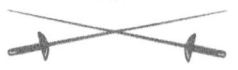

GWENNA

"AND HOW *ARE* YOU DOING, GWENNA?"

Dr. Riggs peers at me from the tiny rectangle of my phone screen. It's a wonder the WiFi even reaches down to my little library nook, but Caliburn seems to have top-of-the-line networking even if the vast majority of its systems are paper-based. I was half-hoping the call wouldn't go through, half-hoping I'd have a good excuse not to show up to this "check-in" appointment.

But here we are.

I clutch my scarf in my hands, out of frame so he can't see how tense I am. It was still there, undisturbed, waiting for me, when I returned to the library the next day. So I've mentally claimed the alcove as mine. Enough evidence that it won't be disturbed, and neither will I.

"Fine," I say. "Great."

I resist the urge to pull my knees to my chest and sit with my heels on the edge of the seat like a little hedgehog. I consciously channel every ounce of my focus into sitting normally, acting normally—content but not *too* happy, a bit bored but not aimless.

"Great?" Dr. Riggs repeats. He adjusts his glasses.

This is his only real gambit, therapy-wise: repeat what I say to myself and force me to explain. Sort of astonishing it costs $300 an hour for a conversation I could have with a mirror, but it's not my call.

"I like my classes," I say. That much is not a lie. I do like my classes—love them, really. It's the *everything else* of college that's proving to be such a challenge.

The other girls. The boys. The...whatever it was I saw in the lake.

Precisely the sort of things I'm trying to conceal from Dr. Riggs.

"I'm getting to study some really interesting stuff," I go on. "I did pretty well on the placement exams, so I skipped right ahead into Latin 302, and our professor has us examining texts from—"

"How are you adjusting socially?" Dr. Riggs interrupts.

I swallow the rest of my sentence, a sour taste in my mouth. What a weird way to phrase it, I think. *Adjusting*, like I'm a bra strap or a seat belt. Couldn't he just ask "Are you making friends?"

Then again, perhaps better he doesn't ask that directly. Because I'd have no way to give him the answer he wants without lying.

As it is, I choose my words carefully.

"I haven't had much time," I say slowly, picking up a strand of hair to fiddle with before dropping it immediately—*no nervous tics or tells, Gwenna. Come on.* "Mostly I'm just focused on the work."

Dr. Riggs purses his lips. Another classic tactic—judgmental silence, inviting me to fill it with further confessions.

"Caliburn's not really a party kind of school," I go on. That, too, is the truth.

"Social doesn't have to mean parties," Dr. Riggs says evenly. "Isn't Caliburn famous for its events—formal dinners, things like that?"

My stomach clenches, and my fingers tighten around the cashmere of the scarf.

He's not wrong. In fact, I've got the R.S.V.P. card for tonight's dinner in my bag—freshly dropped in my mailbox this morning.

"Yes," I say. And then, because I don't know what's come over me, "Actually, I'm going."

The lie makes Dr. Riggs brighten. "Really?" His voice is milder, almost pleased. "I'm happy to hear that."

I nod, forcing a smile. "Yeah. It...should be nice." There's a theme, I vaguely recall—something foreign and fancy. Specific enough that I can invent some details after the fact. A white lie, that's all. No one ever needs to be any the wiser.

"Your mother will be thrilled to hear it, I'm sure," Dr. Riggs adds.

Least of all her.

"Yep," I agree. *Hearing it should be all that matters*, I think.

He shifts his gaze downward, making some notes, then looks back at me. "I'm sure you two keep in touch," he says, "but for full disclosure, I will be sharing my session notes with her—"

"I know," I say. It's part of the deal. Always has been. And now that I've successfully fed him a satisfactory morsel of untruth, I'd like to get the hell off this call. "That's fine."

"Good." Dr. Riggs gives me a tight smile. "We'll continue to keep this up, but for now, it seems like you're on the right track."

"Great," I say hurriedly. "Thank you."

I mash the LEAVE SESSION button as quickly as could be considered polite, and instantly tuck my knees up to my chest. I'm breathing heavily, like I've just run a marathon, and the need to bury my face in the softness of the scarf isn't helping me draw in oxygen.

It hasn't been the best couple of days. Not by a long shot.

But it also hasn't been the worst.

That's a pretty high bar to clear.

And if I can keep this up…
I just might make it.
So long as I can keep Dr. Riggs and my mother content, anyway.

My heartbeat back in the realm of normal, I lift my head and blink away the fuzziness in my eyes. There's no hope of my studying right now—I need something to eat, maybe some water, a turn around the quads to clear my head. I sit back up properly, gather my notebooks and texts and small stack of flyers and announcements from my mailbox, including…

The cream-colored card stands out on top of the photocopied notices for clubs and donation drives.

September Formal Dinner
Saffron & Salamanca: A Voyage to Spain
Proper attire required. Fees to be withdrawn from student bursary account.
R.S.V.P.

I run a finger over the embossed letters, idly, yet as I do, a low sense of dread starts to build in the pit of my stomach.

Like I'm forgetting something.

Fees to be withdrawn from student bursary account.

Oh, shit.

My account is linked to my mom. She's the one putting in the funds.

And if the fees *aren't* withdrawn…

She'll notice.

Other parents might not pay that much attention to detail, but other parents aren't corporate M&A attorneys with a background in forensic fucking accounting.

Goddammit. I all but crumple the thing in my fist, choking back a wail. Instead, I just shove my bag onto my shoulder and stalk out towards the staircase.

I'm fuming, fuming but panicking, trying to think of some

way I can substantiate my lie as I go up and up and up the stairs until I'm storming through the main-level secondary landing, the one by the copy machines and printers, and nearly run into someone.

Someone tall.

"Whoa there."

It's him—the one with the piercings. The grad student.

He catches me before I trip and fully eat shit on the polished floor. I tug my elbow back.

Kai. That's his name. He's holding a sheaf of papers—quiz sheets, it looks like, a few more softly shuffling out of the humming photocopier beside us.

"Sorry," I mumble, swiping hair out of my face. "I just—"

"Well, if it isn't Wednesday Addams." He smiles. "In some kinda hurry, aren't you?" He sets down the quizzes, folds his arms, and leans against the stationery cart, legs out at *just* such an angle that it's impossible for me to pass without stepping directly over him, like I'm fording my way across a log-strewn stream.

I don't answer. The question's fully rhetorical, an obstacle as annoying as his body blocking my path.

"Heard you're kicking King's ass in Emrys's class," he goes on. "About time someone gave him a run for his money. I'd watch your back if I were you."

At that, I shuffle in place, suddenly self-conscious. Did Kingston tell Kai about me? Do I…mind if he did?

Seeing my non-response, Kai backs off. "Kidding, of course. King wouldn't hurt a fly. Probably." He chews his lip ring as he smiles, a move that makes me wince.

And when I do, his smile fades.

"Something wrong?" he asks.

"I…no."

It's not convincing, not at all. Like I burned all my lie-fuel in the virtual session with Dr. Riggs and now am running on empty.

And Kai doesn't suffer fools. That much is obvious. His eyes go from my face to the R.S.V.P. card clutched so tightly in my hand I've left a dent in it.

"Ah," he says. "First formal dinner jitters? Don't worry. Apparently there's enough free wine to keep everything nice and lubricated, socially speaking."

For a moment, curiosity supplants my anxiety, and I lift an eyebrow. "Apparently?"

"Well, so I've heard. Because, you know. The risk of debauchery. Not something befitting us holy rollers of Camlann." He presses his hands together in a little mock prayer. "But I bet you'll have fun."

Something about his certainly is unnerving. "I'm not going," I say forcefully. So forcefully, in fact, that Kai looks taken aback.

"Could've fooled me," he says, glancing again at the R.S.V.P. card. He tips his head. "Why miss out?"

"I..." My mind flicks through myriad excuses, plausible, nonsuspicious reasons I wouldn't bother getting dressed up and dining by candlelight. "I don't have anything to wear."

It's not *un*true, at least, if not the real reason. My wardrobe hardly has anything that would be considered *proper attire*; I'm not even sure I own a pair of tights without a run in them.

But as soon as I say it, his expression changes. A sidelong grin pulls at his lips, his eyes alight.

"Well, that's easily fixable, isn't it?"

He straightens, steps directly in front of me—close. Too close, really, just an inch or so of space between us that feels warm with the heat of his body yet flooded with the cool, rich scent of his cologne. His eyes flick up and down my form as he digs for the phone in his pocket, whips it out and starts swipe-typing with one hand.

I stand, frozen, the situation unreadable and my instincts giving me no clue as how to exit swiftly.

"What are you—"

Kai interrupts me, looking up. "You're what, 34-26-37?" He frowns, tips his head a little more. Smiles. "Make that 36-26-37."

Are those...my measurements? I fold my arms over my chest. "What the fuck are you talking about?" I blurt out, the overload of adrenaline in my veins overriding my need to be polite.

Kai ignores the question.

"Here. Hold this." He passes me the phone and pats his jeans pockets, his jacket pockets, then fishes a hand inside for a wallet, from which he extracts a card that he then holds in his teeth as he replaces the wallet with one hand and gestures for the phone back with the other.

"Thanks," he says, removing the card and holding it at arm's length to study the number. He glances at me again. "I'm gonna say...dark colors. Long sleeves." His gaze drifts to my turtleneck. "High necklines."

"That's...what?" I stammer, piecing together what's going on. "You can't just...buy me clothes."

"Me? No. I'm broke as fuck," Kai says, his grin widening. "But Daddy Pendragon's got a black card, and was stupid enough to put his foster son on the credit line."

With one final tap of the thumb, he nods.

"Done. Package from Neiman's coming to Broceliande Hall by 5 p.m. Wear your favorite and keep the rest."

I'm too stunned to speak. Too *confused* to speak, really.

"Better get that R.S.V.P. in, though," he adds, nodding at the card in my hand. "Don't want them to give away your seat."

Finally, I find my voice. "Why would you...why did you do that?"

Kai strolls back to the stationery cart, retrieves his stack of photocopied quizzes. Shrugs.

"To make some people angry. And maybe to make you happy, huh?"

Papers in hand, he reaches out and gives me a little *tap* on the top of my head.

"Give 'em hell, Wednesday."

I CAN'T BELIEVE I'm doing this.

I cannot believe I'm doing this.

The thought runs through my head like a drumbeat, like a pulse, as I scuttle across campus a few minutes before six p.m. Above me, the sky is a wild orange and purple, the kind of sunset you only get when a day of pounding rain breaks into a balmy, almost sunny late afternoon. On the colorful backdrop, the full moon is rolling out from behind a tree.

Campus is dark, but alive; figures are moving from residence halls and houses in the slow, considered steps of twenty-year olds wearing tuxedoes and ballgowns after a few pregame servings of Schnapps. Me, I did no pregaming, and even got ready alone. Morgan's nowhere to be found, and I have no way to contact her—no cell phone number, no...I don't know, forwarding address?—so I assume I'll either see her at the formal dinner or she'll reappear in her own good time.

I hitch up the skirt of my dress so the hem doesn't drag over sticky, wet leaves, and pick up the pace. Which isn't easy, in the matching (I think?) high heels that I'm wobbling on.

It's probably for the best, anyway, that I came back alone, because the order Kai put in for me turned out to be...substantial. Six—six!—plush garment bags hanging to the side of the mailboxes, all so surprisingly heavy that I struggled to get them all up the stairs myself.

But I managed. Got them up. Unzipped the bags. Read the note.

Best wishes for a stellar evening!

—*The shopping team at Neiman Marcus Boston*

That's a two-hour drive at *least*, meaning they'd booked it to get these here in time. And...

Voices come into range as I near the dining hall, snatches of conversation I can distinguish, and I instinctively straighten my spine as I enter the observable area around other people.

That's the thing. The dress makes me feel...conspicuous. More than I usually do.

All six of them were gorgeous. Luxurious. Nicer than anything I'd ever owned or worn, and Laura Vale didn't skimp on her daughter's wardrobe. These, though, were next level. Heavy crushed velvet, satin smooth as sealskin, fairy-fine embroidery on yards and yards of tulle. Italian names on silky labels.

But in the end, I knew which one was right. Valentino—a name I know only insofar as it's synonymous with fancy and expensive. Tiers of red silk chiffon, a swirling collar up to my neck, long sleeves. Layered, almost sculpted in places, yet light to wear. Comfortable.

Almost.

My ankle gives a precipitous wobble, and I stumble a few steps forward.

Can't say the same for the shoes, though.

The tide of dinner-goers is thickening, more and more bunches of students drawn up the steps like moths to the golden lights of the hall, and the clock on the face of the chapel steeple is inching is iron hands toward 12 and 6.

I suck in a deep, deep breath, pick up my skirts, and plunge in.

Immediately I'm struck by how *un*like the dining hall it feels. Granted, Caliburn's facilities are luxe on a normal day, but this is elevated to a degree I didn't think was possible outside of Oxford or Cambridge. Billowing hangings in Caliburn red sweep from the middle of the ceiling to the side wall, catching the glow of candles—candles!—in the brass chandeliers. The tables have been pushed together from individual islands into four long banquet-style seatings, set with a tablescape of votive lamps, sprigs of olive and rosemary, and bright bunches of marigolds and dahlias. Instead of trays, chairs are individually set with places: gold-rimmed china, linen napkins, a dutiful array of flatware, place cards. And at the far end of the room is a dais: a high table—for faculty, presumably.

I stand like a rock in a stream, taking it all in, as people swirl around me—waving to friends, jostling to places, laughing. It's all very…convivial, very collegiate, despite the formalities.

There's enough free wine to keep everything nice and lubricated, socially speaking.

Kai's voice springs unbidden into my mind, and I grimace in acknowledgment. If I'm going to make it through the evening, I might have to avail myself of some of that.

As I stand there, I catch a glimpse of a familiar figure gliding in through the arched entryway: tasteful purple gown, expertly smooth chestnut-colored updo.

Elena.

I fist the chiffon of my skirt, then let it go.

Yep. Definitely having the wine.

Before Elena can notice me—thank God—a bell sounds from somewhere unseen, and the murmurs and laughter dwindle down to a soft hum as people weave their way to their seats. They're divided by year, I quickly realize, and the first-year table is farthest to the right, so I pick my way over, reading over shoulders and scanning for the capital G and V of my names like I'm reading minuscule in Emrys's class all over again. At last, I find it —almost all the way at the end, which is when I realize (of course) it's alphabetical by last name.

Which, unfortunately, puts S just a few Ts and Us away from V.

Across the table and two seats over, Elena stares at me. No

narrowed eyes or wrinkled nose, just pure...astonishment, I suppose. I choose to ignore her—as much as you can ignore a heat-seeking missile, anyway—and pull my chair out.

That, for whatever reason, gets a reaction. Elena laughs, at once harsh and musical, and I stop, freeze in place.

Did I mess up already?

I don't need to wait for an answer. Another bell rings—deeper, this time—and that's when I realize everyone is still standing. Motion stirs at the front of the room, and I slink awkwardly out of my half-seated position and stand behind my chair as a pair of figures emerges to stand on either side of the head table platform.

Familiar figures, I realize, my breath catching in my chest.

It's them.

Kingston, Kai, Lanz, and Callahan. Not dressed in tuxedoes and bow ties, but in some sort of...black doublets, with high necks and wide epaulets. Wordless, they each take a side, in pairs—Kingston and Lanz on the left, Kai and Callahan on the right—and draw swords high into the air. They stand like that—silent, still, one hand held firm at the small of the back—and hold the blades up as the faculty and deans to process to the head table, the whole room silent but for the shuffling of academic robes.

"Benedictus benedicat," comes a sonorous voice from the head table. It's the dean of the undergraduate college—a serious-looking man in dark-framed glasses who I only know from brochures.

Around me, heads bow.

Grace. Of course. I duck my head as whichever dean finishes his brief prayer.

"...Dominum nostrum, amen."

All at once, life returns to the hall, movement and sound.

But when I look up, the four of them are gone.

Not something befitting us holy rollers of Camlann.

So they can come to hold up swords, but not stay longer than that?

I don't get it.

I don't get a lot of things about this place.

Immediately, a flock of stewards appears from the side doors, interrupting my thoughts: some bearing tureens of soup, others with wine decanters.

"Crema de Mariscos con Azafrán," one says to me, suddenly at my left elbow, and proffers his holdings. "Saffron seafood bisque with cream."

"Thank you," I say, self-consciously, as he serves me a portion, sliding a thin slice of garlic toast beside it, and again when a different steward appears at my right and pours my glass neatly half-full with white wine. Drinking age be damned, I suppose.

Conscious of my earlier faux pas—but in fairness, who the *hell* would've expected a sword ceremony before dinner?—I look around at everyone else to follow their lead. But things appear to have relaxed somewhat, with conversations springing up between seat partners and music—faint, Andalusian-sounding—playing from somewhere.

I gulp the wine and pick at the soup. The food's not bad—it's excellent, actually—but my stomach is too twisted with nerves to have much appetite.

Wine, though...

I take another healthy sip. *It's not like I have to drive anywhere, right? And it's not like anyone's really going to talk to me.* I take another. And another.

A prickle of realization creeps over my skin, and I turn. Across the table, Elena seems to have noticed me.

But all she does is smile.

"It's so nice to see you out here, Gwenna," she says, her tone as warm and bright as the sun-colored marigolds dotting the tablescape. "I didn't think you'd be here."

"And yet, here I am," I say, equally evenly. Maybe it's the wine, or maybe it's the dress, but I'm feeling…bolder. Feistier. A little looser than usual.

And I like it.

Elena takes a dainty spoonful of bisque.

"That's such an…interesting dress," she says, nodding at me. Credit where credit is due: the pause between the indefinite article and the adjective is *just* too long to be accidental, but still too short to be audibly impolite. Masterful bitchiness. I almost want to golf clap for her.

"Thanks," I say. For a split second, I consider name-dropping the designer, but reconsider; if the conversation steers toward fashion, I'll be quickly exposed as a fraud. Instead, what comes out of my mouth is: "It was a gift."

Elena coughs, and the boy to her left—a red-faced guy with strawberry-blonde hair whose whole head appears to be converging into the same color—snaps to her with concern, but she waves him off.

"Spicy," she murmurs, smiling, and pats her mouth with her napkin. "Quite a gift," she says, once she's recovered. "Maybe I need better friends." She tilts her head and laughs a little.

To my right, a steward is refilling my glass, like he's appeared from nowhere, and I smile my thanks. Take a sip. And then, to Elena, a broader smile. "Well, the Pendragons are quite a generous family." I give the ruffle at my wrist a little fluff. "Kai in particular."

Bam. Direct hit. Elena's eyes go wide as the salad plates. *Wee-woo, wee-woo, you sank my battleship.* I resist the urge to literally cackle. I know it's petty, know it's deeply stupid even to care, let alone stoop to her level, but right now, I'm helpless. I can't resist my own bad instincts.

Besides, I think, with another strong pull of my wine. *She almost left me to drown.*

After a moment or two, Elena mumbles some conversational segue, turns to the red-haired, red-faced boy, and the discussion swirls and flows around us as the soup course winds down and the stewards whisk away bowls and spoons. No one talks to me, not really, but I listen on neighbors, nod along as if I'm participating rather than eavesdropping, and sip at my wine. Through the peaked windows, I can see the sky has gone a deep sapphire, the full moon pearl-bright against it, and I wonder how late in the night this will all go. Wonder when I'll get back to my dorm, wonder if Morgan will be there—*and why isn't she here?*—and how I'll ever manage to explain away my new wardrobe.

Salads—blood orange, frisée, toasted almonds—come and go, and as the main dishes roll out, I notice Elena excuse herself—for the bathroom, presumably, although I find myself wishing it were for good. The redheaded guy stumbles to stand and help her seat back, while I sample my *merluza a la vasca*—cod, apparently, in a white wine and herb sauce.

By the time Elena gets back, I'm properly tipsy. Just past that point of no regret where I realize I should have stopped half a glass ago, but it's too late for me to do anything now.

She settles into her seat, smiling graciously as the stewards appear, white-jacketed, pouring more for all of us, and I'm no longer in any position to refuse.

"So," she says, leaning in, her forearms against the table, just a few inches above. Her elbows, perfect manners, not to be considered rude. "How about we play a little game?"

She arches her eyebrows up, and people around us exchange glances and murmur.

"Oh, come on," she says. "It's fun. My cousin at St. Mary's College in Oxford says they do it all the time. You just have to make sure the deans don't hear."

"I'm game," says the red-headed guy.

"No pun intended," I mutter into my wine glass. He either

doesn't hear me or doesn't get the joke. A few others murmur agreement.

"Excellent," Elena says. She sits back primly, smiling, and lifts her glass. "Never have I ever." She sweeps a look around. "Everyone know the rules?"

I almost want to snort. Is she serious? What's next? A round of beer pong on the long tables? But I don't really care.

"You go first, Chet," she says, elbowing the redheaded guy.

He goes, if it's possible, even redder in the face. "Um," he says, "never have I ever, uh…"

"Fucked on the first date!" calls one of his buddies from down the table.

Chet goes pure crimson, and everyone around us laughs. We've crossed the line from an academic proceeding to college students again, albeit in all the fancy trappings of a swanky soiree.

"Yeah, yeah, okay," Chet says. "You got me."

"You know the rules," Elena says, looking at all of us in the eyes. "If you've done that, you have to drink."

A few swigs from people around us. His titters as friends recognize unspoken truths about their nearest and dearest. I, of course, don't need to take a drink. I haven't even…well, it doesn't matter. I wouldn't say I'm fully a virgin, but certainly don't need to take a drink in this case.

"Go, go," Elena says, gesturing at the girl across from her.

"Um…" The girl twiddles the end of her hair, sucking her teeth nervously. "Never have I ever hooked up with two guys in one night." She throws a sidelong glance at her friend down the table, who laughs, a little embarrassed, and throws back the rest of her wine glass.

I may not be well-versed in parties, but I'm starting to see the pattern. It's less about what you haven't done, and more about what your friends have, and how you can get them sloppy drunk on their own indiscretion. The game circles around, mercifully in the opposite direction from me, as confessions are solicited, or offered, and with pride.

I start to think about what I'll say when it's my turn. *Never have I ever gotten less than a B on a language exam. Never have I ever had a curfew because my parents knew I would never leave the house because I had no friends. Never have I ever*...My thoughts trail off as a slight shift tilts itself under the legs of my chair. I flatten my palms on the table for purchase. Look up at the chandelier.

The wine, I think. Way too much now. And it's coming on all at once, like a bunch of ice cubes rushing from the bottom of the glass, hitting me in the face.

I swallow, my mouth suddenly dry, and my throat feels tight behind the impressive red collar of the Valentino dress. There's ice water, I realize, and I take a sip, but it does little to assuage the thick feeling in my mouth and throat. I've been drunk before, but this is...I'm not sure. Different. Banquet drunk, I suppose.

The girl on Elena's other side is thinking, "Never have I ever..." She drums her fingers against her jaw. "Had sex while my parents were home."

Plenty of drinks at that. Even Elena takes a little sip, looking the tiniest bit embarrassed, although I feel like it's for show. "Only halfway," she says. "It doesn't really count." But she scoffs, tosses her head. "My turn?" she asks.

Everyone nods. I do too, except that my head feels heavy when I do it, rocking back and forth like my brain is sloshing with its own momentum. *Jesus, Mary, and Joseph, get yourself together.* I know the stewards are quick on the refills, but can I really be this trashed? On wine? It's not like I don't have a full stomach. I gorged myself on that fish. And I got seconds of the garlic toast. I even had a real lunch today, more than just an apple or almonds.

And still, I brace my thumb and forefinger against my temple, gently rest my elbow against the table, manners be damned. Things are spinning, fading, sliding. *I need to get a grip.*

"Let's see," Elena says, biting the tip of her thumb. It's obviously fake consideration. I can tell. She knows exactly what she wants to tell all of us and is just making us wait for the theatricality of it all. Which, considering the state of my head, my body, I don't appreciate at all.

Somewhere, in another universe, stewards are coming around with dessert plates, some sort of small chocolate cake that smells bitter and coffee-like, with a cinnamon-freckled cream dolloped on top of it. But I can barely think about dessert, let alone the sweet-smelling port that they're dosing out into snifters.

"Never have I ever," Elena says. "Never have I ever. Oh, I know," she says, her voice too perky, too certain. It makes my stomach feel like a block of ice before I even know why. "Never have I ever been locked up in a mental hospital."

A few gasps, some uneasy giggles, and she's looking right at me. Soon everyone else is, too.

"I promise," she says, her voice distant, echoing. Her face, more a general area than something I can pinpoint.

I move my hand from my temple to the table again, press the other one next to it, pushing down, trying to be steady.

"Cross my heart and hope to die," Elena says, and draws a cross right above her heart, on the tan, expansive skin beneath her collarbone.

Right where my scar is.

Nobody moves. Nobody even laughs or says anything, let alone drinks. But Elena doesn't take her eyes off of me.

"Shouldn't you take a drink, Gwenna?" she says, her voice cool but friendly, non-confrontational. "Or was that something you were trying to hide from everyone?"

I can't answer, won't answer. My tongue is too thick, my temples are pounding.

Before I realize what I'm doing, I push off on the table, stand up, the chair scooting behind me, and the men in the general vicinity leap up from their chairs, showing sloppy decorum, but I wave them away.

"No, it's..." I try to explain. "I'm going to..." I lurch to the side, clutch one of the chairs for balance.

"Oh my God," I hear a female voice whisper, "she's drunk."

I'm not, I think. *I mean, I am, but something's not right.*

"I have to go," I mutter, I think, or at least I hear the words in my head, as I take loping, uneven steps down the length of the table, to the sound of ghoulish laughter, and out the arched doorways, to the foyer, and out into the night.

I gasp for air.

It hurts, burns to breathe, and nothing feels stable underneath me, like trying to walk across a treadmill that keeps changing direction, and these stupid fucking shoes aren't helping. I've been tipsy before, been drunk once or twice, actually, enough to rush back home and quietly vomit into my bathroom toilet, hoping my mom would never hear. But this feels different.

This feels...

Maybe I'm sick. Freshmen come down with things all the time, don't they? Mononucleosis, the flu. Meningitis.

I press a hand to my forehead, suddenly clammy, and realize I'm sweating all over. Sweating in this beautiful dress that I don't deserve to have, my stomach churning up the gourmet food I didn't even want to eat, my feet teetering beneath me, and I stagger along the cobblestone path toward Broceliande, and room 326.

Somehow, I make it to the room, just as my stomach gives a heavy lurch. I barely make it to the bathroom sink. Wine, bile, something, whatever it is, it all comes up. I wretch, feverish, wobbling, my knees giving out, and I catch my reflection in the mirror, pale as powder, sweating, lips flushed, eyes bloodshot.

It wasn't just wine, I realize.

Someone gave me something. *Slipped* me something.

All at once, it feels impossibly hot in the bathroom. I swerve back into the bedroom, but that's no better. It's stuffy. Nauseating.

I need air. Cold night air. I latch onto the idea like a starving man in sight of food, and all but sprint down the hallway, the skirts catching between my legs, the hem nearly tripping me as I fly down the stairs two or three at a time, barely seeing anything. I sprint, pell-mell, out into the cold, and my stupid, slender high heel catches on something I can't even see.

Pain shoots up my ankle as I tumble to my knees in the ivy of the courtyard. My fingers find purchase, dirt and vines, and I clutch at them, desperate for something real, something grounding.

Somewhere at the edge of the universe, I hear footsteps. A voice.

"Gwenna?"

I lift my head barely. My vision is swimming, pouring over itself like spilled ink.

"What are you—oh my God."

I'm about to topple forward, but a hand steadies me. He catches me, his arm firm and steady on my shoulder, and the last thing I see is the full moon and pair of bright blue eyes.

Then darkness.

SIXTEEN

LANZ

I SLAM into the door of Camlann House with my full body weight.

And hers.

She's like a furnace in my arms, a tangle of limbs and red silk. I can manage, but she's heavy with her muscles slack. Her forehead is dotted with sweat. But she's breathing.

No one appears to be on the first floor—which, thank God. Maybe it was stupid to bring her here, but it was either that or crash into Broceliande Hall and surprise all of its female residents, and somehow I didn't think that'd be a good idea.

Instead, she's here. In my arms.

"I've got you," I whisper.

She says nothing coherent. Just murmurs something and nestles her head against my chest.

My heart kicks at the movement, pulse skittering into every limb. It's an accident, I know, a reflex—she hardly knows who she is, let alone who I am.

But...

But she's so incredibly *lovely*.

And God help me, I could hold her like this forever.

No sooner do I think it than my arms tense, buckling a little as I strain to stay upright, keep her balanced. I *can't* hold her forever, not like this, not physically.

Slowly, slowly, I walk to the living room, to the velvet couch. There, I lower her, even slower, more careful, release one arm from behind her shoulders and the other from under her knees so that her head lolls onto the pillow.

As I do, the edge of her jaw trembles, her teeth giving a faint click-click-click.

Chills. She's cold.

In a single move, I whip off my jacket, stripping my arms out of the sleeves so I can lay it over top of her. It's not a great blanket, but it's the best I can do right now.

Now I'm breathing hard myself. Look down at her, her breathing steady but shallow, her skin paler than usual.

What happened to you, Gwenna?

I'd seen her at the formal hall. I couldn't *not* see her, standing out in that red; even if my eyes didn't seem to snap to her like a magnet every time, I wouldn't be able to miss that dress. It's...I don't know things about women's clothes. Different. Nothing like the sleek gown that Elena had on—I wasn't looking, but Elena never seems to miss a chance to force me into catching a glimpse of her. This is...sort of an old-fashioned style, I suppose. Lots of lace, and layers. But it suits her. Even though she'd look good in anything.

Morgan, I think. My first instinct. Except Morgan's not even here. It's a full moon. Morgan's out...witching. Whatever she does on these nights. And why would she do anything to her roommate, anyway? Maybe...

Food poisoning? But no, the odds of that are close to nothing; Caliburn food is top-tier, and the formal dinners even more so. The only way for the food to poison someone is if it had literal poison in...

Oh, my God.

The pieces slide into place before I even fully realize what the picture is, and I clutch at my hair. Elena. She was sitting close enough to Gwenna—I know she was, because she was staring at me the whole time we were there, and I had the bad luck to be facing the student tables. She wouldn't...

I tear at my hair again, pure fury coursing through me. "How could you?" I mutter and look at Gwenna's almost sleeping form on the couch. I can't just leave her here, but if I can find out what's wrong with her, at least I can figure out how to help. I bend over, tucking my jacket a little more securely around her. At least that's what I'm telling myself. Not that I want to go let loose on Elena.

I cross campus in what feels like a minute, practically sprinting with a burning feeling at the back of my throat. Disgust. That's what it is. Disbelief. My shoes ring on the cobblestones as the quads lie empty—everyone either tumbled back to their dorms after the formal haul or cozied up in Porter's for a nightcap, the official after-party location. And that's where I head, all but punching open the double doors to the main building and swinging around the worn basement steps two at a time.

I burst through the wood-paneled doors and narrow my eyes in the dim lighting. It doesn't take long to find her through the stale air of the pub, a few clusters of students in black tie formal lounge in the booths, laughing low—and she's right there in a corner booth, candlelight playing off her hair as she laughs with her friends. She's relaxed even as her gaze is as sharp as ever, and something about that fuels the fire in me even higher.

Quickly, obviously, someone notices me: her friend Claire—the blonde one—nudges her and nods in my direction. I don't wait for Elena to look up; I stride across the pub, my steps ringing on the stone floor, ignoring the hush falling over the tables.

I stop before her at attention. I am intent. "What did you do to her?"

Elena leans back a little, shifting her pint glass from hand to hand, her eyes wide. "Do to who?" she says.

I grit my teeth. "You know who."

"Oh, your little girlfriend?" Elena laughs.

"She's not my..." I clench my hands into fists and loom over the table. "Are you serious, Elena? I'm not interested. In you. In... in anyone." I fumble only slightly. "You know that. You've always known that. Why would you think something like this is okay? Poison?"

Her eyes flash. "It wasn't *poison*," she says. "Not in the sense that it'll kill her." She licks her lips. "A little ground-up Dramamine. She'll be fine in time."

I don't care when she'll be fine. She shouldn't be not fine in the first place. I tense my grip on the table. "Why would you think this is okay? Just for a stupid crush?"

Elena's smile goes brittle. "A stupid crush," she repeats. She snorts. "Don't flatter yourself." She leans forward, the candlelight turning her features sharp and shadowed from below. "That girl is a menace."

Her tone takes me aback, and I withdraw a little, confused. "What?"

"She is," Elena says. "She set the fire, Lanz. She ruined everything."

"What are you talking about?" I say, low, slow, dangerous.

Elena glances at Claire. "We looked her up," she says simply as she sets down her pint glass. "The swim test prank was mean, I'll admit it. But I noticed that she had all these, I don't know, burns on her arms, scars. And I thought, that was weird. So Claire here"—she nods at her friend—"looked through a few of her things from the admission file. And that's when I realized, Gwenna and I are from the same little suburb of Philadelphia. Only her parents are high-powered attorneys. And mine," she says pointedly, "are a shift nurse and a building inspector."

She takes a deep breath in through her nose. "I was going to go to Stanford," Elena said. "My parents had been saving their whole lives. I studied my absolute ass off. I got in early. Everything was ready to go." Then she swallows, her voice catching a little, and starts again, stronger. "This church in my town just… just burns down to the ground with a girl inside it. They never say who it is, and I never find out—but it was obviously her fault because her parents were connected."

"That can't be true," I grind out. "You're lying."

"Lying?" Elena laughs. "Why would I make up a lie like that? Why would I?" She clenches her fist, and I realize a tear is sparkling down her cheek in the dim light of Porter's.

"Everyone said it was an electrical fire," she begins. "That it was just *bad wiring*. That it wasn't to code and *someone* should have caught that in the inspection." She gives a small, cold chuckle. "The fact that the mental case, diagnosed pyromaniac daughter of two powerful lawyers just happened to be in the church at the same time? Oh, just a weird little co-inky-dink. But surely couldn't be her fault. Surely." She giggles, but there's no mirth in it. "Except it has to be someone's fault, right? Hm? And it doesn't seem to matter that the building inspector actually did nothing wrong. That he had a business and a family to support. Nah, who cares?" She shrugs. "Fuck 'em! Let them drain their life savings in legal fees fighting the negligence charges, right?"

The tears are pouring down her face now, her voice almost ragged.

"Oh, baby." Claire pouts and hands Elena a cocktail napkin, but Elena waves her away, swiping at her cheeks, and suddenly she's all composed again. She looks at me, eyes hard.

"That girl ruined my life. She's a psycho religious freak. She's dangerous and she shouldn't be here. She shouldn't be near people at all."

Suddenly the pub feels stifling. Conversations pick up again, swirling around me like smoke as my mind races.

Could it be true? I don't know where Gwenna's from, or Elena—just that Elena came here on a swimming scholarship, a late add to the team. That's what Callahan told me. Burn scars—I've never seen Gwenna's arms. I barely know anything about her, beyond that she's brilliant in French and has my entire heart in a chokehold without even knowing it.

Elena seems to have calmed down. She drains her beer with theatrical primness, sets the glass down, and slides out of the booth. " So go save her if you want," she says as she brushes past me. "But don't be surprised if she burns you to the fucking ground." She leaves, leaving only the flickering candle behind her as her friends scramble to follow.

I stand alone, the music and laughter rising around me like a taunt, the normalcy of everyone else's lives carouseling around me. I have to go back.

I barely mark crossing campus this time, only regaining consciousness when I'm back in Camlann House. Rush through the door, to the couch, to her—

But she's not alone in here.

"What the fuck is going on, Lanz?"

SEVENTEEN

KAI

FIGURES. Fucking figures. I step outside for one measly smoke break and suddenly there's an unconscious girl on our couch.

Lanz gapes at me, looking somehow stupefied and keyed-up all at once. "I...she..."

"Yeah, go ahead," I say. "Explain. I'm *reallllly* looking forward to *this* little tale."

Between us, Gwenna lies loosely on the couch cushions, asleep—I think—but breathing, definitely breathing, and unless her blood pressure has dropped precipitously since I checked her pulse two minutes ago, she's definitely alive. There's a slight dark circle on the pillow under her cheek—sweating? crying? I have no idea—but she doesn't seem like she's in active danger.

Not sure I can say the same for Lanz, though.

"I was just...I was out on campus, and she ran into me, and she...she passed out," he stammers. "So I picked her up, and—"

"And you're just gonna let her sleep down here?" I finish for him.

"You wanted me to just barge into an all-female dorm with an unconscious girl in my arms?" he cries.

I see. He has a point there. But still...

"What are we going to do with her?" I ask. "Did you think that through? No, of course you didn't," I answer my own question. "You didn't think any of this through. So I'm going to have to fuckin' *fix* it for you."

I sidestep to the couch and kneel down, weight in my heels, and slide one arm under her shoulders, the other under her knees. She's not exactly dainty, but I'm strong, so.

On an exhale, I hoist her up.

Lanz's eyes go even wider. "What are you—"

"What's going on?"

I jump, but it's just him—Callahan—coming down the stairs. Takes one look at Gwenna in my arms and Lanz's burgeoning freakout and raises *both* eyebrows—maybe the most expression I've ever seen out of the guy.

"Oh, you know," I say breezily—or breezily as I can, holding an unconscious coed in a designer dress. "Just shooting the shit."

Callahan stares. "Is she…"

"She's fine," Lanz says quickly. "Or she will be. She just…" He runs a hand through his hair. "She needs a place to sleep."

"As I've been *saying*," I enunciate, sagging under her weight for effect. "Can you fuckin' strategize here, please? Where am I putting her?"

Cal and Lanz look at each other. Then at me.

"My room?" I say. "Absolutely not." Many reasons for that, of course. But I go with the innocent one. "It's filthy. I haven't washed my sheets in—"

"I'll take her," Lanz says hurriedly. "I mean…" His face flushes. "She can have my room. I'll…" He glances at Cal.

"Sure. Bunk with me." Cal's face doesn't change.

"*Thank* you," I say. "Now, can we all scatter to the four winds and clear the area?" I'm already going to get a reaming from Luther, and possibly Kingston, over the shopping spree. The last thing I want is another problem they can blame me for.

Because they will. It'll always be me.

Neither of them moves.

"*Now*," I bark.

That works. They scatter.

And I walk her, quietly as I fucking can, up the stairs.

Lanz's room is, in fact, much cleaner than mine—his bed is actually made, for one thing, which leaves me to kind of shove the covers back with my foot so I can set Gwenna down more or less on the sheets.

Her breath flutters over my arms as I lower her down, pull back my arms. I stand a second, panting a little, and look at her.

At her dress.

Fuck. She can't sleep in that.

I mean, she can, but...

I eyeball the swirls of silk, the corset sides of the bodice. It can't be comfortable. And...I mentally think back to the itemized receipt the shoppers had sent me. If this is the Valentino, that's a $7,000 dress. And while it would really drive the point home to spend all that money and then ruin what it bought, I don't want to. Not for her sake. Not if she liked it enough to pick it and wear it.

Honestly, I wasn't even sure she would do it when I made the offer. Just liked the idea of fucking with Daddy Pendragon's head. But now...

I stare at her there, thinking through my options. Probably something she can wear in Lanz's bureau. Just have to get her in it. And out of this.

I'd have to get her out of this.

Shit. Shit. As gentlemanly as I can force myself to be, with every fiber of my self-restraint on point, I still feel...awkward about this.

Gwenna stirs a little, pulls her head from the pillow as she rolls over, eyes still closed.

"Too hot," she murmurs.

Oh, for Christ's sake, I think. I'm really going to do this. Really going to undress a girl who I can't touch not only because she's unconscious and unable to consent, but because I have to be a pious, chaste little swordboy for the foreseeable future.

I swallow hard, my throat suddenly dry.

"Hang on," I whisper, "hang on."

I chew the inside of my cheek. *How the fuck does this thing come off?*

Gingerly, I ease her shoulders forward a bit, looking for a zipper at the back, and mercifully, there it is, although not without a series of tiny buttons the size of a pea leading down to the pull-tab from the...turtleneck part of the top, or whatever it's called.

"Shit," I whisper through my teeth. I crouch by the bed and start in on them, fumbling their slippery surface through my fingertips, suddenly clumsy as a goddamn puppy. Each one needs to go through this infinitesimally tiny loop of silk fabric, and it takes me a good five minutes just to get all seven of them undone. But I do, and the red lace falls back, revealing the pale nape of her neck.

I swallow again.

Look but don't touch, Kai.

Lord knows I've seen women in states of greater undress than this. Seen them naked as God made them, and gotten to touch them to boot. Run my fingers over every sweet curve and soft expanse of skin, inhaled their scent, tasted them.

But that was before. And this...this is all that and more.

Instinctively, blood rushes to my cock, because I'm a fucking animal.

I yank myself back.

Come on. No.

I think of boring things. Of scoring matches. Of French verb conjugations. Of fucking anything until the heat of my pulse cools down.

Then I reach for the zipper.

It's small and fine, and I have to brace my left hand against the top as I pull down with the right to keep it from snagging. But it slides down the extent of her spine easily, all the way to just above her tailbone. She's wearing a bra, thank the Lord, and her panties are nothing for display. Black, but a practical kind of black that nevertheless makes my throat feel like sandpaper.

I pull back a little, bite my cheek harder, strategize a bit, then gently push her shoulder so that she's rolled onto her back. From there, I lift her left arm, easing it down and out of the sleeve, and...her skin.

I suck in a breath.

It's not smooth and pale anymore. It's kind of...mottled. Rippled. All the way from her wrists to above her elbows.

Like she's been hurt.

Instinctively, again, I avert my eyes. Like I've truly seen something I have no business seeing.

Explains all the long sleeves.

Heart hammering, I delicately repeat the process with her right arm, then peel the top of the dress down to her waist, over her hips, down her legs and off.

The whole time, I train my gaze on the dress itself, the clothing, the bunches of red, the gentlest movements so as not to disturb her. Not to look at what I shouldn't.

But good God, is it difficult.

There's just millimeters of this gauzy stuff between my fingertips and the skin over her ribs, her hips, her legs. And heaven knows I've been tested before, but this is next level.

Dress removed, finally. I roll it into a ball and throw it on the floor—Valentino be damned; dry cleaning exists. I turn for Lanz's bureau and rummage through it, extracting the first clean T-shirt and pair of sweats I can find. Then I blow out a low breath and begin the process in reverse, easing the sweatpants up her legs, getting the waistband over her knees, and finally over the crest of her hips, and into place, ignoring the thin, visible strip of black that stays at the top.

The shirt's more difficult. I have to bunch it up around the neck, so it's like a ring in my hands, and then sort of shove it over her head, like she's a giant doll. Guide her arms through, awkwardly, but in her half-conscious state, she helps me along. My breath catches as she gives her shoulder a little shrug, easing the material into place.

If she wakes up, sees me, I'm absolutely fucked. There's no good explanation for this.

Lanz, sure. Callahan, definitely. Kingston—well, he'd never get himself in this position to begin with.

But me, Kai?

No one would believe me.

I start to pull the hem down, and I'm so focused on *not* seeing anything in the kill zone that I can't help see something else.

Faint, but unmistakable.

A scar. On her chest.

Not an ugly one, like from a car crash. Not even all puckered and painful looking like the ones on her arms.

Two pearly lines, carved right over her heart.

A cross.

"What the *fuck*," I say out loud, before I can stop myself. Anger, bitter and hot, surges up my throat. Because that's not from an accident. Whoever did that wanted to hurt her.

To mark her.

And I want to kill whoever would do that.

Cool it, Kai.

Not now. Not…yet. Or possibly ever.

Instead, I just tug the shirt down, over the soft liquid space of her stomach, and take a step back, biting my lip hard, clicking the ring against my teeth.

She looks...comfortable enough. Hopefully less hot, anyway. Better for sleeping

I curl my fingers in tight to my palms, digging the nails into the flesh.

There's my good fucking deed for the day, I think. *Hell, this should count for more than a day, maybe a month.* I breathe out hard and breathe in slowly, and as I do, catch the faintest edge of her scent—not anything perfumed or artificial, but clean, warm, the smell of soap and human girl.

The most of her I'll ever be able to take in.

I don't know where that thought comes from. I shake out my hands, give the room one last look, and leave, shutting the door just firmly enough not to wake her.

EIGHTEEN

GWENNA

I WAKE up from dreams of fire with a gasp.

Sweat drenches my body, my neck, and I sit up, heart pounding. The light is gentle, the sheets are soft and cool, and the room…

The room is not mine.

Consciousness slams into me like a tidal wave. Flashes of last night: the formal hall, the dress, the wine, the stupid shoes and my painfully throbbing ankle.

My arms go loose where they're propping me up, and I fall back into the pillow.

And now I'm…where am I?

I take a few unsteady breaths. It smells like sandalwood and spice. Masculine, quiet. Sunlight pours through a wide window with a narrow seat and cushion.

And there's just this one bed. Like a real bedroom, not a dormitory. A few feet a way, on the floor, I see a mass of red silk, and that's when I realize I'm in different clothes: a T-shirt, sweatpants, too big and baggy to be mine.

A boy's room. I'm in a boy's room.

I draw the blankets to my chest and look around. Context

clues. Textbooks. Clothes. And then I see it. A framed photograph of a dark haired boy with bright blue eyes and a man who looks almost the same. His father, presumably.

Lanz. I'm in Lanz's room.

My skull clenches. *How did I…?*

I close my eyes, pulling my memory back in time. The walk, the room, the bathroom. I threw up, needed air, went downstairs, ran into someone. Him.

I open my eyes again. That doesn't answer much, but it answers enough.

The terrible thought seizes my mind.

Was I…

As soon as it comes in, I banish it just as easily. There's no way, I think. I just can't see that happening. Can't see him doing that. Besides, who would assault someone just to dress them in pajamas?

All of a sudden, I spring out of bed, like a sudden impulse has come to life in me, and land with a wince. My ankle *hurts*—not broken, I don't think, but twisted pretty badly. Still, I pull the blankets back in a single tug, smooth them, and slip to the door. I have to not be in there, I think, get out of here.

But once I'm out on the landing, my breath catches.

The house is ridiculous. Vaulted ceilings, two balcony-like hallways—one of which I'm standing on—that sweep into a massive wood staircase leading to a huge entry hall. Above, a skylight lets in honey-warm morning light and everything smells like cedar and wood smoke.

This is Camlann House.

I pictured something nice. Premium quarters for the star athletes. But this—this is like a mansion and…

…and I shouldn't be here.

Carefully—gingerly, on my ankle—I pick my way to the stairs, the half staircase down to the main landing, and then the grand sweep down to the hall, the whole thing like I'm walking to dinner on the Titanic. I look left and right: a study room to the left with bookshelves and armchairs, and more of a living space on the other side, a couch and a massive fireplace almost big enough to stand in, with a coat of arms standing guard atop it. Swords crossed, purple shield, Latin motto.

"Well, hello there, sleeping beauty."

I jump nearly a foot in the air at the sound of the voice. It's low, rough, masculine, and familiar. Kai.

"I, um, hi," I say quickly. "I don't—" I don't even know how to finish that sentence. I don't know why I'm here. I don't know how to explain this.

Kai, for his part, seems equally perplexed but unbothered. He looks me up and down at the T-shirt, the sweatpants.

"You joining the squad or something?" he says, smiling. "Because I hate to tell you, but fencing's single-sex here at Caliburn."

I look down at the T-shirt that does in fact say *Caliburn University Fencing*.

"No, I just…"

I press a hand to my forehead, take a wobbling step back.

Because I'm wearing short sleeves. On top of everything else. I might as well be naked.

"Whoa, whoa, easy," Kai says, and crosses the hall to steady me.

If he noticed the burn scars, he hasn't shown it. But how could he not? I pull away from his hands like a reflex.

"My bad." He goes palms-up. Cocks a look at me. "Hungover?"

"Something like that." My head is pounding in time with my ankle.

"I've got just the thing." He gestures for me to follow, takes a step.

I hover a moment, uncertain.

"Coffee," he explains.

Fuck me, I think. It had to be coffee. The one substance that could get me to stay.

I'm sold.

Limping, I follow Kai through the living room to a back arch door that leads to a kitchen. More huge windows. A giant stainless steel fridge. A massive island with stools. And pantry cabinets that are, when he opens them, perfectly organized.

"You can sit," he says over his shoulder. "You won't get arrested."

"What about you?"

Kai snorts as he pulls down a mug and fills it from a coffee pot that's tucked in the corner.

"Be the least of my problems right now."

He hands it to me.

"Technically no girls allowed," he says. "But I think we can make an exception for almost dying."

"Almost…" I trail off, my single sip of coffee going ashy in my mouth. "What?"

"You…" He blinks. Like he's calculating. Seems to change tack. "You didn't wear that to the formal hall, I hope." He eyes me up and down.

"No," I say. "I…" I don't even know where to start. I need another slug of caffeine to get my brain working. "I wore the red one," I say, "with the lace."

"Mmm," Kai says, nodding his approval. "I know."

He pulls out a mug of coffee that must be his, takes a long drink, and fishes a pack of cigarettes from his back pocket, sticking one between his teeth.

"Relax," he says, "I won't light it. So long as you're here, anyway."

He pins it between his index and middle fingers, rests his hand on the counter. Almost as if he's waiting for an explanation.

"I went," I say, "and then I ran out, and I tried to go back to my room and…"

Suddenly it all pours out of me. The dinner, no one speaking to me, Elena disappearing and coming back, the drinking game, getting sick, passing out—

And then I pause, realizing I've said too much. But Kai holds up a hand.

"You don't need to explain," he says. "If you're here for innocent reasons, I'll take it on good faith. Lord knows we're all about that."

It hits me. He's not pressing me, not judging, letting me have my own space in this room, even when I'm very much not supposed to be here.

And it warms me inside, just a little bit.

At least until a heavy tattoo of footsteps pounds closer from the living room.

"What did you do?" It's Kingston—his expression cold and dangerous, levied right at Kai. He sees me, I can tell he sees me, and yet he won't look at me.

Instead, he's taking measured, fury-filled steps across the kitchen toward Kai.

I've never seen Kingston like this, never seen him feel any kind of strong emotion. It's disarming, so disarming I almost forget that I'm very much not supposed to be here—and I don't even know how I got here in the first place.

"Are you serious?" Kai scoffs. "For once, nothing—"

"Don't!" Kingston growls. "Don't lie to me this time. I know that you—"

"Okay," Kai says, putting his palms up. "Okay, I should admit —the charges to daddy dearest's card? Those were mine."

Daddy dearest? They're…brothers? I dart my eyes from one to the next. They don't really look anything alike, other than being tall, strong, and white. The similarities end there, especially temperamentally.

"I don't even care about that," Kingston mutters. "That's his problem to deal with—with you. I meant her." Now his eyes turn to me; that warm, enveloping stare paradoxically freezes me in place.

"It wasn't him," I say. I don't know Kai well, but he did spend God knows how many thousands of dollars of his father's money on me, and I don't like people being falsely accused of things besides.

"Wasn't it?" Kingston says, pivoting back to Kai. "So what, she just decided to break in in the middle of the night? Sure, a likely story."

"*It wasn't him,*" I say, my voice harsh and loud in my raw throat.

Kingston and Kai both stare at me now, and I shiver, unused to being held in place by two men who look like that, who look at me like that. Kingston blinks, presses his lips together, folds his arms.

"Then, what are you doing here? Pardon my asking."

"Hang on, hang on," comes a voice from outside the room. Another set of footsteps—a quicker clip, almost panicked. Lanz rushes in, breathless, his dark hair sticking at all angles, bare-chested and in a pair of sweatpants. I'm so astonished I forget to look away, out of modesty.

And I have to say, I never thought of fencing as a sport with impressive physique behind it. But Lanz—Lanz looks good. Not absolutely jacked, but long, lean muscles carved from his shoulders down to the flare of his waist, the V just disappearing into the top of his gray sweatpants. Gray sweatpants. I look down at my legs. They're identical. They could be a uniform, I suppose, but—

"It was me," Lanz pants. "I—it's a long story."

"I believe we've got time," Kai interjects mildly, picking up his coffee.

Lanz glowers at him, swallowing and catching his breath.

"I found her outside," he says, "last night. Outside Broceliande. She couldn't stand. She fell over. She looked sick. I didn't know where else to bring her."

And then Kingston spins, with ferocious precision, toward Lanz.

"So you thought the best solution was to drag a half-conscious freshman girl here? Do you know what would happen if someone found out? If they'd seen you? Out all night with…"

"He wasn't out all night." I didn't even hear Callahan come in, but there he is, in a T-shirt and basketball shorts, his glasses on. "He slept with me. On the floor," he clarifies, nodding at me. "She was in his bed."

Lanz's cheeks are flushed and pink. He throws a long look at Cal, then back to Kingston.

"They tried to poison her," Lanz says.

My heart drops into my stomach.

"They did?" I say, at the same time as Kingston. He slides a look at me for a half second before going back to Lanz.

"What do you mean? Who's they?"

"It's—" Lanz looks at me again, and the pain I see in his eyes is stunning, shocking, like he feels terribly badly for me even though he doesn't even know me.

"Elena," he says. "Elena Shalott—she has some kind of vendetta against Gwenna, and—"

"I'm not trying to steal you from her," I interrupt. "I mean, you're not even hers. I don't know why she thinks that."

"It's not that," Lanz says. "She says she's from the same town as you. Nearby. Where there was a church…" He chews his lip, eyebrows held high, waiting for me to react.

And I don't. I can't.

My body has gone cold.

"Does anybody want to explain?" Kai says after a moment, tapping his hand with a cigarette against the counter. "Or…"

"It's not my story to tell," Lanz cuts in. I know he's looking at me even though I can't look up from the counter. "There was an… accident. A fire."

I clench my fists in my lap and stare hard into the marble, as if I could crack it open and find a hiding place, just with the power of my gaze.

I can feel it. All of them staring at me.

And I can't read minds, but I know for sure what all of them are thinking.

Did she?

I wonder the same thing.

Here's what the official report concluded.

A combination of faulty wiring, outdated sprinkler systems, and poor ventilation left the church a veritable tinderbox. It was only a matter of time before an accident like this happened. And it was an incredible stroke of bad luck that someone was inside at the time.

Here's what Dr. Riggs theorized.

After the divorce, I started sleeping less and less, and whatever sleep I did get was less than restorative. This chronic state of exhaustion left me more vulnerable to latent psychological issues breaking through. At the same time, as sleep treatments failed and the insomnia only seemed to get worse, I became attached to the idea that my only salvation would be through divine providence, granted through prayer—a result, he claims, of too much Catholic school. Finally, I reached a breaking point in the form of full-on spiritual psychosis—a not uncommon form of dissociative break, often preceded by a fascination with things like ritual, purity, and religious doctrine. Comorbid disorders, such as pyromania, are atypical but not unheard of.

St. Catherine's was certainly full of candles.

And here's what I remember.

Waking up surrounded by fire, my skin melted halfway down my arms. Bleeding.

But no pain. Never any pain. I could watch the pieces of my body shrivel and burn as easily as watching TV. Like it was all happening to someone else.

The cure to all wounds.

The vessel of vessels.

"I don't want to talk about it," I say, short and clipped.

"Fair enough," comes Kai's voice. "Everyone's entitled to their secrets."

To my surprise, no one objects.

Slowly, slowly, I raise my head.

"But what does that have to do with Elena?" Kai goes on.

Lanz breathes out hard. "If what she told me is true, then...it's personal for her. What happened."

This—this I don't know.

Don't understand.

"What do you mean?" I ask him. "I don't even know Elena. Didn't, until I came here."

"She..." Lanz hesitates. "She said her dad was a building inspector? And he...they lost everything. The legal charges."

Realization carves into me like a dagger.

The person they found liable for the fire. For the *accident*. The building inspector whose name I only knew by initials from sealed court proceedings, who Mom only referred to as "him" or "the responsible party."

That was Elena's father.

And it ruined him.

I ruined him.

"I wouldn't be surprised if she tried to hurt Gwenna again," Lanz goes on. "Worse."

At that, Kingston snaps into motion.

"Then you shouldn't be here," he says. "Not at Caliburn. Not for your own safety. Not for…"

"What?" I say it so loudly my voice cracks. "Leave? What—"

"You've already been targeted. Made seriously ill." Kingston's voice drops to a dangerous calm, his eyes locked with mine. "You think that's nothing? Or are you calling one of my most loyal team members a liar?"

"I'm not! I'm not." I tighten my hands into fists again. "I'm not doing that," I say, "but I'm not leaving. You can't tell me to leave. I won't. This school is all I have." The words crack as I speak them —not something I meant to say aloud, but it's too late now.

Four pairs of eyes bore into me.

Something wells up inside me—humiliation, panic—and it's too much. I stand up abruptly, the chair falling behind me. "I have to go."

I wrench myself free, dart out of the kitchen, through the hallway, out the front door, into the quad that's deceptively sunny and happy and green—a perfect collegiate day like it's trying to taunt me. I squint into the sunlight, the pounding of last night resurging in my temples, the pulsing pain in my ankle shooting to my heart with every step.

Poison? I think. *That can't be right. Even if she…*

But if she knows, then…

No. That doesn't mean I have to…

But if they know, then …

I'm not crazy.

I can't leave. I can't.

The quiet of the early morning canvas makes everything feel exposed, tripwired. As I cross to Broceliande Hall, I mentally rehearse, prep myself: shower, change, maybe slip out for a cup of coffee at Holy Grounds. Lay low—the lowest I've ever laid. Go to my place in the library and hide in my alcove.

I round the corner to Broceliande and slow my steps.

There's a crowd gathered outside. Girls in pajamas, everyone whispering frantically, eyes wide, and glances darting everywhere. There's a tangy, acrid smell in the air. Heavy, familiar.

Smoke.

I break into a run, ankle be damned. The crowd parts for me, almost like it was expecting me.

And I race into the hallway and up the stairs, leaping, flying, until I get to the room, our room. And Morgan's there, but not inside, just at the door, hanging back.

She turns at the sound of my footsteps, and her eyes go wide.

"Gwenna," she gasps. "You…oh thank God, you're all right. It didn't…"

"What didn't?"

Instead of answering, Morgan just takes a step back, her arms clutched to her chest. I advance a half step at a time and look into our dorm room.

Or what used to be our dorm room.

Because now all I see is…nothing.

At first, I'm confused, wondering if I've lost consciousness, blacked out entirely, because that's all there is around me: black.

But slowly my brain parses the information: not black.

Gray.

Gray everywhere, like a blanket of snow, or a blanket of…

Ash. It's ash.

Everything—my clothes, my books, my comforter and blankets and pillow, everything that Morgan owned—someone burned them up and dumped the ashes in the middle of the floor. And on top of it, a single sheet of paper with a handwritten line:

See how you like it.

NINETEEN

GWENNA

AROUND ME, Holy Grounds swims and buzzes in indistinct shapes. I'm sitting hunched over, wrists pinned between my knees, the best invisible-girl posture I can manage, and try not to cry.

It's over, I think. I barely made it two weeks. And now it's over. I'll have to go home, sit on Dr. Riggs's stupid couch, endure the punishing glares from my mom, the threats, the eye-rolling—

Or maybe this time they'll go through with it. Maybe this time they'll really and truly lock me up—not just temporarily. For good.

I'll never go into the library again. To the chapel. To Dr. Emrys's class. To any of it.

In spite of myself, a choked sob comes out of my throat.

"Gwenna?" says a voice from outside my cocoon.

I freeze. I'm not alone, obviously, and at the one moment where I truly, desperately, physically need to be alone and unseen, and untouched and almost non-existent. I swallow hard, my throat swollen from all the tears I'm holding back.

"Are you alive?" comes Morgan's voice a little more gently. The slight edge of humor disarms me so much that I actually relax for half a second, but I don't answer. I can't; I'm not even sure if a yes would be accurate.

"I got you tea," she goes on. "It'll help you feel better."

Doubtful, I think. If Dr. Riggs's battalion of veterinary grade pharmaceuticals weren't enough to fix what's wrong with me, I'm not sure how a cup of Lipton's is going to do the job. But at the same time, someone got me tea, and that's more than I deserve. More than I've ever gotten, anyway. It's comfort rather than trying to solve anything. I swallow again, pushing down the ache in my throat, and emerge, just barely, from my pretzel position.

Morgan sits backwards in one of the armchairs. Her hair's in a high ponytail, a loose sweatshirt hanging off her shoulders. "Good morning, sunshine." Her sarcasm is dry as a bone.

I blink, don't say anything, but sit up a little more. I'm still in the T-shirt and sweats—Lanz's presumably—but the clanking radiator and the sheer heat energy of my panic has me sweaty, my hair sticking to my neck. Between that, my bare feet, and the raw eyes from crying, I must look like an absolute lunatic—which, of course, I am—and now everybody knows it.

Morgan, though, doesn't react. She just tips her head to the side.

"Tea?" she asks, swiveling around and holding out a mug the size of a soup bowl made of some earthy, hand-thrown pottery and smelling like...I'm not sure. No kind of tea I've ever had. I wrinkle my nose out of reflex, so taken aback by the smell that I almost forget what's going on.

"It's herbal," she says. "I had them brew it special—my own blend. But it's not poison, I swear." She winces, realizing what she's said. "Too soon?"

I shake my head dumbly. Joke about it, don't joke about it, it doesn't matter.

"Okay," she says, but it doesn't sound like she believes me. "Anyway, I put loads of honey in it, too."

I reach out a hand—then two, when I realize how big the thing is—and take it from her. *Even if it is poison,* I think, *who cares?* It'll make me feel better, do nothing, or end everything.

The first sip is earthy, with a hint of grass and a flowery sweetness at the end that I can't put my finger on—honeysuckle, maybe, or passion flower. I wouldn't call it...good, exactly, but it does make me feel better surprisingly quickly.

"Attagirl," Morgan says, as she purses her lips and stares at me like I'm a child she's waiting to finish her dinner. I resist rolling my eyes and take another big sip. It's weirdly the perfect temperature—not hot enough to burn, but not that tepid, microwave-level heat that you get in cafeteria tea.

I don't want to talk, because talking just reinforces that I exist. But Morgan doesn't seem concerned with what I want.

"How are you feeling?" she asks.

I narrow my eyes. "Why do you care?" It comes out harsher than I mean it to. And Morgan's brow furrows.

"Jesus, I'm sorry," she says.

So am I. I want to slap myself in the forehead, but I'd have to let go of my tea to do that.

With shaking hands, I set it on the edge of the armchair and hunch over myself, staring into my lap.

"No, I..." *Fuck,* I think. I look up. "You're being really nice. You've been a good roommate—"

"*Have been?*" she asks, cutting me off. "What do you mean? Am I about to die or something?"

"No, I just..." I hesitate. "I mean, I can't stay here." My voice cracks as I say it. "Obviously."

"Obviously?" Morgan scrunches up her face. "I think not. You mean just because Elena's a bitch? I mean"—she lowers her voice—"allegedly." She stirs her own cup of tea with a dainty spoon and a scoff. "Word is they're saying one of *my* candles started the fire. And I'm like, *please*, I am *nothing* if not careful about fire safety—"

"Did the candle write the fucking note, too?" I interrupt.

Morgan pauses. Then laughs.

"That's what I'm *saying*," she mutters. She sips her tea. "You could raise a stink about it to the college, you know. Press them to—"

"No." I cut her off swiftly. I'd thought of that, too, but immediately rejected it. Anything that could make its way back to my mom—an inquiry, an official investigation—will only add insult to injury. Majorly. I can't.

"Mm." She casts a glance around the shop, doesn't push back. Anyone who *was* staring at us has politely retreated. "Well, I guess my point is, no matter what they decide, you can't let her chase you out of here. Don't give her the satisfaction."

It's not that, though, I think. *It's—what even is it? How do I explain this whole thing?*

Morgan waits in silence, as if patiently expecting more from me, but there's nothing more to give. Just an ache in my chest and the crushing sense of doom. And resignation.

"Is it true?" Morgan asks, her voice lower.

A few feet away, the espresso machine squeals and hisses. I dig my fingernails into my palm.

"You want to know if I did it?"

"Not in so many words," she replies. "But...I'll admit I'm curious."

I swallow, nod. "It wasn't on purpose," I say. "It was...I was going through something. I wasn't...right. But it's not like I was out there with a can of gasoline and..."

Morgan holds up a hand. "I believe you." She stares into my eyes. "And I believe you didn't know Elena's dad had anything to do with it."

Unbidden, tears flood my eyes. I scrub at my lash line furiously, hating how weak I'm acting. "Of course I didn't. My parents—they just wanted it all to go away. Didn't want to have a crazy daughter." *Sorry about that*, I think bitterly. *Wish not granted.*

"They said I could come here, but—"

I hesitate. Should I tell her the whole truth?

Morgan nods, tips her head at the mug. "Another sip," she says, "for your throat."

Meekly, I obey, like a little kitten accepting some milk. And after another sip, I do feel calmer.

"They said I could come here," I start again, "but if I couldn't hold it together, then...then..."

The last word wobbles.

"They'd send you away," Morgan finishes. "Somewhere where you'd have a roommate even crazier than me."

I smile, even as another tear finds its way out of the corner of my eye.

"I don't want to go," I say, almost choking on the words.

"Hey, hey." Morgan covers my hand with hers. "It's all going to be okay, okay?"

I nod, not believing her, and too late realize that her eyes have followed her hands.

To my arms. The burns.

Because I'm still wearing a T-shirt.

I breathe out, hard.

"So that's..." Morgan says. She doesn't have to finish the sentence.

"Yes. It was bad," I say, not meeting her eyes. "Skin grafts."

It feels strangely good to show her the scars—well, the burn marks, anyway. The other part, the scar on my chest—

I don't think I ever want anyone to see. Ever, ever, ever.

"Do they hurt?" Morgan asks, interrupting my thoughts.

"No."

"You know, there are treatments that—"

"I've tried everything." I cut her off.

Morgan opens her mouth, seems to reconsider, and closes it. Thank God. I don't want to hear another girl going on about her miracle essential oils or K-Beauty scar cream. I've spent enough time in those internet rabbit holes, and I'm not up for more disappointment.

"I'm gonna have to go home," I mutter, more to myself than to her. A half-formed list of chores floats into my mind: packing, train tickets, calling Mom and Dad...

Oh, God.

"No, you're not," Morgan says sharply. "You're not going home. You're going to drink your tea, first of all. *Now.*"

I'm too shocked at the force of her command to disobey, and gulp another mouthful. It really is good—not tastewise, exactly, but in how *calm* it's making me feel. It's efficient, almost chemically efficient, and too late, I remember what I saw from Morgan and Kingston my first day here, and I wonder if there's some sort of CBD infusion or mushroom microdose or God knows what else lacing this tea.

Oh well. In for a penny, in for a pound. If I'm going to have another mental breakdown, I might as well be tripping balls while I do it.

"I'm not going home," I repeat, testing out the words on my tongue.

"Correct." She nods her head resolutely. "You're gonna...let's see. Take a day to recuperate, lay low, whatever you want. Tomorrow, too. Then you're gonna get up, you're gonna drink some strong coffee, and you're gonna go to class, and—"

Maybe it's the tea, or maybe it's just that my body is out of adrenaline and can't pump out a stress response anymore, but I suddenly feel—not *good*, not even *better*, but not *bad* either.

Like maybe I almost have a friend. Someone taking care of me.

Someone who's cool and doesn't seem bothered by the fact that I'm officially psycho.

Which...in and of itself is kind of a red flag.

Right?

I stare at Morgan until, finally, she notices, and does a quick double take.

"What?" She paws at her face. "Do I have something on me?"

"You're acting so...*normal*," I say. It's all I can think to say.

She cocks her head back my way. "And?"

And your roommate is the campus lunatic, I think. "You actually feel safe having me for a...roommate?" I can't bear to say the word *friend*. Can't bear to jinx it.

Morgan laughs. "Shit, I feel *safer*." She considers. "Although... yeah, we don't really have a room. The house matron said they'd try to find some vacant singles or something in the second- or third-year halls, but..."

She trails off, eyes fixed at something over my shoulder. I frown, but Morgan just nods, and does a little "turn around" gesture with her fingers.

So I do. And find myself facing Callahan.

"Gwenna," he says simply.

My heart goes from 60 to 100 in a single second. "Yes? What?"

A thousand half-formed possibilities stream through my mind: they're officially coming for me for trespassing. I owe Kai thousands of dollars for dresses I can't afford. They're having me thrown out of school against my—

"Come with me," Callahan says. "Kingston says you're staying with us now."

TWENTY

CALLAHAN

IT'S strange to have a girl in Camlann House.

We didn't speak on the way across campus, and now that we're standing inside the house, I feel obligated to break the silence. Kingston didn't give me many instructions—he never does—but I am supposed to show her around.

She's staring—staring up, which is the first place you'd stare if you'd never really taken this place in before. I know I did when I came in here last year. Even after however many years in churches and Catholic schools, having archways and columns and chandeliers in the place you're supposed to *live* is something different.

And I don't mean to be staring—not at her, not at anything around Camlann House—but it's hard not to.

Because it is strange to have a girl in Camlann House.

Especially a pretty one.

I don't know why I notice or even can tell that she's pretty, but she is. Even when she's clearly exhausted and wearing Lanz's sweats. Something about the set of her lips, the curve of her throat, the long hair streaming over her shoulder.

It's nice.

"This is the front hall," I say after a moment, just to say something.

She—Gwenna—looks at me. Draws her brows together. "So I see."

Right. Obviously. *She's a girl, not an* infant, *Callahan.* I mentally smack myself in the forehead.

"Lots of swords," she observes, eyes flitting from one set of crossed blades to another, the displays mounted on the paneled walls.

"Yeah," I agree. I stuff my hands in the pockets of my jacket. Give my head a shake.

I'm supposed to be showing her around, I remember.

I take a few steps forward and indicate the room to our left. "Living room."

She follows my lead, drawing closer and peering into the space, taking in the heavy leather armchairs and sofas, the Persian rug, the massive stone mantelpiece. Then she fixes her gaze on me.

Her eyes are really green.

"Are we just naming rooms now?"

"What?" I say, taken aback.

"Front hall, living room," she echoes. "No offense, but…I *can* tell that's what these are. And I have been here before."

"Right." I nod, breathe in. I'm not used to giving color commentary or context, but I suppose I can try. "Of course. Um, this is where we hang out, usually, if we're not in class. Or studying. Or practicing."

"So basically never?"

The joke catches me off guard. "Ah, yeah. We are…pretty busy, I guess." I scratch the back of my head. "But it's a nice space. And sometimes we'll light a fire if…"

Too late, I realize what I've said. I feel my face go red. "Sorry. I—"

"It's fine." Her tone is polite, distant. I kick myself.

"Let's, uh..." I escort us out of there and try to stay on task.

We cover the library, the kitchen, the dining room—

"Breakfast is at seven," I say, gripping one of the high-backed chairs as light streams through the leaded-glass windows. The table up here is simpler than the Black Table. Still an expensive antique, but nothing showy. "Lunch at noon. Although usually we all take it to go or just grab something on campus. Dinner is... whenever practice is over."

"You all eat here, too?"

"We have a chef." I wince as I say it. It's still a little foreign, even to me—sure, I've lived at Camlann over a year now, but I'm still the kid who spent summers bussing tables at the Milton Hoosic Club. In my mind, I work *for* the chefs, not vice versa.

Gwenna just nods. But frowns as she does it.

"Sorry. Just...this is a lot," she says. "You all just...live here? Like this?"

I shove my hands back in my jacket pockets. "We don't have a choice."

Confusion colors her features.

"It's just how the team has always been," I say—the simplest explanation I can offer. "And Luther Pendragon makes sure we get what we need."

She nods.

"We won't really be around to bother you," I reassure her. "Most of the time we're in the salle. The fencing hall," I add, when her confusion lingers. "Where we practice."

Gwenna blinks. "You don't practice in the gym?"

I shake my head. "The salle's here, on the ground floor—the walk-out level towards the lake."

She looks over her shoulder, to the hall that connects us back to the kitchen, the two closed doors that lead downstairs.

"So that's the salle," she says.

"On the left," I agree. But as soon as I say it, her gaze drifts to the door on the right.

The door down to the lowest level of all.

My chest seizes.

"That's nothing you need to worry about," I say quickly. "Here. Let me show you your room."

There are more bedrooms than there are swordsmen, God knows why—the house is just too big for only four residents. We've already laid claim to the best rooms—Lanz and I on one side of the landing, Kingston and Kai on the other—but the smaller one, the one Kingston said to give her, isn't bad by any means.

Silently, I open the door for her. She enters silently, taking it in.

"Small," I say, "but there should be plenty of room for your stuff."

From her place at the window, she shoots a look at me.

"What?" I say. Did I say something wrong?

"*Stuff*," she repeats. "*What* stuff? My room burned down, remember?"

I shuffle my weight from foot to foot. "Kingston…said he'd take care of it."

I nod at the closet, and her mouth falls open in surprise.

I may be a Knight, used to living here with all the luxuries and conveniences of Camlann House. But I'm still not used to *this*—money, gifts, like it's nothing.

And neither, apparently, is Gwenna.

It's a full wardrobe. Perfect. Complete. *More* than complete. And definitely top-tier stuff. Sweaters and pants, tidily folded. Blouses and skirts, hanging smooth and unwrinkled. A dozen or more pairs of shoes, still in tissue-paper-filled boxes.

Slowly, she puts a hand to her mouth.

"This is…" She pivots to me, slowly. "It's too much."

I swallow. "It's from him."

She blinks. Peers at the closet again. Tiptoes to the dresser, opens a drawer. Widens her eyes. Shuts it again.

"So does he…know my bra size?" she says, tipping her head at the dresser. "Or just guessing?"

"I…"

I have no idea. I don't even know what sizes bras come in. Small, medium, large?

"He might have asked Morgan?" I guess.

That makes her smile. And it feels nice to make her smile.

Except it's not just that.

It's…her.

I'm just doing what Kingston asked. Ordered. Get her here, so we can protect her.

But she's not some scared, shy little thing. She's not little at all, actually, maybe five-eight or five-nine. It's more that…compared to us, our stuff, she almost *looks* small, in the space of one of these high-ceilinged rooms. Delicate among all the sturdy masculinity.

And that's…different.

Powerful, in its own kind of way.

Gwenna's back at the closet. She lifts a blouse by its hanger, surveys it. Replaces it. Takes out another.

"You don't like it?" I ask.

"I didn't say that." She says it without looking at me, turning her attention to the shoes. Picks up a boot, studies it: black, leather, thick soles and buckles. Good for a New England winter. "More practical than what Kai got me, that's for sure."

She drops it to the floor, starts to ease in the toe of her left foot, but winces and stops.

Without thinking, I step to her side, offer her an arm. She looks up at me, quizzical.

"I thought…you were losing your balance," I manage.

She laughs a little, tucks hair behind her ear. "I'm stable. Physically." But she still clasps my forearm, steadies herself as she lowers her body to sit on the desk chair. With her settled, I instinctively duck down to retrieve her shoe, dropping to one knee to reach for it.

"Thanks," she says, and it's only once I follow her gaze that I realize I'm still holding the boot, still kneeling at the foot of her chair. Another little smile. "You...planning to help me with that?"

She's kidding—I'm pretty sure she's kidding. But when I look up, I almost lose my balance, even kneeling.

Because she's watching me. Not like Lanz. Not with hunger.

With expectation.

"Well?" she asks. Calm. Measured.

Like she knows I'll obey.

And the worst part is...

She's right.

"Sure." I nod.

Just to be helpful. Just to be efficient.

Just—

My fingers tremble as I undo the buckles, tug at the zipper, my throat is dry. Her foot—bare, delicate, pale—is warm under my palm as I ease it into the shoe, her ankle lightly shaded with bruise. I can smell the clean edge of her soap, maybe even her skin, and I'm so worried I'm hurting her, but she doesn't move. Doesn't flinch. As if I'm just...supposed to be here.

Kneeling.

Touching.

Serving her.

God.

I blink. She's saying something, and I'm not listening.

"Sorry?" I say, my heart hammering at the front of my ribs. The shoe. I finish up the fastenings, quickly and clumsily.

"It's...nothing," she says. "A joke. I was just asking if you always take such good care of your guests."

"I...don't know," I say. "You're my first."

Heat creeps up my neck before I even realize what I've said. What it sounds like.

Oh, God.

But if Gwenna notices it at all, she doesn't show it. Just thinks for a moment.

"So yes, then," she says at last. "By definition, you do."

I hadn't thought of it that way. But I suppose she's right.

"If the shoe fits," I say.

Her whole face lights up when she laughs. "And, in fact, it does." She presses her lips together. "Thank you, Callahan."

I nod. Nod again.

Then remember I'm meant to speak.

"My pleasure," I say.

And it is.

Even if I don't know what, exactly, she's thanking me for.

AN HOUR LATER, the air in the salle is thick and heavy, the stillness only broken with the swipe and clash of metal on metal.

Late-afternoon sun pours onto the piste as we spar back and forth. Lanz's hits are sharp, aggressive; his footwork quick and deft. My parries are solid, but my feet feel like lead in my shoes, almost dragging along the piste, and my focus is everywhere and nowhere.

En garde, allez, halt.

"All good?" Lanz lunges, thrusts the epee tip right for my shoulder, but I dodge.

"Fine."

I shrug, deflect a strike. Loosen my sword hand and instinctively rub the rings together—thumb and index finger, trying to ground myself.

It doesn't work.

Lanz retreats, circles me. He's breathing hard—it's been hours now. And I think he can tell I'm wound up.

"Take five?" he asks.

I nod. "Sure."

I need it, too.

He nods back, and loosens the collar of his lamé, shaking his head to cool off and dragging a wrist over his forehead before peeling off his glove and discarding it. His cheeks are flushed, his lips parted.

I'm staring. The blood pulsing through my whole body like it never has before, so hard and fast I'm surprised Lanz can't hear it echoing in the salle.

And maybe he does. Because his bright eyes find mine. A knowing furrow in his brow.

Oh.

"Here?" I ask. He looks around, over either shoulder; shrugs.

We're alone.

I can only nod.

He bites his lip and grabs for me.

I kiss him—familiar, practiced, hot. Shuddering as soon as our mouths meet. He rips at my lamé, prying the covering from my chest and skating his hands over bare skin. I gasp a little, and he edges me backwards, gentle but firm, until the backs of my knees hit the bench and he's pushed me to sitting. Lips and teeth nip their way down from my shoulder to my waist, and I clench in anticipation, for him to surge up, straddle me.

He doesn't, though.

Instead, he eases my legs wide with his own.

Then drops to his knees.

I sit up straighter, realizing. That's...not what we usually do.

Not that we've discussed it. Who's into what and everything. On some level we *should*, I guess. But we haven't. Just went with what felt right.

Maybe I'm just a natural giver.

"Hold on. *Hold—*" I shudder as his lips brush the top of my fencing knickers, the low waistband the only thing between him and my sensitive skin. "*Stop.*"

I push him back by the shoulders, hold him firm, pinning him there on his knees. He raises his head, soft confusion written on his face, and—

And his eyes. Those eyes.

I've always loved those eyes.

They're the first thing I noticed about him. That bright blue.

But here, with him kneeling before me like this, they strike me again. Anew. Looking at me not directly, not eye-to-literal-eye, but from below.

In supplication.

Begging.

And giving me no way to say no.

My cock goes iron-hard.

"I just...you don't have to," I murmur. "Let me—"

"I'm good." Lanz shakes his head. "I want to."

"But—"

"Don't argue," he bites out. "You need this."

And presses a kiss to the cusp of fabric right under my hip.

A moan floods out of me. He isn't wrong.

"Good boy."

Oh, God.

His hands are quick, fingers deft, as he works the fastening and pulls the pants to my knees, letting my cock spring out. But my gaze is only on his face: determined, but unsure, maybe, hesitant.

A tremor of guilt flickers in my chest even as I feel a drop of precum beading on the tip of my cock.

Has he done this before?

Then he sucks the head into his lips and my muscles buckle.

Never mind. Don't care.

I'm gone. Obliterated. Lost in a headrush, whited out by pleasure. Struggling to think, to *be*, as he pumps up and down my shaft.

My fingers grip the wood for desperate purchase.

It's...he's...

I've sucked Lanz off God knows how many times at this point. Stroked myself late at night thinking about him, muttered his name as I came into my own hand. But this is...

This is...

His right hand clamps me beneath his sliding lips, and his eyes flutter shut.

Fuck me.

It's heaven.

I close my own eyes, let my head fall back, a growl I didn't know was in me rumbling out as he finds a rhythm. It's so good, too good. I'm both dying for release, needily quivering for it, and desperate for this feeling never, ever to end.

"Unh." The sound kicks out of my throat, and impulsively, my sword hand shoots out, grips that thick black hair of his.

As I do, he pulls back, just a little.

Looks up at me.

Those eyes.

And then flicks his tongue again.

I'm done.

I explode into his throat, come so hard my thighs are quaking and I nearly slide off the edge of bench, but Lanz doesn't let me, pushing his left hand to brace my hip even as his right works me, rubbing firm and swift until what feels like every drop has pulsed out of me. Even then, he doesn't let go, cinching his lips warm and tight as the blood slowly beats out of my cock and back into my body.

I blow out a shaky, shaky breath. Lanz rocks back on his heels, thumbs at the corner of his mouth—a gesture that could get me half-hard again if I weren't bone-exhausted, and gives me a smile. Nervous, even shaky.

"How was I?"

"Great," I rasp. "You were…" I blink, hard, press a palm to my damp forehead. Need to catch my breath. "You've never done that before?" I pant.

"Nah." He half-smiles and looks away, shaking his head. "Did okay, then?"

"You…" I can't form sentences. "Jesus. That was…"

"Nice, right?" He laughs softly. "Always been one of my favorites. Or was before—"

He catches himself.

Before me. Before this.

I'm suddenly cold. Goosebumps prickle over my naked chest. I tug at the waistband of my fencing knickers, shrug my lamé back into place.

"So you got around, huh?" I ask. I need to find my epee. Look around us for wherever I dropped it.

"Are you asking me if I was some kind of manwhore?" Lanz laughs again, softer this time, and stands, hands uneasily on his hips. "Because trust me, I was not."

"But you got head," I say. "From girls."

The blunt words surprise me as much as him. But I've said them now.

No taking it back.

Lanz shifts his weight. Scratches the back of his neck. "Yeah. Sure. I mean, a few times. High school."

"Oh yeah?" I still don't look at him. Where the hell is my goddamn weapon? "How was it?"

"Come on, Cal." Lanz sighs softly. "Don't—"

"No," I say, forcing my voice into lightness, casualness. I turn to look at him, pasting what's meant to be a grin on my face. "Just curious."

    I wait a second. Two.

    Then I ask.

    "Was it better?"

    I stand. Wait. And Lanz frowns, a real frown.

    "Not...it...neither," he says. Sighs. "It wasn't better, it wasn't worse. Just...different."

    "Different how?" I push on. Unable to let go.

    Because now I'm wondering. Now I can't stop wondering.

    About Lanz and girls.

    About girls.

    About deep green eyes looking up at me instead of blue ones.

    "I don't know, Cal!" Lanz throws up his hands. "Just *different*. Okay? And it doesn't matter now anyway. You wanna find out so bad, quit the team and go find a girlfriend." He blows out a hard breath. "I'm...taking a shower."

    He stalks off, and I stay behind, motionless except for my thumb rubbing over the rings on my first two fingers.

TWENTY-ONE

GWENNA

I HALF-EXPECT Kingston to say something in Latin class.

Hell, I fully expect it. The situation is too unusual, too *weird* for him *not* to say something.

And yet…he doesn't.

Not to me or about me or even in my vicinity, despite the fact that we are once again sitting next to each other, the only two people no one else wants to be nearby, albeit for wildly different reasons. The fact that I'm in real clothes again—a deep purple crewneck sweater and a black corduroy skirt that had the tags demurely sliced in half to omit the price—doesn't make it any more comfortable to be near him, either.

Especially with no recognition from him.

Instead, I get a solid forty-five minutes of lecture on variations in orthography across England, Ireland, and France, the lights dim so Dr. Emrys can slide transparencies onto an overhead projector, blow up quill-scratched letters and phrases onto the pull-down screen and explain in detail what they mean.

"And this one?"

Emrys removes the transparency with a flourish and replaces

it with a new one: a pretzel-looking squiggle from, according to its footnote, an 11th century book of hours.

"That's an ampersand," someone calls from the back.

"Mm, indeed," says Emrys, his face lit up in eerily harsh orange light from the old-school projector. "And its name means?"

"Um…that's just what it's called?"

"*Et per se et*," comes the deep voice to my left. Kingston. "It's a combination of the letters in the Latin word for and: E T. *Et per se et*. Hence the word ampersand." I turn imperceptibly, but can't make out any of his features, let alone his expression.

"Exactly," Emrys cries. "Et. You see how it forms the letters E and T?" He points. "Such a familiar little flourish, just a piece of Latin hiding in plain sight even to this day."

I'm fascinated, of course, because I'm a hopeless geek. Who would have thought that Latin is hiding in our iPhone keyboards?

Kingston, though, does not seem as tickled by the trivia, despite the fact that he's literally the one who pointed it out. He doesn't seem affected by anything, really.

Even his new housemate being a girl.

It's spooky. Almost supernatural.

Emrys switches off the projector, its humming sound rattling to silence, and restores the overhead lights. "Well, that's enough tedium for today, I suppose. Review the photocopies I've made for you and perhaps I'll give you a quiz next time." He shrugs, as if he hasn't really decided yet. "Ah, and—Mr. Pendragon, Ms. Vale? If you don't mind…"

He gestures towards his desk. The rest of the room packs up, shuffling papers and muttering about coffee, while Kingston slides his single elegant notebook into his leather satchel and I shove together all of my various belongings.

Even standing at Emrys's desk, Kingston only acknowledges

my presence with the barest of glances. And this time, for some reason, it pisses me off.

So you'll help me, but not show me any human emotion?

"You wanted to see us, professor?" Kingston says.

Us. Despite my pissed-offedness, something about the plural pronoun makes me shiver a little.

Like we're a team.

A unit.

An…anything.

"Ah, yes, yes, my illustrious champions." Emrys pushes his reading glasses further up his face and cranes his neck as the last two stragglers depart the classroom. Once they've definitively disappeared, footsteps barely audible, he turns back to us and procures a fat leather folder from within his desk drawers.

"For you two," he says. "Your prize."

I stare at the folder. Stare at Emrys. Stare—or glance—at Kingston.

No one says anything.

Fine. I will.

"What is it?" I ask.

"A text, of course," Emrys says. He gives the top a little pat. "A new project for you two to tackle."

"Our prize is more work?"

Kingston's words are blunt, even if his tone is polite. And I have to say, I agree. It's not like we don't already have loads of homework for this class—not to mention all the others.

"The finest prize there is." Emrys nods. "More to read."

Kingston's jaw ticks. I bite my lip—intrigued, but confused.

"So what are we supposed to do with it, exactly?"

"Why, transliterate," Emrys says. "Same as it ever was. We've just gotten a true treasure trove of new manuscript material—I'm sure your father has told you, Mr. Pendragon—"

Kingston's grip on his bag tightens imperceptibly.

"—and now the fun begins." Emrys nods. "As you two are my bright stars, I've awarded you the chance to take on this sizable chunk. *And* you'll have until Monday to complete it."

"Monday?" The stiffness drops from Kingston's voice, replaced by genuine disbelief. "We fence Sainte-Odile this weekend."

"Good thing you have a colleague, then," Emrys says. "Many hands make light work."

"I need more time," Kingston insists.

"And yet there is none to be had." Emrys's voice takes on the slightest edge, the tiniest bit of firmness, and it's enough—somehow, it's enough to cow even Kingston Pendragon. "What is human life if not one giant, immovable deadline? Best to learn to work efficiently." He claps Kingston on the shoulder and all but shoves the folder of papers into his chest. "Now, if you'll excuse me. I've been told there are biscuits in the faculty lounge."

With that, Emrys sweeps out, coat over his arm and briefcase in hand, leaving just me and Kingston alone.

I wait for him to move. He doesn't.

"So…"

"I won't be able to work on this until Saturday," Kingston says. "Night. Before then, I need to focus."

"O…kay," I say. "We can start then, I guess." I eye the thick stack of papers in the folder—it'd be tough to get through all of them even with a full three days. But I'm not about to contradict Kingston.

"Good. We can meet in the library." He slides the folder into his bag—not without some difficulty, given how thick and unevenly stuffed it is—and heads for the door.

"Kingston, wait."

Once again, I'm struck by how strange it feels to say his name out loud—to him. And maybe he realizes, too, because he stops immediately short, his eyes instantly locked on mine.

"Yes," he says. And then adds: "Gwenna."

Direct. Decorous. And…firm.

The sound of my own name has never given me butterflies before.

"I just…" Where do I even start? I pluck at the hem of my skirt—my *new* skirt, the one *he* bought me. "You had Callahan bring me to Camlann House. To…live with you?"

His mouth hardens to a line.

"Do you have anywhere else to live at Caliburn?" he asks at last.

"No," I admit. "But—"

"Is there something wrong with your room?"

I bite back a groan of frustration. "*No,* but—"

"Then there's nothing to discuss." He buttons the front of his overcoat, those golden-brown eyes right on mine. "Don't miss the meet tonight."

TWENTY-TWO

GWENNA

I STILL DON'T KNOW what to think about Latin class, or about Kingston in general, when it's time for the fencing meet. Campus has fallen to dusk, and the walk to the field house is almost shrouded in shadows. Fortunately, Morgan agreed to go with me.

"Not exactly my first," she says.

"Really?" I say.

"Oh sure," she says airily, linking her arm through mine. "I got dragged to plenty of these back when Kingston was still coming up. Guess *my* hobbies weren't ever worth wasting *his* time on," she grumbles. "At least back then."

"I see." I realize I don't even fully understand their whole setup. "So, wait," I ask her, "you've been in this little blended family since…"

"Feels like forever," she says."Toddlerhood at least. My mom was the side piece."

"Oh," I say. "Congratulations?"

Morgan cackles with laughter. "She'd love that. But yeah, got her claws into a rich one and brought me along with. That meant spending a lot of my formative years watching boys play with swords. At least until I finally got my way and they packed me off to boarding school."

"There are worse ways to spend an evening," I say. Like a... formal hall, for instance. "How long does this thing last?"

"In this case?" Morgan says. "Not very long. These guys make quick work of their enemies."

We step into the field house, and although it's ostensibly a gym, it sure doesn't feel like it. The floors are polished wood, and the walls are paneled rather than cinderblock. There are steel beams crisscrossing the ceiling, but they're all disguised in draped banners, almost like the ones at the formal hall. The windows are arched in typical Caliburn style, crisscrossed with latticework showing just the bleak expanse of the cold winter lake. Bleachers are set up around the edges and a single long strip of play area, I suppose, laid out in the middle of the room. There's a table of judges, some sort of electronic scoring equipment, and the air smells like adrenaline, steel, and excitement.

On one side of the room hangs the familiar Caliburn banner, its crest and colors vibrant as ever, and on the other an unfamiliar one, green and yellow.

"The Université de Sainte-Odile," Morgan says. "Quebecois, very snooty, or so I've heard." She looks around, sweeping a gaze over the bleachers. "Don't look now, but you are public enemy number one out here."

I believe her. I only flick my gaze sideways to the bleachers, but I can feel the intensity of dozens of pairs of eyes on me. Elena's made quick work of spreading rumors around the campus.

I hate this. I hate being seen, hate being perceived at all, especially by this many people at once. But Kingston wanted me here. And I don't think I had a choice in the matter.

At least I could bring a friend.

"Pick a seat, any seat," Morgan says, in a low tone so only I can hear. "I don't know that any one is gonna be any better than any other."

"Fair enough," I grumble back, thinking idly about quick exit strategies. I nod toward a gap in the second row on the opposite side, near to the stairs up.

"Works for me," Morgan says.

As we cross the boards of the floor, my boots squeaking along the polish, I hear someone yell out, "Check out Ash Wednesday!" And a ripple of laughter sounds through the crowd. My cheeks go hot, but I keep my shoulders back and head high, the way Mom always claimed would give me confidence. It didn't work in middle school, and it isn't working now. But the only way out is through.

Morgan and I take our seats, a good three empty spaces between us and the rest of the crowd, but that's probably for the best. I try to look for a bright side, try to be excited about something, and I realize I never have been to a fencing match—meet?—so that'll at least be something.

"So what exactly are the stakes here?" I say to Morgan. "Like an NCAA thing, or…"

"I don't think so," she says. "Caliburn's in a pretty small league, only…" She scrunches up her face. "Twelve or so schools, I think? They do this different kind of fighting, hence the small squads. Three swordsmen, three weapons, three bouts, that's it. Anchor scoring, multi-weapon relay."

"I see," I say, even though I'm not really sure what most of those words mean in context.

Just in front of us, the team from Sainte-Odile is warming up, wearing their padded fencing attire with the high necks and broad shoulders, rigging themselves up to the wires that I suppose are the electronic scoring system. From somewhere in the back of the stands, I hear laughter getting louder and louder until someone calls out boisterously.

To me.

"Hey, I was just wondering," he says, the smirk on his face tamped down unsuccessfully, "if you, uh, liked Alicia Keys."

"I don't know," I say. "I guess she's fine. What does that have to do with anything?"

"Oh, you know," he says, his breath beery, "because *this girl is on fiiiiiiire.*"

Oh my God. My eyes shimmer with a hint of tears, the back of my throat catching. It isn't funny, even though he and his friends are cracking up. I tense my jaw and focus on the announcements, trying to drown them out.

A man has taken center stage, or the equivalent, and commanded attention, getting the crowd to murmur into quiet.

"My distinguished guests, Caliburn students, and those of our visiting opponents," he says, "it is my pleasure to welcome you to the opening match of this year's fencing season."

Applause. Cheers, and a few hoots from the small visitor section of Sainte-Odile.

"My name," he says, "is Luther Pendragon, a trustee of the college and a proud fencing parent"—a smile flickers over his face—"as well as a former swordsman myself."

"That's your stepdad?" I whisper to Morgan.

Her face remains impassive. "Unfortunately." She sighs. "I mean, he's my mom's type. Rich. So that helps." She shrugs. "He and I aren't exactly close, in case you can't tell."

I dart a glance to the corner where Kingston is sitting, with perfect posture. His eyes locked on his father, that unyielding stare. "I suppose he's more of a father-son type?"

"In a manner of speaking," Morgan mutters. "Liked having a son so much he took in a bonus one as a foster kid."

Kai. That's right.

"As you know," Luther booms, "we at Caliburn, as well as our colleagues at Sainte-Odile and the rest of the league, fence a unique style. This style is derived from the French school and is, as we would consider it here, the purest form of the sport. It is about excellence, dedication, and singular focus." He smiles. "Three bouts, one swordsman per weapon, first to eight points each. Victory goes to the team with the most total points across all bouts combined."

"In other words, no quitting just because you're ahead," Morgan adds, to me. "Even best two out of three won't cut it if you lose really badly in the third. Third bout's where you really wipe the floor."

I guess that makes sense. Otherwise, why bother even *having* a third bout? "Who goes third?"

Morgan scoffs. "Who do you think?" She mimes putting a crown on her head.

Oh. Duh. I glance at Kingston, but his eyes are trained directly on his father.

"And with that," Luther says, spreading his palms wide, "I wish you all success and a fine display of swordsmanship."

He backs away as the dean of the divinity school takes his place, murmuring a prayer. As he does, I watch the four swordsmen—Kingston, Kai, Lanz, and Callahan, in practiced order—fall to one knee, their foreheads pressed to the hand holding their swords upright. Sainte-Odile does the same. And for a moment, I'm struck by how genuinely...reverant the moment seems, as opposed to some perfunctory little pause before a sporting event. It's moving, actually. All of their eyes closed. Certainly better than something corny like the national anthem.

And all too soon, it's over.

"First bout," calls the official. "Saber."

In front of me, the first swordsmen are taking their places. Kai. Hulking, tall, bouncing his weight lightly from foot to foot, looking fired up as if smoke's about to come out of his nostrils. The other swordsman, in Sainte-Odile Green, is stone-faced, but

Kai seems unable to resist a smirky little grin. He murmurs something only the two of them can hear before he slips on his mask, and then the official gives a signal.

"Swordsmen to your places," he says. "En garde."

Wordless, instant, they both spring back into position. It's elegant and swift, almost balletic: their sabers poised at each other, tips angled just above target range.

"And...allez!"

Kai explodes forward, slashing straight for the head—fast, relentless. His opponent, about half a head shorter but just as solid, deflects—*no*, parries, I think—cleanly, retreating just enough to duck the next cut, his blade whistling through the air in a counterattack.

But Kai pulls his arm back just in time. Silence—no buzz from the score box, no point.

They pull apart briefly, breathing hard, but not for long. Undaunted, Kai launches forward again, goes for a head cut—or, no, *feints* a head cut, but drops, snaps his wrist and whips his blade up and across to hit the other guy right in the side.

The buzzer sounds.

"Touch left," calls the scorekeeper. "Point to Caliburn, 1-0."

Cheers from the crowd, which Kai barely registers, just circles again and shakes out his legs.

This time, Kai barely rests before he strikes again. Left, right, left, down, up, in. Buzz, a point.

"En garde—allez!" Slash, slash, clang, buzz, a point. It's 2-0 Kai, then Sainte-Odile comes in with a skimming touch and the score tightens. 2-1. 3-1. 3-2. 3-3. I can almost sense the frustration coming from Kai, the need to be quicker, more decisive about it. At one point. his opponent signals, needing a breather, some water. Kai is offered the same, but he waves it off, simply paces a circle like a caged tiger, rippling with energy.

"5-3, Caliburn," restates the official. "Swordsmen, take your places. En garde. Ready? Allez."

This time, it's fast and brutal. Kai springs forward and whips a head cut home—hard.

The crack of blade on mask echoes through the salle. The Sainte-Odile fencer stumbles back, clearly rattled, and pulls off his mask. Above his eyebrow, a thin line of blood trickles from a fresh, crooked gash.

The official throws up his hand. "Halt!"

Gasps go up from the crowd, but Kai merely shrugs—and at that, the official all but storms onto the strip, a yellow card in the air.

Now Kai's ripping off his mask too, cocking his head and spreading his arms in disbelief. The ref ignores him, checking the mask, the wound, the blade.

"What's going on?" I whisper urgently. "What happened?"

"Too much force," Morgan says. "You're supposed to score, not crack their skull open. A head cut like that and you could put someone's eye out."

My mind flashes to the silk patch on Luther Pendragon.

"Yellow card means they won't throw him out," she goes on. "But only if he doesn't fuck up and lose his cool about it."

A tense few moments pass as the Sainte-Odile sabrist is examined. Someone produces a bandage, applies it. Questions are murmured, heads nod.

"Swordsmen will reset," the official calls at last. "Places."

A sigh of relief ripples through the stands—a few cheers, even. Kai runs a hand through his sweat-slicked hair and grins like he just got away with something—which, I suppose, he did—before slamming his mask back into place.

"En garde. Ready?" Two short nods. "Allez!"

Now the Sainte-Odile sabrist goes for broke. He leaps and lunges, slashing at the air and slicing inches from Kai's body. But

Kai moves, ducking, rolling, arching backward and up in every direction. His opponent is undeterred, tries again, the blade moving so fast I can barely track it, but Kai repels it like a magnet, left when it's right, right when it's left, down, down, up, over.

I realize my fists are clenched in my lap. It's tense.

And then...then Kai lifts his own blade. A feint left, then right, then right again, but—no, he strikes, swift and direct, and the edge of the blade hits square in the chest of Sainte-Odile's sabrist.

Buzz. The final buzz seems to sound just a little bit longer.

"Touch," calls the official, "bout to Caliburn, 8-5. Caliburn leads 1-0 in bouts, 8-5 in total points."

The crowd erupts in cheers and hoots, and I clap too, more stunned than excited, in awe of what I've just seen. From what I know of Kai, and that admittedly isn't much for someone who's technically now my roommate, he didn't seem that disciplined. But what I saw just now, that takes strength and skill that doesn't come about by accident, even by natural talent. He was impressive.

"I know, right?" Morgan says. "Swords are cool."

I have to admit, she's right.

"Bout two," calls the official. "Epée, to your places."

I'm about to ask Morgan which of the guys is up for epee, not that I can quite tell the difference between the two weapons, but I don't need to. The swordsman that steps onto the piste is unmistakably Callahan, impossibly tall, implausibly broad, and I wonder how he'll manage to move as quickly and as nimbly as Kai did just now.

"Swordsman to your places," calls the official, "en garde."

Immediately I realize there's no reason to wonder. Callahan's on defense almost immediately—the other swordsman is much smaller, smaller even than Kai's opponent, and what he lacks in size he makes up for in speed—but Callahan dodges the lunges easily, almost as if he's waiting for the guy to tire himself out—and then, on the next attack, extends his own blade.

Buzz. A single light on the scoring machine. Callahan caught him on the wrist, like it was nothing. His longer reach paid off.

"Touch right," calls the official. "Point to Caliburn, 1-0."

When they resume again, I wait for a burst of action, but none comes—not from Callahan. His advances are cautious—smaller steps, lighter blade motion—and he controls the distance masterfully, maintaining even space between them with deft steps, and I find myself wishing I had the vocabulary to describe it, to put words to this kind of dance-like sport, to know exactly what makes Callahan so *different* from Kai and yet just as good.

"Touch right!"

There's a buzz. Callahan's blade point flexes slightly against his opponent's shoulder. They pull apart. His opponent nods in recognition, which Callahan returns. They take their places again.

"Allez!"

This time, the other swordsman is too quick, and Cal not fast enough. With a swift lunge, the Sainte-Odile swordsman bores a hole through the air and right into Callahan's side, buzzing on the score system. I let out a little gasp, clutch my hands to my chin, and then feel silly.

Next to me, Morgan chuckles. "Relax," she says. "They can lose a point here or there. They're not going to lose the bout."

And she's right. The smaller Sainte-Odile fencer finds his rhythm, cuts through the distance Callahan's been so careful to preserve, nocks up a score on his hand, then his foot. The crowd tenses, but if the pressure makes it to Callahan, he doesn't show it. I get the sense that Callahan's style is more strategic, intellectual, than Kai's. Less barnburner, but still gets the results.

And sure enough, the next two points are his, and then a third, followed by a long exchange of thrusts and parries that culminate with a narrow point for Sainte-Odile.

But after that, it's like Callahan locks in. Point, point, point. He makes it look easy, almost motionless, and it's clear that his opponent is getting tired. Soon he's a point away from victory, running the poor guy up and down the strip, wearing him out until at last—

Zzzt.

"Bout to Caliburn, 8-6. Caliburn leads 2-0 in bouts, 16-11 in total points."

The applause is loud once more, but more measured this time, almost cautious. I clap hard, genuinely impressed at Callahan—and Kai, too—but look to Morgan for guidance.

"They're good, right? Two bouts to zero?"

She squints, wavers a *kinda sorta* hand in the air. "Yeah, but. Sainte-Odile could still pull it out if they dominate foil. If they come out, like…" She does the math quickly. "Eight points to two, they'd win by point total."

I nod, processing. Realizing what that means.

We have to win the next one.

"And now, foil," calls the official. "Swordsman, take your places."

This, I know, is Kingston. The only one who hasn't fought yet. A shiver runs down my spine, and my eyes flick to the VIP box, where Luther, to my surprise, isn't hunched over with intense focus, or even clapping harder for his son. He's frozen, unmoved. Simply ready, as if it's a done deal, and he's only waiting to see just how it will unfold.

"Swordsmen, take your places," says the official. "En garde. Ready? Allez!"

It's quick. Kingston advances decisively, lunges, but his opponent deflects. Both blades flash and bend in the clash.

Buzz. Two lights. A pause.

"Attack no, riposte yes. Touch left. Score 0-1."

"What's that mean?" I hiss urgently.

"Foil's right-of-way scoring," Morgan says. "Only one of them can score at a time, and apparently Kingston's attack was no good. Just the riposte—the counterattack, basically."

"Allez!"

They're moving again—quick, intense, feet flying fast. My eyes dart from the clash on the strip to the score box lighting up, barely able to keep a bead on the action but still sensing a kind of sinking energy. Not quite panic, but close to.

"Touch right," calls the official. "Score 2-4."

"Oh," Morgan murmurs. "Oh oh oh. I don't like it."

I glance at her. "What do you mean?"

"He's in his head," she says, eyes forward. "I can tell. He's just a little too slow to move. He's overthinking it."

I look back at the piste. Nothing about this appears slow to me, unless you consider a lightning strike slow, but still, a point to Sainte-Odile. It's the first time they've had the edge, I realize.

And I don't like it.

"Swordsman, take your places," says the official. "En garde. Ready? Allez."

Kingston lunges this time, fast, forceful, like he's making up for lost time.

Except it's too much. Because when Sainte-Odile counters, Kingston's overextended. Unbalanced.

I don't know what I take in first, the sight of him hitting the ground or the hard thud of his fall. But my reaction is the same: a chill, painfully swift, rushing at once down my spine and up my neck.

The crowd gasps.

"Kingston!" someone yells.

"Time," calls an official, their voice sharp but impassive.

Immediately, Lanz and Callahan, followed by Kai, leap off the bench and rush to Kingston's side on the piste. He comes upright, but wrenches off his mask, his face contorted in pain that even he can't manage to hide.

I look at Morgan. "Is he going to be okay?" I whisper, "What happens now?"

"I don't know," she says. "We'll see, but if he's too badly hurt…" Her eyes dart to her stepfather, and mine follow suit.

If anything about Luther Pendragon's attitude has changed, it doesn't show physically. And *that* is even more chilling than watching Kingston fall. His son just took a hard blow, wrenched his arm, from what it looks like, could be injured badly enough to take him out of the match, never mind doing anything else, and he's sitting as placidly as if he's watching the grass grow at a golf course.

I look back to the strip. Kingston's gotten back to his feet, and Lanz leans in. He gives his head a little shake, but Kingston seems to be insisting, nodding. The official takes two brisk steps to both of them, listens, nods. He returns to his microphone.

"Pendragon out, substitute Dell'Acqua."

A gasp, louder this time, reverberates through the field house. The Sainte-Odile fencers look at each other in disbelief. Even one of the scorekeepers lifts his eyebrows.

"What does this mean?" I say to Morgan.

"They're putting in their alternate," she says, "just like it sounds. Lanz is taking over. I think he's the one they have doing all three weapons, just in case something like this happens."

Kingston's face is somber, but he forces a smile as he nods to the crowd, gives a short, stiff bow, wincing again as he does from the pain in his arm. He turns to Lanz, his left arm at the small of his back, and Lanz does the same. They each raise their blades in a salute, Kingston with some difficulty. Lanz slips on his mask while Kingston returns to the bench. He sits on the edge next to Kai, who looks at him with an expression I can't quite read. Angry, disappointed, smug? Maybe all three.

"Why wouldn't he...go get medical attention, or something?" I say to Morgan.

"Because he's an idiot," she says, rolling her eyes. "And because there's this whole tradition. You don't leave the salle until the match is done, no matter what. Literally even if you're dead—they just leave your body there and carry on."

Jesus. "That's grim."

"Swordsman, take your places," the official says. "En garde. Ready?" He pauses a second longer, waiting for Lanz's nod. "Allez!"

I am absolutely captivated.

I can't help it.

Lanz and Kingston might be the two most physically similar of the team, but their styles are entirely different. Lanz's whole posture is tense, and he explodes forward into two lunges. A quick two touches. It's like his opponent is confused, needing to adapt, but it doesn't take him long. He pushes forward, gets Lanz towards the back of the piste. And even though I can't see his face with the mask, it almost seems like Lanz is flustered. Touch. Touch. Sainte-Odile has the advantage again, but barely. Lanz walks in a slight circle, shaking his limbs out.

Come on, I think. *Come on, you can do it.* I'm surprised at how much I care, how much I'm invested. But this close, with Kingston hurt, we can't lose.

"We can't. I know we can't," Morgan says.

I blink. *Did I say that out loud?* No, I'm certain I didn't.

But either way...

"Allez!"

This time Lanz's rhythm is different. He's faster. Quick flashes of blade, a tight feint. Direct thrust.

Zzzzt.

"Touch," calls the official. "Bout to Caliburn, 8-7. Final match score: Caliburn wins 3-0 in bouts, 24-18 in total points."

The bleachers explode with cheers. Lanz stands still for a minute. Stop. And when he takes off his mask to shake his opponent's hand, his face is utterly shocked, like he can't believe he did it.

Believe it, I think. I'm so proud of them and I don't even know why. Maybe it's just the sheer joy of watching people with talent execute something flawlessly, or almost, I think, looking at Kingston. Maybe it's the team spirit of the place catching up with me. Or maybe it's just that…

"See?" Morgan says, clapping herself. "Like I said. Swords are cool."

I'm about to agree, when—splat.

Something soft and wet smacks and sticks against the back of my neck.

"Look out below," someone yells, laughing.

"Oh my God," Morgan shrieks, "are you okay?"

"I…don't know," I say. I'm stunned more than anything, and clutch at the back of my head to figure out what it is. My fingers sink into it with a little stick.

It's chewing gum. But not just a single wad. A whole ball, like someone had been chewing and spitting and chewing and spitting, specifically to build this projectile.

"Jesus, Gwenna." Morgan wheels around. "You absolute shitheels! What the fuck is wrong with—"

"It's fine," I hiss at her, "it's fine. I'll just…there's a bathroom in here, right?"

"Yeah," she says. "That door over there, hallway to the locker rooms."

"Thanks."

Biting the inside of my cheek, I rush across the field house, fighting the stream of people exiting, presumably headed to Porter's or dorm rooms for after-match celebrations. I follow the signs for the women's lockers, fling myself in front of a sink, and rake at my hair with my fingers.

I get it, I think furiously. *Okay? I get it. You hate me. I hate me. I should never have fucking gone out and paraded myself in public like this. Should never have gone fucking* anywhere *after what I did.*

Shame floods through me like liquid fire, and I pull harder on the hair, yank more desperately at a knot that will never come undone.

Even if it was a fucking accident.

I still did it. Somewhere inside me was the capacity to be that destructive.

Elena didn't deserve what happened.

Her father didn't deserve it.

No one did. *No one did.*

Except me.

I pull at my hair, pain lacing my scalp.

Then I pull harder.

I deserve this.

I deserve this.

I deserve this.

In one final yank, the strands rip from my head.

It hurts, *burns*, but it's gone. Done. And I feel…

I don't feel better.

But calmer, maybe.

Like I'm done for now.

I square my shoulders, blow out a breath, toss the ugly clump into a trash basket and dare to survey myself in the mirror. The damage is hidden—or hidden enough.

Not like anyone who looks at me will care.

With a hand towel, I wring all the water I can out of my hair, then deposit it in a laundry basket. I linger a moment, my breathing returning to baseline, my heart squeezing less and less frantically.

Something skims off the edge of my chin—a drop of water, not from my hair.

There are tears in my eyes, I realize. I'm crying.

I need to get out of here.

I could wait until everyone leaves. Or I could just get it over with and hide.

Resolved, I push through the swinging door—and into something.

Someone.

TWENTY-THREE

LANZ

"GWENNA," I say, breathless, "Hi."

I'm...overwhelmed. Flustered. I can't believe I did it, can't believe I pulled off foil at the last minute like that, and against Drummond from Sainte-Odile, who's a senior and no slouch.

But my excitement fades, *plummets*, as soon as I take her in.

"Gwenna," I say again. "What's wrong?"

She shakes her head, says nothing. But her eyes are red and swollen, her expression tight, and her hair is hanging damp over her shoulders.

"Nothing," she manages at last. She tips her chin up to face me, and it's even more obvious that she's lying. "It was just..."

Realization hits like a sledgehammer. My voice turns to stone. "What did they do to you?"

She presses her lips together. Lets out a shuddering breath. Mutters something I can't hear.

I lean in, heart pounding. "Say again," I ask gently.

"I said, what *didn't* they do?" She hugs her arms around herself, slowly shaking her head back and forth. "Never mind. Forget I said anything."

Adrenaline, pure and uncut and already primed from my time

on the strip, surges in my veins. "Those bastards," I grind out. "I'm going to kill them. I'm going to—"

"Wait!"

She reaches, grabs at my wrist, and just the brush of her fingers is enough to hold me in place.

I wait.

"Don't," she says. "You'll…it'll just make it worse."

I clench my jaw. "No. Not if I make it clear that—"

"*Lanz,*" she says, and her voice is so firm and resolute that it startles me. "Please."

No sooner does she get the word out than a fresh round of tears takes her over.

"I…Gwenna." Everything in me slackens, collapses, desperate in my need to comfort her, and before I can think, I've wrapped my arms around her, taking her shaking form to my chest and holding her still.

And she lets me.

I am more awake and alive and alert than I think I've ever been. My entire being is focused on being here, with her, *for* her. Slowly, gradually, I lift a hand to stroke the back of her head, and my fingertips meet damp hair, snarled in tangles so fierce I almost hiss at the sensation.

Gwenna startles. Like it hurts her.

Like *I* hurt her.

Just by touching her head.

"I—" My heart rate skyrockets. Thinking *now* she'll push away.

But she doesn't.

Just rests her head back against my chest.

Breathes in. Out. In.

And fuck me, but it's intoxicating.

"Shh," I say. "It's okay. You're okay."

Nothing else matters. Nothing else exists—not fencing, not

Camlann House, not the vow or the quest or anything beyond this girl and whatever she needs that I can give her. I want to hold her tighter, deeper in my arms, stroking her head and keeping her safe for as long as she needs. As long as she'll let me.

"I...God." She pushes away, gently, scrubs at her eye as she slowly shakes her head. "I'm sorry. I'm a mess. I'm...I'm fine."

"You don't have to be fine," I murmur. That gets me another head shake, firmer.

"I do," she insists, "and I am. Now." She exhales. Blinks. Looks up at me, and her expression shifts, just the smallest bit, like she's just now piecing together what just happened. "I...you..." She blinks again. "Oh my God. I'm throwing this...this *pity party* and I didn't even say congratulations."

A pang grabs at my chest. *Who cares about my stupid fencing victory?* I want to say. *I would've forfeited the whole season just to keep you from feeling like this.*

But a smile breaks across her face, so genuine and excited, that I can't help but feel excited too.

"Granted, I know zero percent about fencing," she says, giving a watery laugh. "But that was..." She shakes her head. "Wow."

"Yeah?" I can't help but ask.

"I mean, it was, and you were..." She shakes her head. "I've never seen anything like it."

I can't handle it. Can't handle even the barest words of praise from her.

My heart is pounding. My *head* is pounding with being near her, with the thrill of actual, literal victory, victory that *I* claimed with *my* sword.

And standing there, even in the dim light of the field house hallway, she looks...radiant. Looks every inch the woman destined to break my heart and leave me to die.

Ever since I learned about the Dell'Acqua curse, I'd imagined what she'd look like—the woman who'd be my undoing. I always figured she would be beautiful, but in a sort of generic sense. Some vague assemblage of supermodel parts, bouncy hair, clear skin, white teeth. But now that she's here and real and flesh and blood, she's different. Not what I expected, or knew I wanted.

She's better. She's everything.

And as I look at her, my mind starts spinning with excuses. Explanations.

I have to. I had to. I couldn't not.

It's too much. My traitorous body seizes control.

I pull her to me, lift her chin, and kiss her.

The instant our lips touch, I know it's wrong. Know that this is indeed what will damn me for all eternity.

But my God, is it good.

Sweet, soft, easy, warm.

Everything. Everything I wanted.

And then it's over. I pull back.

"I," I stammer. "Oh my God, I didn't…"

"It's fine," she says, her cheeks a little pink. "It's…" She tucks a hair behind her ear.

"Just…I'm excited," I ramble on, "and I…we won, and you're here and…"

"Lanz?"

My stomach drops.

It can't be—

But I turn, and there he is.

Callahan. Freshly showered, holding his equipment bag over his shoulder.

Waiting for me.

And no mistaking what he's seen.

"Cal," I say. "Callahan. I was just…we were just…"

"You don't have to say anything," he says. "Don't worry about it. But we should…"

"Yeah, I…" The pit in my stomach has turned to a churning,

the excitement of my victory now stirred up into a kind of fresh terror and self-loathing.

And it's all too much.

"I've got to..." I can't string two words together. "I'm sorry. I—"

That's all I can manage before I run.

Run like an absolute coward. Away from her, away from Callahan, away from everything.

TWENTY-FOUR

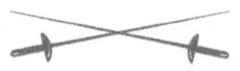

KINGSTON

"THAT WAS A DISGRACE."

My father's voice is as pitiless as it is cold. I stand in front of him, the fire in his townhouse living room flickering light across the oriental carpet, my arm hanging heavy in the black sling that loops around my neck.

"I cannot tell you," my father goes on, pacing, not looking at me, "what it is like to stand there and watch my son allow that abomination of a performance."

"It was a mistake," I say quickly. Nothing to deny there. I don't look at him, stare at the ground instead.

"Obviously," my father drawls. "That's all you have to say? You agree that what you did was beyond the pale?" He gives a low snort. "Your powers of observation are to be commended, Kingston."

Father's house in Sarrasford is nothing elaborate. High quality, of course, but only the necessities. Brownstone, three floors, sleek furniture. Mallory is notably not here—presumably either in New York or in Boca or God knows where Morgan's mother likes to get up to spending the family fortune. This house by Caliburn is all

Luther, all masculine energy, all the things that should be my birthright and that I clearly failed to make good on.

And yet, at the same time, there's something strangely comforting in it. The ritual. Knowing that any failure, all failures, are met with this. That I can count on him in that regard.

"That's it?" my father barks, spinning on me. "You come here to tell me what I already know?"

"You told me to come here," I say simply.

It's the wrong thing to say. He narrows his good eye at me, closes the space between us.

"I should strike you for that," he says, voice low and lethal. "But it's unseemly to hit a man when he's already down." His gaze falls to my arm. "How long?" he says.

"I don't know exactly. It's just a sprain."

"We'll find out how long," he says, "and then take half that time. Dell'Acqua was fine, but we can't afford to have you out of commission permanently. It's too risky."

"I know that," I say, but my tone must be too strong.

"I want nothing but rehabilitory exercises for you," he says. "Between now and the next match, that's it. Eat, sleep, and work that arm back into shape. Have I made myself clear?"

I bristle. I'm not a child. I don't need to be told how to take care of my injuries.

Or I don't *now*.

Where were you when I was bruised and beat up from all those practices as a kid? I think. *Where were you when Kai would pound the shit out of me after I beat him? Where was your insistence on rehab, your attention?*

But I don't say any of that.

Instead, I do what I do best. I parry.

"What about studying?" I say. "Don't I need to do that?"

His mouth hardens into a thin line. "Of course," he says

tersely. "I figured that goes without saying, but if you need it all spelled out—"

"I don't," I say. "I just wanted to affirm, because Dr. Emrys has selected me for a special project."

That gets his attention. His expression changes, not softens exactly, but loses some of its keen edge.

"Has he?" he says.

"Yes," I say. "We did excellent work on a team project in class, and so he's given us an original text to—"

"We," my father interrupts. "Another student?"

I dip my head. "Yes," I admit. "She's quite accomplished."

"She?"

Damn it. I hadn't meant to reveal that. Now, or ever.

But I can't unspeak what I've said.

So I pivot.

"Correct." I curl my lips. "A female student. Caliburn has admitted them since the 1900s, you know."

"Don't be smart," he snaps back. "You know why I'm asking." He turns to face me full on, his one eye boring into me. "Is that going to be a problem for you?"

My blood rushes hot in spite of myself.

"No," I say as evenly as I can manage. "Why would it be? Have I ever showed signs of being tempted before?"

"Have you ever lost this badly in a match before?" my father counters.

I have nothing to say to that. I clench my jaw.

"It won't be a problem," I say. "I'm keeping her close so that I can work twice as fast."

TWENTY-FIVE

GWENNA

SATURDAY NIGHT and the library is quiet as a mausoleum. Just the way I like it.

Yet I'm still on edge, despite the quiet. Because I'm not here by myself. I'm here loaded down with notebook papers and dictionaries, reference guides and glossaries, waiting for—

"Gwenna."

I look up into a pair of golden-brown eyes.

"Hi," I say, the word almost sticking in my throat.

"Hi." Kingston meets my eyes, but just briefly. And he looks... rough. Nothing in his behavior gives him away, no cracks in the facade, but physically, he seems different, somehow.

The arm hanging in the sling doesn't help, either.

He shoots a glance around the library, at the various late-night studiers propped up on elbows and yawning into their textbooks, blearily picking at keyboards and scribbling on looseleaf. As he does, a few of them turn, almost magnet-like, to take him in: mighty Kingston Pendragon, the fencing star laid low.

He doesn't need to say it. I can practically read his mind.

Too many people. Too many eyes, observers.

"I know somewhere we can go," I say, low enough so just he can hear. "This way."

I brush past him towards the side of the room, through the passageway with the stationery cart and copier and down to the service staircase, down from the A-level to B1 and then B2. It's dark when I swing open the door, and I fumble to the right for the timer switch on the wall, giving it a good crank when I find it.

"Archives level," I say. "No one ever comes down here. Hence the...lighting on a timer."

Kingston doesn't say anything. Just nods, taking in the racks of moveable shelving, the dim, dark walls, the warm, dusty air that comes without thousands and thousands of yellowing pages and minimal ventilation. "Where should we set up?"

"Here." I walk him to the side of the room, to what I've started to think of as my private table, and set down my coat and bag. I tug at one of the narrow table drawers and remove some spare notebooks and pens I left down here last time, along with my copy of the Pocket Oxford Latin-English dictionary. All the while, Kingston stares, like it had never occurred to him that I might have any sort of secret dealings outside of his awareness, no matter how mundane, and a wave of embarrassment washes lightly over me.

What kind of weirdo school obsessive keeps a cache of translation materials at the ready in a basement level of the library?

Be normal, Gwenna.

Too late.

With a final glance back at the staircase door, Kingston sets his own bag on the table. I take a seat, but he stands a moment, considering, and I realize a beat too late that he's still wearing his coat

"Oh," I say. "Here. I can..."

I jump up, step to his side and curl my fingers under the

camelhair collar. He doesn't speak, doesn't look me in the eye, just inclines his head slightly as I slide the coat from his shoulders. It falls into my arms in a heap, still faintly warm from his body heat.

"Thank you," he says softly. His eyes are lowered, his lashes practically sweeping his cheekbones, and it occurs to me that this might be the first time someone's ever done the all-powerful, ever-so-chivalrous Kingston Pendragon a small favor.

Because clearly, he isn't used to it. The slight tinge of pink in his cheeks is testament to that.

Well, the honor is all mine, I think sarcastically.

Or half-sarcastically, anyway.

Because up close…

Strong jaw. Straight nose. *Cheekbones.*

…up close he's not so bad.

All at once, Kingston moves, pulling out his chair with his left arm and settling in. I fold his coat and drape it over the back of another chair, almost reluctant to let it go, and take my seat. From his bag, he produces the folder of papers from Emrys.

My heart sinks.

It's in terrible shape. Not physically—the facsimiles are good, well rendered and crisp—but the lettering is…well, it's barely lettering. Serpentine, rippling, almost curlicues—there's no sense of individual letters, let alone words.

Kingston must share my dismay, because his golden eyes go wide. "This is…"

"Awful," I agree.

He presses his lips together. "I was going to say *challenging.*"

I blow out a breath, not quite hard enough to be a snort. "All a matter of perspective, I guess," I say, throwing my hair over my shoulder to lean closer. Then I frown. I grab the first sheet of the stack and pivot it around, so that it's facing the opposite way.

"What are you doing?" Kingston says.

"I'm trying to read it," I say. "What do you think I'm doing?"

"You're reading it upside down now," he says, and rotates it around with his left hand. "There."

A small burst of indignation flares at the base of my neck. "No"—I turn it again—"*this* is the right way." I give it another turn. "*This* is upside down. For me," I add. "For you, it's right ways up."

A frown, definitive and firm, draws across Kingston's handsome face. "I don't think that's correct."

I set my jaw. "Well, I do."

He blinks at me. Then again, leaving his eyes shut a fraction of a second longer than necessary. Exhales hard—hard enough to be a snort, if you ask me.

And starts writing.

"Kingston!" I cry, almost forgetting we're in a library—albeit an all-but-abandoned part of it. "What are you doing?"

He barely looks up. "I'm transliterating, *Gwenna*."

I don't care for the way he says my name. Certainly not for the way it *feels* to hear him say it.

Not one bit.

I clutch my pencil, throat suddenly dry.

"But…" I crane my neck at the paper. "But it's *upside down*. For you, I mean. It won't make any sense."

"It *will* make sense, because this is the correct way to read it." He all but slams his pencil down and looks me dead in the eyes. "Look. You can help, or you can leave, but I will not waste my time arguing with you. Do you understand?"

He's so sharp, almost harsh, that I temporarily forget how to speak.

But when his eyes meet mine, they're not hard with fury or even annoyed.

They look…desperate.

It's too intense. I blink first. Look away. Heat crawls up my neck, and I take an inordinate amount of time tearing a sheet from my notebook, arranging it to write on.

And still...he's wrong.

I sneak a look up to glower at him. It's five minutes to midnight, we've already lost an entire day for this assignment because of his need to focus on this fencing match—which, at the risk of sounding cruel, does not seem to have mattered, in the end, for him, given that he got hurt—and now he's just steamrolling over the fact that the text is literally not readable from where he's sitting?

I would rather die than give him the satisfaction. *Especially because he is wrong.*

I sit up straighter.

"No, you're right," I say, forcing my voice to be calm and even. "We'll both give it a shot, and eventually it'll be clear which way is up."

"Agreed," Kingston says, without looking up.

"Fine," I add, needlessly except for my crushing insistence on having the last word.

I pick up my pencil and write.

It's miserably slow. Painstaking. Lots of stops and starts, checking against various reference sheets. But it's also...kind of satisfying in its slowness, like cross-stitch or whittling or something else cozy and deliberate you'd do to relax.

And...it's nice, being here. In the library. Working.

Even if it is with Kingston.

"Done." I put down the pencil, push my paper a few inches away to actually read what I wrote now that I'm not just focused on finding letterforms and spacing.

"What is...beneath," I murmur slowly, "is...just as...that which is above. And what is above is just as that which is beneath."

Huh. A little tautological, but it's grammatical—a real sentence. Triumphant, I look up to see Kingston's reaction.

He straightens. Lowers his pen. And turns his own paper around to me.

Quod est inferius est sicut quod est superius, et quod est superius est sicut quod est inferius.

The same thing. The same exact text.

"What?" I pull his sheet closer. "How?"

It's then that I notice his handwriting isn't its usual perfect penmanship, but shakier, more labored...

He's writing with his left hand. Because his right is in a sling. My heart squeezes a little at the realization, and I immediately feel like a jerk for gloating.

Of course you finished first, Gwenna. He literally can't go any faster.

"I told you," he says.

"And *I* told *you*," I retort. "I guess we're...both right."

He nods, frowning at the paper. Turning it one way, then the other.

"The same thing from either side," he says—unnecessarily, I think. Then he pins his eyes on me. "What does it mean?"

"It means...it means what I just said," I say, not following. "It's not that complicated of a text."

"But what's the *point*?" Kingston says, a little sharper. "What is it telling us?"

I tilt my head at him. "It...means that what's above is below, and vice versa?" I frown. "I don't know what you're asking me."

Kingston curls back in his seat and blows out a breath, which, combined with the stony look on his face, makes him look like an overgrown, sulky little prince.

He mutters something I can't quite catch.

"Sorry?"

"Waste of time," he says, loud enough for me to hear. Then he's on his feet, pushing the chair back in place, and grabbing his jacket. Doesn't bother to put it on, or ask for help, just throws it over his arm and leaves, the door to the B2 level swinging behind him.

Stunned, I sit in silence, until—

Click.

The timer shuts off. And I'm left in darkness.

TWENTY-SIX

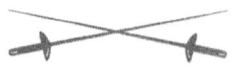

LANZ

EARLY SUNDAY MORNING, very early, and the chapel is cold and hushed. Not even the rectory staff is here yet to set up. No movement except for the gentle play of dust motes in the colored shafts of light streaming onto the flagstones and me.

I've been kneeling so long that I'm losing feeling in my feet. My fingers interweave on the bench in front of me. And yet I haven't asked for a single damn thing—forgiveness, understanding, wisdom.

I can't.

I woke up early as usual. My body's too accustomed to our early morning warm-ups, but it's Sunday, the one day we have off from those, and so I figured...I figured this was where I needed to be.

I messed up, I fucked up, big time. I shouldn't have kissed her, even if I liked it, even if she liked it—which, there's no way she could have—and I fucked up even more, because we got seen.

I've never been big on confessing my sins. Self-awareness is good, I guess, but the whole self-flagellation thing is a step too far for me—I torture myself plenty in my own mind. I don't need to invite God or a priest to step in as well.

But right now, I need all the help I can get.

The problem is, I just...can't make it all line up. Temptation, sin, wickedness, adultery—the words don't mean anything to me, don't apply to where I am, to who she is.

She's not darkness; she's light. She's not degradation or corruption; she's...a higher standard.

I shouldn't have kissed her, I know that much. And yet I also know that if I were ever going to kiss her again—which I won't— I'd have to be twice as worthy and three times as good as I am now. A better fighter, a better knight, a better man.

But Jesus. If this is what winning does to me, then I'm a goner. If this is what happens when I'm put to the test, I'm failing at every turn.

I let my head fall to my fingers and tense my jaw, when suddenly, I hear footsteps—a gentle rustle of movement to my right as someone slides in next to me, kneels.

I don't need to look up to see who it is. Callahan.

It's still silent, but a different kind of silence than before; the incense-scented air feels taut, electric, thick, even though it's cold and dry in here. I press my lips together, run my tongue over my teeth.

Cal speaks first.

"Praying?" he says.

"Trying to," I mutter. "Can't think of any words to say."

Cal gives a low chuckle.

"Should have been raised Catholic. Say Hail Marys in your sleep."

He's got a rosary in his hands, I notice now. I've never seen that before.

But then again, I've never been in this kind of situation either.

I clasp my fingers together a little more tightly and tip my chin up to look at the rose window and the stained glass scene beneath it—the altar silent and draped with a red cloth, the arches of the choir loft looming shadowy.

I made a mistake. Or several. Maybe. Does it count as more than one if it was a single action? Or was it even? Have I ever been doing the right thing? Or is this all just a selfish quest to get freed from my own fate? Is that why I treat the vows like an escape hatch, Cal like a loophole?

He won't talk, either. I know that much about Cal. Calling him a man of few words would be a generous overstatement.

"Are you...doing okay?"

That's the best I can manage. Best I can phrase it in a semi-public place where we could be overheard. I can't meet his eyes; I can't look anywhere now, except for the very center of the rose window—the hundreds or thousands of multicolored facets, winking and gleaming as somewhere in the east the sun is rising.

"Fine." Cal's tone is even, controlled, and I realize how hollow my own words sound compared to his. He never lies, except by omission. Never is anything but stalwart. He doesn't seem so plagued with inner turmoil. "You?"

"I don't know," I reply at last, genuinely uncertain. I can practically hear Cal swallow. He's put his hands up on the bench too, stringing the rosary beads through his fingers—even if he's praying, he's doing it silently. "The pressure got to me, or not—the pressure, you know how it is after a bout like that. It's nerves, I guess. Just….adrenaline. Hard to stay focused. You know."

Cal shakes his head. "Not really."

Right. Of course he doesn't know. Cal's...intent. Dedicated. I've known that since the moment I met him, written all over him, the way he walks, talks, holds himself. I never could have been like that—never would have been able to pledge myself to waiting for marriage, for Christ's sake. The Dell'Acqua curse notwithstanding, I fall hard and fast.

Not Cal. Even when he's stumbled, he's never fallen.

And his next words send an arrow straight to my heart.

"Is there anything I can do?"

"No," I say quickly. *Fuck, God, no, Cal.* "Don't...say things like that. You don't need to do anything. To...change anything."

He knows what I mean. I know he does.

"I'll get back on track," I go on. "I just..." I scratch the back of my head. "Momentary lapse."

Cal doesn't move for a moment. Then he nods.

"Okay." He looks at me, directly, for the first time in minutes. "I know how much this means to you."

I don't know what *this* he's even talking about.

But no matter what...he's right.

The light from the stained glass window plays across his face, and unable to stare at him any longer, I look up at it too. Beneath the rose window is a tableau of the Last Supper—serene disciples, a table piled high with food, and a shining gold chalice in the middle.

I have to shake my head.

"They don't even know if it's a cup," Callahan says.

"What?" I turn to him, frowning.

He nods just barely at the stained glass.

"The Holy Grail. It's disputed. Could be any kind of object. Lots of people think it's the same as the Philosopher's Stone. Or a place. Garden of Eden, Fountain of Youth, Lost City of Atlantis."

Oh. I don't want to talk about this now—logistics, semantics—but this is what Cal does, I've noticed.

Changes the subject. Gets down to brass tacks.

Anything but talk about feelings.

"Huh," I say. "Go figure."

"Yeah." Cal's voice is low. "Do you think..." He pauses. Continues. "Do you think this is all worth it?"

I chew the inside of my cheek. I don't want to lie to him, but I don't know if I can tell him the truth. Being one of us knights has been—I hate to overstate it—but basically what brought Cal back to life. It gave him a purpose after losing his parents, the swim team. It gave him, as terrible as it sounds, me—something to live for. If I tell him what I think, what I've *been thinking*, it could destroy him and—selfishly, I admit—it would destroy me, meaning that everything I'd worked for was just an excuse.

"I think it's something that needs to be done," I say. "And if we're the ones to do it, then we have to do it."

It's not an answer to his question, not really. But Cal says nothing in reply. For a moment, I imagine the tension dissipating—that we won't have to talk about the one thing I know we're both thinking about, or at least that I'm thinking about enough for the both of us.

"Does she change anything?"

God damn it.

"No," I manage.

It's a half-truth again.

Because the whole truth is, I can't let go of what I'm feeling for Gwenna—the magnetic pull that she has on me. It feels like the only way to rid myself of it would be to carve my soul out of my body somehow. Let it all go at once—the curse and my life. Which, I suppose, is how it works.

And yet, it hasn't changed how I feel about Cal. It doesn't make me want him less or care about him less.

That's why I have to answer the way I do.

"Well, well, well." The cracking of boots startles both of us—me so much I nearly jump out of the pew.

"Isn't this a nice little surprise." Kai cocks his head at us as he advances from the back of the nave. "Here I am thinking I'll have the place to myself to clear my conscience over nicking that Sainte-Odile guy, but what am I to find but Callahan with Pretty Boy on his knees."

The barest flash of panic goes across Callahan's eyes. I see it. I feel it.

"That what you're here to confess?"

Neither of us says anything. Kai's expression shifts from smirking and smug to curious, intrigued—as if he might have hit a nerve and could pry more out of us.

No, God, no. A one-time lapse is, well, one thing. But a continued...whatever-it-is-that-Cal-and-I-have. Affair? I don't even know what to call it. That would be something else entirely.

And for Kai to find out...it'd be almost as bad as Kingston finding out.

No, I think, *worse*.

I have to throw him off the trail, and fast.

"I kissed Gwenna," I blurt out.

The admission hangs in the stillness of the morning air. But it works.

Kai's eyebrows leap up, his mouth slightly open, total surprise overcoming him.

"You *what*?" he says, almost spitting the T at the end of the word.

"It was after the match," I say. "Adrenaline, excitement, I don't know. She gave me a hug and I just—" I loosen my shoulders, raised my hands in defeat, like the pathetic excuse for a man that I am. "I wasn't thinking. I couldn't think. And so I'm just here to..."

Kai waves a hand in the air. "Hold on to your panties." He draws a quick sign of the cross over his chest, curls his hands to his breastbone, closes his eyes, and says the quickest prayer I've ever seen.

"I can't believe you," he says, and there's no teasing in his voice anymore—just disgust, so raw and undiluted that it actually surprises me, even from Kai.

"Everyone makes mistakes," Callahan says, and my heart squeezes to hear him defend me—defend me against the very thing that I know hurts him three times as much as it could ever hurt the integrity of our code.

"Cram it, Ms. Rachel," Kai says, then turns to me. "Does Kingston know?"

"No," I say quickly. "And he's not going to find out. I'm here. I got forgiveness. I'm…I'm good."

But the look on Kai's face doesn't go away. Like I'm a worm. Like I'm reprehensible.

"You don't understand," I say. "It was…"

"Of *course* I understand," Kai says, fierce but cold. "Of *course* I do." He spreads his arms wide. "You think I don't have trouble with these vows? Me, of all people? For Christ's sake." His scowl at me is next level. "You shouldn't even be on this team, *Lanz*."

My name, not Pretty Boy or some other demeaning nickname. I don't know what to say because I don't know that he's wrong.

"Don't tell Kingston," I say quickly. Begging. A pathetic 10-year-old caught up past his bedtime. "Please, I just…"

Kai puts up a hand to silence me.

"I won't," he says. His eyes dart up to the stained glass. "Stays between you and God. And"—he glares at Callahan—"big guy here, I guess." He swivels back to me. "But you know why I won't tell?" He advances, jabs a finger barely an inch from my eyes. "Because you can't keep a secret for shit. And I have a feeling it's just a matter of time before you slip up again and fuck all of us over."

With that, he spins on his heel and leaves.

TWENTY-SEVEN

KAI

I CAN'T BELIEVE IT. I can't fucking believe it.

I slam the door to Camlann wide open, after stalking up the steps. Indignation, fury, coursing through every fiber of my being.

That little shit, that little baby-faced, blue-eyed twerp of an alternate, steps in for one fucking match and thinks he's the Wilt Chamberlain of fencing?

Fuck. That.

The door gently taps itself shut behind me, and even the small, inoffensive sound pisses me off so much that I turn and crane-kick it right in the crossbar.

"Fuck him," I say out loud.

I scrub my face with my hands. I didn't sleep last night, couldn't sleep last night, thinking about her here, and then realizing she wasn't here, and waiting for her to get back from the library. And for what? So that I could keep Lanz's pretty little side piece all perfect and unharmed for him. Fucking Christ.

I need a gallon of coffee, a lava hot shower, and the world's sloppiest blowjob.

Guess I'll have to settle for two out of three, *like I always do*.

I storm to the kitchen and slap together the coffee maker,

jabbing the on button on my way to the stairs. I pause at my bedroom to peel out of my jacket and chuck it at my bed. Spin around and bang the door to the bathroom shut too.

I strip off my jeans and T-shirt, barely even glancing at myself in the mirror. I don't hate the way I look. Hell, I've basically been customizing my appearance ever since I had a good enough fake ID to get me my first tattoo.

But right now, seeing myself is a reminder of everything I'm not.

The shower in the house is a lot more spacious and accommodating than the one down in the locker room by the salle, with deep terracotta tiles, two shower heads, and a low bench that I can't see any discernible purpose for beyond…something sex-related. Nevertheless, there it is.

I step into the water and hiss as the scalding stream hits my sore muscles. I rub at my neck, traps, as much of my lats as I can reach, roll the muscles out. I'll recover. Didn't push myself too far, no injuries or anything, but for now it's gonna hurt.

Sainte-Odile bastard's gotta feel even worse, though. And that's what counts.

With the kinks gotten out, I stand there a second, waiting for the water to burn all the pissed-off out of me.

It doesn't.

I close my eyes, scrub at the sockets.

He kissed her. Of course he did. Weak little moony-eyed shit. Bet she liked it, too. Girls always go for that puppy-dog thing. Swooning for him, sighing, licking those pretty little pink lips of hers…

…and now I'm hard.

Goddammit.

It's unfair. Unfair that that soft little fuckboy got to kiss her and unfair that now that's all I can think about. My imagination's overclocked on a good day, and I have too much information to feed it—too many visuals seared in my memory from the other night, when I had to get her out of that ridiculous dress.

My dick twitches as the water pounds down around me. As if to say *not going anywhere. Better deal with this.*

Masturbation is…kind of a gray area, from what I gather. Very don't ask, don't tell. Never interviewed the other guys on their schedules or anything, but I'd be shocked if they aren't beating off at *least* every few days.

Anyway. If I make it quick, it barely counts, right?

I breathe out hard and brace my left hand against the shower wall so my right can get to work.

Won't take much, I immediately realize. As soon as my eyes are closed I can see her, smell her, practically fucking taste her, and my dick throbs so hard in my hand I actually feel a little dizzy. I sink my teeth into my lip and rub faster. Harder.

Green eyes. Flushed cheeks. Dark hair flowing over all that pale skin, knotted in my fist to pull her back and—

Knock, knock.

"*Fuck.*"

I clutch the wall, eyes open, heart pounding like fucking apoplexy.

I don't mean to scream, but the sound actually scared the shit out of me.

"Sorry," comes a voice.

Her voice.

Oh, fuck.

I clear my throat, drop my traitorous idiot dick, pinch the bridge of my nose and beg for the shower to drown me somehow.

"I was just…I left my hairbrush in there, and Morgan's coming to pick me up in a few minutes—"

"I'm…" My voice sounds weirdly strangled. Fuck. I clear my throat another dozen times. "Yeah. Gimme a sec."

I wrench the water all the way to cold and stand there until it's...done its job. Then I shake myself like a dog, smack myself in the face, and yank a towel from the stack.

When I open the door, she looks...

Goddammit. She looks so nice.

"Oh," Gwenna says. "You didn't have to...I could've waited for you to finish."

For. Fuck's. Sake.

She had to say that.

I grip the towel in my fist so hard I'm going to break a finger.

"S'all good," I manage. "Just not, uh...used to close quarters with a lady."

I step aside, stupidly, to let her slip in and grab the hairbrush. Good thing I didn't know it was in there or I might have tried to smell it or something like the absolute pervert that I am.

"Thanks." She ducks back out.

"Mi baño es tu baño," I say. "Literally."

I'm antsy to get back in, shut the bathroom door and shove a washcloth in my mouth so I can rage scream at how fucking stupid I am, when—

"Hey, Kai?"

I skid to a stop, door ajar. "Mm?"

"I, uh..." Gwenna looks at the floor. Then up at me. "I never said thank you for the dresses. They were..." She blinks a few times, and I wait, mentally filling in the adjective: *expensive, over the top, indulgent, expensive, impressive, expensive...*

But she doesn't go with any of those.

"...really thoughtful." She shakes her head. "I mean, you were."

I just stand there, clutching my towel. "Oh. Uh."

Thoughtful enough for you to end up getting poisoned, I think. But I know what she means.

And it's nice.

Kind.

Too kind.

"I think the words you're looking for," Gwenna says, with just the hint of a smile, "are *are you're welcome.*"

I swallow. "You're welcome."

Anytime, I add silently. *You are welcome anytime, Gwenna Vale.*

TWENTY-EIGHT

GWENNA

THE ORACULAR CURIO IS A CRAMPED, labyrinthine shop packed floor to ceiling with glass jars, dried herbs, and books with titles like *Fung-Tastic: The Curative Power of Mushrooms* and *Moon Sisters: Awakening the Wild Woman Within.*

I feel perplexed, intrigued, and unsure where to look first. And a little nauseated from the overwhelming blend of smells.

But Morgan seems, well…right at home.

"Ugh, finally," she sighs and steps inside with the confidence and direction of a doomsday prepper walking into a Costco. "I need *everything.*"

I glance at what appears to be a small, gold-plated bird skull on top of one of the bookcases.

Hopefully not everything, I think.

Sarrasford's pretty small and humble as towns go, but it has all the necessities—a coffee shop, a dive bar or two, a pizza joint, and even a few quaint little New England-y shops along the main street, of which the Oracular Curio is one: an "alternative art gallery and home goods store."

When Morgan asked what I was doing on Sunday, I had to

admit that I had no plans, and I wasn't about to spend the entire day loafing in Camlann House, not after the match on Friday and especially not after my study session with Kingston.

So when she subsequently asked if I wanted to hop a ride to town with her for some shopping, I said yes before even thinking through what I was agreeing to.

And now, even though we're in what is quite possibly the most bizarre shop on the entire Main Street, I feel...oddly relaxed. Peaceful. Like a normal college student in a normal, charming college town. The sky is clear and blue despite the few flurries of yesterday, the air is crisp and smells like pine sap and woodsmoke, and I'm bundled into a thick cable-knit sweater (black, of course) and knee-length peacoat that have me feeling like Rory Gilmore's long-lost goth twin. In a good way.

"All right, let's see," Morgan says as she produces a shopping basket from out of nowhere and starts dropping things in from what seems like random shelves—little shards of crystals, piney-smelling sticky globs of resin, a few spray bottles with labels I can't quite make out. It's such a strange assortment of stuff contrasted to her low-cut, cream-colored sweater and heatless curls, clean girl meets evil sorceress.

"Good to see you again, my dear," says the woman behind the counter, who could be forty, sixty, or a hundred, with dyed red hair the color of a stop sign and what looks like three individual shawls draped over her shoulders.

"You too," Morgan yells back as she drops candles into her basket: one, two, three, four. "God, I know I'm going overboard, but I'm literally starting from scratch. Don't judge me."

"Not judging," I say. "Is your room nice, at least?"

She shrugs. "Imagine our old room, but just with me in it, and you basically get the idea. Stuck on a hall with a bunch of third years, but they'll just have to get used to me."

"I did," I say. "Wasn't even that hard."

"See," Morgan says, laughing, "I'm a fucking delight." She slides her eyes in my direction. "How's yours?"

I pick up a geode with a sparkling blue center that makes me think of hard candy and examine it, tilting it this way and that.

"It's...different," I say. If I'm being honest, I don't want to think too hard about it—the proximity of all of them, the considerable upgrade to my living space, the catered meals and entire wardrobe of replacement clothes. Like if I stare at it too closely, it'll vanish.

Fortunately, Morgan doesn't push. I squint into the glimmering hollow of the geode and change the subject. "Should I get this for my room?"

She, too, squints at it. "Depends. Does it meet the Camlann House rules? Can't be bringing bad vibes around the perfect swordsmen." She laughs.

I replace the geode on the shelf, letting my fingers linger on its bumpy surface. There really is something about this place—the Oracular Curio in particular, with its jewel-green walls and moody vibes, but Sarrasford in general, and certainly Caliburn—that's...unusual.

"Is it just me, or is everyone around here kind of obsessed with, like, relics and rituals and magical shit?"

Morgan doesn't turn around from wherever she's rummaging. "Are they?"

"*Aren't* they?" I glance up at the pressed-tin ceiling, which has a series of suncatchers in the shape of the evil eye dangling from tiny hooks.

Morgan just shrugs, still fixed intently on a vial of essential oils. "Who knows? Academically intense schools attract nerds."

"Yeah," I agree. Although, this stuff, and to be honest, a lot of the stuff at Camlann House, goes beyond sheer geeking out.

Besides, I wouldn't really call Morgan a nerd. Or Kingston. Or any of them for that matter.

"You really think *you're* a nerd?" I say, eyeing her up and down, "let alone, like, Kingston or Kai?"

Morgan sighs. "Yeah, well, they're a special case. Luther's obsessed with excellence, so I guess an ordinary Ivy League wasn't going to cut it. That plus the whole fencing legacy thing." She rolls her eyes. "I mean, he wasn't satisfied with one kid being a prodigy. He had to literally go acquire one to, I don't know, double his odds or something."

I frown. "What do you mean?"

"Kai," she says. "You didn't know?"

I shake my head.

"He was straight-up a foster kid. Luther was doing some kind of charity fencing clinic and saw this kid with a terrible attitude and a wicked talent for swords—or so I've been told. I was off at the South Salem School for Girls by then." She shrugs again. "From then on it was a fast track to the Pendragon townhouse and all training all the time."

"Oh," I say. That certainly explains more of it. Certainly why he and Kingston look and act absolutely *nothing* alike. "So Kai was just naturally good at fencing and...just like that, he's adopted into one of the most wealthy and powerful families on the East Coast, if not the country?"

"Yep," Morgan says. "Some of us snuck under the velvet rope with our gold-digging mothers, and others just had dumb luck, I guess."

I laugh, even though it still doesn't quite add up to me. I mean, good to be talented at fencing, I guess, but so much so that you actually recruit someone to be in your own family? No wonder Kai's not so crazy about Kingston or the rest of them.

"Okay," Morgan chirps, "stop me now or else I'll max out my entire credit line."

I blink and look down at her basket, which is suddenly filled to the brim and visibly dragging her arm away from her body. "Jesus, Mary, and Joseph," I whisper. "Is there anything you *didn't* buy?"

"Like I said, I'm starting from scratch." She moves it to the counter, not without some difficulty, and the red-haired woman starts gingerly taking it out piece by piece and punching the prices into an adding machine. Old-school here too, I see.

"And with these, Morgan dear?" She holds up a black candle with a black wick. "Do be careful that—"

"I know, I know," Morgan says, cutting her off—a bit harshly, I think. "You don't need to lecture me about *fire safety*, Lucinda."

The heaviness in the last two words must be some kind of hint for the woman to back off, which she does. I'm silently grateful for it.

She produces a black credit card with a flourish and hands it to the woman, who painstakingly transcribes the card number by hand.

"Thank you, stepfather," Morgan whispers, pressing two fingers to her lips and blowing a kiss to an invisible Luther before taking the card back. "And thank *you*, Lucinda."

"Anytime," the woman burbles. "Oh, and this is a lovely choice," she adds, holding up a small rectangular box—a tarot deck, I realize. "The last one we had, too."

Now it's Morgan's turn to frown. "I do *not* remember putting that in there," she says. "And God knows I have plenty. You can just put that back."

But the woman shakes her head, waggling a finger in the air. "Ah, ah, ah, my dear, you know the rules. If a deck finds you, then you desperately need it." She pops it into the tote bag with the rest of Morgan's loot. "No charge."

Morgan opens her mouth as if to protest, then snaps it shut. "Fine, fine," she sighs. "What's another to add to the collection?"

"You know how to read tarot?" I say. I'm impressed, although not surprised.

Morgan scoffs. "Oh, it's not that hard."

"Don't be falsely modest," chides Lucinda. "Morgan's got a great talent for the cards."

"Yeah?" I say, kind of intrigued now. Having grown up largely friendless, I'd never gotten into the whole Ouija board, MASH, light-as-a-feather-stiff-as-a-board kind of slumber party stuff that a lot of other girls did. I'd certainly never had my fortune told. "Can you do me?"

"Oh yes!" Lucinda insists, giving a happy little clap of her hands. "Go on now."

"Sure." Morgan cracks open the box with the tips of her long lavender nails and expertly snaps the cards, sending them arcing from one hand to another like she's a Vegas dealer.

My eyes go wide. "Holy shit, Morgan. When do you find time to practice that?"

She shrugs, shuffling deftly. "Like I said, just a little hobby. Now focus your mind on a question you want an answer to."

"Okay," I say.

Where do I start? I think, but I close my eyes and focus and try to let something come to me. Lucinda, meanwhile, clears a little space on the counter, looking on with intrigue.

"We'll do just a quickie mini-cross spread," Morgan says, flipping the cards out into a kind of compass formation: north, south, east, west, and then one in the center.

Morgan frowns. "That's...I don't know what that is." She looks at Lucinda. "Have you ever seen that?"

Lucinda shakes her head, earrings swinging wildly. "Very curious."

"What?" I say, my heart lurching. "What is it?"

"That's the thing," Morgan says, biting her lip and putting a hand to her chin. "I'm...not sure." She closes her eyes and inhales sharply, a little reset. "Okay, so, this is your basic cruciform spread—cross-shaped," she explains.

"I know what *cruciform* means," I retort. "I'm in Emrys's class with your stepbrother, remember? It's from the Latin."

"Right, right, right." Morgan waves a dismissive hand. "Anyway—it's a cross. The intersections of the conscious and unconscious, the past and the future." She makes a little plus sign with her index fingers to illustrate. "As above, so below."

At her words, a full-body shiver courses through me, scalp to toes.

Quod est inferius est sicut quod est superius, et quod est superius est sicut quod est inferius.

"I see," I say, but my voice sounds uneven, wobbly, like I'm underwater. So I focus instead on the cards, frowning, pretending to study them. The illustrations are intricate and curlicued, like woodcuts or engravings, with a decidedly old-fashioned aesthetic: billowing feathers, curling ferns, doublets and ballooning sleeves. Renaissance, maybe? Slightly later?

Kai would know, I think. Then shake away the thought.

"Look at that," Lucinda says, hovering a fingertip around each of the four framing cards in turn. "What are the odds—one of each suit?"

I follow her gesture: *Cavaliere di Spade, Cavaliere di Coppe, Cavaliere di Bastoni, Cavaliere di Denari.*

Knight of Swords, Knight of Cups, Knight of Wands, Knight of Pentacles.

"I don't know," Morgan murmurs again, sounding vaguely irritated. "That's a math question. It's…the knight is the headstrong one," she adds, to me. "They express their suit's essence to the extreme."

"Swords for intellect," Lucinda interjects, "cups for emotions, wands for charisma, and pentacles for groundedness. Air, water, fire, earth."

"Right," Morgan says. "But to have them all in the spread, kind of focused in on the center like that..."

She trails off, her gaze fixed on the center card. That one is less ornate—almost boring, actually, a simple round slab of wood with a column-like base.

The caption beneath it reads, in spidery Italian, La Tavola.

"The...table?" I translate. "What's that mean?"

"I already *said*, I'm not sure," Morgan all but snaps. She looks me dead in the eye, and for the first time since the day we met in our dorm room I see a sharp edge of suspicion in her gaze. "What did you ask?"

Lucinda intervenes with a slight cough. "You don't have to tell her, ah—"

"Gwenna," I say, not looking away from the cards.

"Gwenna," Lucinda finishes graciously. "Morgan, perhaps it's an old deck. You know how the classic *tarocchi* has some variations in the cards that—"

But Morgan is only fixed on me. "What did you ask?" she says again, a bit more gently.

I stare at her, stare at the cards.

What am I doing at Camlann House?

But before I can answer, a soft hum breaks the silence. Morgan's phone, in her back pocket. She shakes to life, pulls it out and gives the tiniest eye roll.

"Sorry," she says. "I've got to take this." She waves the phone in the air, scooping her purchases and the loose cards into her tote bag. "Gwen, meet you for coffee? I won't be long."

I nod, swallowing, hiding the untethered wriggle of panic that's now taken up residence in my chest.

Be normal.

"Great." She whips the phone out of sight, but not so quickly that I can't see whose name came up on the screen. "Hey. I'm getting it now. Can you..."

Kingston.

WITH ITS RECLAIMED WOOD TABLETOPS, stark white walls, and minimalist decor, Eclipse Coffee Lab is decidedly *not* Holy Grounds.

But heads still turn my way when I enter.

Fine, I think, lifting my chin. *It's going to be that way? Stare all you want.*

Armed with my fake-it-til-I-make-it energy, I get at the end of the long line, trying to lose my train of thought in the whistling of the espresso machine and the faint sounds of 70s yacht rock—played ironically, I'm sure—over the PA system.

The letterboard behind the bar informs me that I won't be getting a beverage for less than six bucks, which makes me wince a little—but still, it's caffeine. And I need some kind of pick-me-up after that tarot card incident.

As I'm debating between a macchiato and a flat white, the line shuffles forward, and the guy in front of me flicks a glance over his shoulder. I see him from the corner of my eye, but do my best to ignore him, staring straight at the tiny plastic letters and emitting as many *fuck off* vibes as I can without saying as much out loud.

It doesn't work. He looks again, this time angling himself to look at me more fully, and the prickling sensation of being not just seen, but *observed* creeps up my chest. I give it another few seconds, waiting for social decorum to kick in and for him to deflect his stare, but…nothing.

My fingers start to shake, and I tuck them up inside the sleeve of my peacoat. The line shuffles forward again, more heads from nearby tables turning and more whispers stirring. Somewhere overhead, the soundtrack shifts to a bumping disco track, upbeat and vaguely familiar, but pinging something in the back of my brain that says *danger*.

Another step forward. The guy still stares. And then the chorus kicks in, and I realize why I hate this song.

Disco Inferno.

Burn, baby, burn...

Titters come from the coffee shop crowd as heat climbs up my neck. And this fucking guy is still staring at me.

I can't take it. I wheel on him.

"What?" I say, a tremble in my voice. "Is this your little prank?" I sweep a hand in the air to indicate wherever the fuck the speakers are. "You want to get a reaction out of the crazy pyromaniac girl, or whatever? Cute. Very mature. Points for creativity."

The guy's expression shifts from curiosity to blank indifference.

"I beg your pardon." His lips tilt in a smile—apologetic, but not guilty. "I only wanted to see what all were staring at," he goes on. "I see it's you, and..."

His words are clipped and musical, a foreign accent I can't quite place—Eastern European, somewhere. That, combined with his relatively imposing height and the sharp cut of his brown suede jacket make him feel oddly sophisticated compared to the rest of the largely student patrons—even though he has to be around college age himself.

And he clearly has no idea who I am.

"I...sorry," I stammer. I clench my fists hard. "I thought you..." I wheel my gaze around the room, but everyone's gone back to their conversations and chocolate croissants, no one daring to make eye contact now. "The song—I thought you were making fun of me."

"No." He shakes his head—dark curls, dark eyes, high cheekbones—and I notice for the first time the thin silver chain around his neck with a tiny cross hanging at the hollow of his throat. He turns to the barista, signals for her attention. "Excuse me. Miss?"

She perks her head up, not without glancing at me. I recognize her, vaguely, from campus—stubby brown ponytail and cat-eye glasses.

"She does not like the music," he says, gesturing at me. "Could you please change songs?"

"I..." The barista girl looks caught off guard, like she's torn between this *ever so clever* practical joke and six-plus feet of tall, dark, and handsome asking her a favor.

"Please," he adds again, with a smile. "I thank you."

"Sure," she chirps, and scurries off to fiddle with a screen. Satisfied, he turns to me.

"Hopefully it is better now."

I swallow, my mouth gone dry. The song shifts to something warm and inoffensive—lo-fi, no lyrics—and I feel my head go up and down in a nod, but I'm not sure I am feeling better.

No, I'm definitely not. The ringing is still in my ears. The cold sweat springing up on my chest and neck. Every pulse of my heart palpable.

I'm going to have a panic attack.

"Good." He nods back, holds out a hand, his voice tinny and distant. "I am Alexei."

Pulse. Pulse. My heart has taken over my whole body, my whole consciousness, and it takes me a minute to realize he's introducing himself—formally. I take his hand, feeling slow-motion, like a marionette, and manage to shake it. It's firm, oddly cold.

"I'm...Gwenna," I hear myself say.

He nods—or bows, almost—just as it's his turn at the register. Beneath me, the floor tips sideways. I swallow, desperate, chasing calm and not finding it.

"What can I get for you?" says a male barista.

"Coffee. Black, please. And for you?"

Me. He's talking to me. Alexei. The stranger.

"I…the same." I blink. "Excuse me," I say hurriedly, stepping past him. "I just…excuse me a second."

I push blindly past low armchairs and cylindrical side tables to the back of the coffee shop, where miraculously I find the door marked W.C. right where I'd hoped. I all but fall inside and slam the door behind me, panting in the cramped space of black tile and eucalyptus-scented air.

I'm suddenly hot, too hot, sweating all over, so I frantically strip myself from my coat, needing out of the heaviness and heat. It's still not enough, so I push my sweater sleeves to my elbows, rush to the sink and scoop back my hair, throwing water on my face.

Fingers dripping, I grip the edge of the sink and stare at the silver circle of the drain.

All shall be well, and all shall be well, and all manner of thing shall be well.

Maybe it's the lingering effects of the weird tarot reading. Maybe I'm actually insane and just incapable of getting an actual grip. Maybe it's some kind of immune reaction to a total stranger being generous to me, for once.

Whatever it is, it's powerful.

And yet…it's passing.

Slowly, slowly, the dread ebbs out of me, leaving sheer exhaustion in its wake. My shoulders feel heavy, my breathing ragged like I've just sprinted a mile. But every heartbeat gets me that little bit closer to calm.

Finally, I'm steady again. Or steady enough.

There are no paper towels—just one of those stupidly unhygienic Airblade things—so I pat my face dry with the edge of my sweater sleeve—dry clean only be damned—and bundle up my coat from where I'd shucked it onto the ground. With a deep breath, I grab the handle and push my way back out into the world.

"*There* you are!"

It's Morgan, rushing towards me from the end of the line. "I was about to put out an APB when I didn't see you." She frowns, looking me up and down, and grabs my upper arm. "Are you okay?"

"I'm…yeah," I say. "Now, anyway." I press a hand to my forehead. "Long story. Or, not really, just…"

I think of the guy—Alexei—and look around for him. Nothing —he's gone. But a single cup of black coffee sits waiting on the sideboard.

"I guess that's mine," I mutter, and gently shrug out of Morgan's grasp.

She pouts. "You ordered already?"

"Sort of," I say, threading my way to grab the cup and ducking back to her side. "I, uh, was in line, and this guy starts talking to me—Russian, or something?—and buys me a drink."

Morgan's eyes go wide. "Russian?"

The coffee's way too hot to drink, so I blow on it, nodding. "I mean, I didn't see a passport. I'm just stereotyping based on accent."

"What did he look like?"

"Um, tallish? Dark hair, dark eyes, little cross necklace?" I lower my cup slightly. "Why?"

Morgan snatches the coffee out of my hand so fast she nearly spills it over herself. "Don't drink that!"

I gape at her. "What?"

"You…you can't just drink random unattended beverages from strange guys," she says, darting a glance from the still-sloshing coffee to my face. "Come on, Gwenna. Have some street smarts. Especially after what happened at the formal hall."

She does have a point, I realize. Still, her reaction seems…off.

"Speaking of which," Morgan says. "I need to make one more stop, so—"

I shrug. "That's fine. I'm down for whatever."

Morgan winces. "Yeah, it's...a little ways out of town, is the thing. *But*, good news is, I got you a ride back to campus."

With that, she turns to the door and waves to someone:

Callahan.

TWENTY-NINE

CALLAHAN

I'M grateful to even have a car. And usually, I can ignore the fact that it's a piece of junk.

But now, with her walking beside me, looking at the battered 1990s station wagon between the sleek SUVs and hybrids, it's all I can think about.

"This is me," I say, indicating. Not meeting her eye.

Gwenna nods. "Volvo," she remarks. "Very safe."

I tense my jaw a little as I push the key into the driver's side lock and twist. Say nothing.

"What?"

Her voice startles me. I glance at her.

"I didn't say anything."

"No, but you..." She frowns. "Reacted."

"I'm sorry."

She sighs—actually sighs. "You don't need to *apologize*," she says calmly. "You're allowed to feel...frustrated, or whatever."

"I'm not frustrated," I say. "I'm..."

I don't know what I am. What I feel. Those aren't things I think about.

"People always say that," I finish. "About the car."

Gwenna cocks her head. "Aren't they right? I thought Volvos were, like, notoriously safe."

I lick my lips. "Safety standards have gone up a lot in the last thirty years. Any car on this block is just as safe as this one. This car's safe mostly because it's...solid."

Her eyes flick up and down. Over the car.

Over me.

She shrugs.

"Solid is good."

A burst of heat, unbidden and unwelcome, flares somewhere deep in my belly, climbs all the way to my cheeks. I take two quick steps to her side of the car, pull open the door and hold it there.

She blinks. "Thanks." Then gets in.

I nod, and go to take my seat. The car rocks to the left as I get in, and I slide the key in the ignition as she wrestles with the passenger-side seatbelt.

"Damn, really jammed in there," she mutters.

The heat flares again, fully in my face. "It catches," I say. "Sometimes."

She nods, but after another fruitless yank, lets it go, drops her hands to her lap. "Well, just drive carefully."

Is she kidding? That's not safe.

I reach over the console, my arm across her shoulders, and give the belt a hard tug. It gives with a jerk, then smoothly as I pull it down to secure it.

Gwenna does, too. And her fingers brush mine.

She glances up, eyes wide like she's worried she's hurt me.

"I don't drive without seatbelts."

"Of course." She nods, gives the buckle a little pat. "Thank you."

I nod, grip the e-brake and push it down, then ease us into the street.

Sarrasford's narrow and choked with pedestrian traffic, but only about three blocks of business district, so we're quickly out of the thick of it and onto the winding road back to campus—probably only two miles as the crow flies, but the switchbacks of the hills make it at least a ten-minute drive. I hold the steering wheel at ten and two, keep my eyes on the road for leaping deer or lingering black ice. Wish I had a radio or something to turn on.

A few minutes pass in silence. I signal for the turn that starts the climb up to campus, and swing the wheel to the right, the last strains of daylight streaking across the dashboard and catching the surface of my rings.

"Those are nice," Gwenna says, nodding at my hand.

I tighten my fingers a little. "Thank you. They're a…" I don't know why I started that sentence. Don't really want to finish it.

A beat passes. "A…?" Gwenna prompts.

I chew my bottom lip, eyes straight forward. "A…family heirloom," I finish.

From the corner of my eye, I see her nod. "Ah. Makes sense."

At that, I give her the quickest look. "What's that mean?"

"Just…I didn't see you as much of a jewelry type," she says. "You're very practical. Straightforward. Matter-of-fact."

I shift a little in the driver's seat.

She isn't wrong.

"They're my parents'," I say. "Were, I mean." Reflexively, I rub them together, the wide silver band on my thumb and the thin, delicate gold one on my index finger. "Wedding rings."

"Oh," she says simply. Frowns. "Don't they…get in the way? When you fence?"

"Yes. Sort of." I run my thumb over the thin gold band, feel the way it catches on the pad of my finger. "I guess that's kind of the point. That they're there. A…"

A constant press back on me.

A firm boundary.

A taut leash.

A *restraint*.

"...a reminder," I finish.

God. It's stifling in here. How did I not notice how high the heat was? I reach down with my left hand, turning the manual crank to let in some air. "Sorry."

Gwenna's voice is puzzled. "For...?"

"For...the car gets hot." I pause. "And I don't really like talking about myself."

I expect her to say something polite, *don't worry about it* or *it's fine*.

But she doesn't.

"God, who does?" She lets out a huff, staring out the window. "I don't either. I hate it. I hate just...being perceived in general."

Something about the way she says it—so deadpan, so sincere—pulls a single-syllable laugh out of me.

"What?" she cries, suddenly indignant. "Is that funny?"

"No, it's not..." I shake my head, still smiling. "It's just the way you said it. *Being perceived*."

"Well, it's true," she says, folding her arms. "Sometimes I wish I could just be a brain without a body. Have everything bend to my will around me."

This girl says the strangest things. I'm kind of captivated. "Really?"

"Sure. I mean, what's so great about having a body anyway?"

I shrug. "I like it."

A small, choked sound comes from my right.

Oh. Oh.

The heat is back, pulsing in my cheeks, in my throat, in my... everywhere.

"That's not...I mean..." My knuckles are pure white on the steering wheel, my hands and abs and biceps clenched tight. "I mean I like having a body. Myself. That's all. Not that your body isn't—"

Jesus. I snap my mouth shut. What am I saying?

"Mm," is all Gwenna says. From the passenger seat, she shoots me a look. "Careful, now."

Her voice drops low as she says it, and I freeze, the single command enough to still something deep in me. Like she'd pressed a hand to my chest and said *stay*.

I would. God, how I would.

"Hey, I'm kidding," she says, after a moment. "You're...probably the least at risk for that of the whole team. No offense."

"None taken."

You have no idea.

Mercifully, we're approaching the gates. I swing us through into the side road that leads to the student parking lot, pull us into the reserved spots for Camlann House that are just faintly slick with ice, and kill the engine.

For a second, we just sit there.

"Well, thanks for the ride," Gwenna says, reaching for the door. "Really, you didn't have to—"

Before she can get out, I shoot up out of my seat and jog around the Volvo's boxy snout to the passenger side, grab the door.

"You're welcome." I hold out my free hand. "It's slippery."

She looks up at me, frowning briefly, then takes my hand.

As she does, her fingertips brush my rings.

Doesn't let go.

Stares at them.

"I think it's nice," she murmurs. "For what it's worth. That you wear them." She looks up at me. "Keep doing that."

Her tone is light, but something about it pins me still.

Like I've been *told*.

She's gone before I can respond.

THIRTY

KINGSTON

ON MONDAY MORNING, Gwenna and I stand before Dr. Emrys's desk expectantly.

Class has ended. Another fascinating lecture about the development of punctuation throughout medieval monastic traditions. And I'm ready to turn this in so that we can get to the next thing.

Hopefully something actually meaningful this time.

Emrys is settled in his chair, looking over various printouts of articles, and only seems to notice we're standing there when Gwenna gives a slight cough.

"Dr. Emrys," she says.

He looks up. "Ah, yes. How can I help you?"

"We—" she throws a glance at me, her cheeks pink.

I nod, picking up the mantle. "We completed your assignment," I say. "The one you said you wanted done by Monday?"

I feel my muscles want to tense in frustration, but resist. My arm's out of the sling now, thanks to the concoction Morgan pulled together yesterday, but it's still stiff, and I'm not going to risk anything.

"The…" Dr. Emrys says, but when I produce the sheaf of papers, his eyes light up.

"Ah, yes, my little game."

"It's an ambigram," Gwenna says, the flush still in her face. "It took us a while to figure it out, because the writing was so cramped, but once we did—"

There's something about the way she talks when she's excited about something, I've noticed. It's…infectious, energized, like she stops forgetting to hold back and just unloads everything that's in her mind.

Magnetic. Attractive.

No. Focus.

A sly smile crosses Dr. Emrys's face. "I thought you'd like that," he says. "Very cheeky, the way they turn that little bit of the hermetic text into a literal bit of text painting, eh?"

"Hermetic text," Gwenna repeats.

"Yes." He folds his hands on the desk. "The Emerald Tablet, a masterwork of pseudo-religious writing from the 14th century. Something of a foundational text for modern magical practices of all sorts."

He murmurs a laugh, and I feel heat crawl up the back of my neck. *Careful, old man. Don't reveal any more to her than she needs to know.*

As far as Gwenna knows—as far as anyone knows—he's just an eccentric old professor.

He looks around the room, as if casting for something new to offer us. "Well, now that you've polished that one off, let me see—"

"May I speak with you privately, Dr. Emrys?" I say shortly.

He looks up. "Mr. Pendragon," he says. "What's the matter?"

"I'd like to speak privately," I repeat, looking at Gwenna. "Would you excuse us?" I ask her.

"I…" She blinks, nods. "Of course."

All the light that had brightened her face when she was talking about the puzzle blinks out in a second. Now she...she's curling her shoulders, biting her lip, pushing her way to the door, through desks and chairs.

I wait until I hear the click of the latch before speaking to Emrys again.

"Games?" I say. "Puzzles? We're wasting time. I don't understand what we're doing here."

"I'd say that much is obvious," he says dryly.

God. His refusal to be serious, even now, infuriates me. Before I can even form a retort, Dr. Emrys looks at me with curious, peering eyes. "You've known me for how long, Mr. Pendragon?"

I resist the urge to tense again, thinking of my injury.

"Since I was eleven," I say.

"Yes," he says. "And it stands to reason I've known you just as long, eh? So trust me when I say this. You are far too serious a man, Mr. Pendragon." He tips his chin down at me. "You were serious as a boy, and you've only...hardened since then. In many good ways, to be fair. In discipline and strength and skill."

In everything I'm supposed to be better at, I think.

"But you've lost that sense of play."

"The sense of..." I trail off, incredulous. "Is this just a game to you?" I demand. "The research, the books, the quest. Do you know how much my father has—?"

"Yes, yes," Emrys says, waving his hand. "I assure you, I'm very well aware of the extent of his generosity. Monetarily and otherwise. But you mustn't forget, Mr. Pendragon—" He corrects himself. "Kingston. Play is vital. Play is what keeps the mind open to see what is beyond the surface. You won't find anything if you look only along straight lines."

What the hell is that supposed to mean?

"I sense your frustration," Emrys says. He leans forward a little. "Let me put it this way. If the Grail were hiding in plain sight, don't you think someone would have found it by now? Because, forgive me if I sound condescending, but many, many intelligent men—and perhaps even a few women"—his eyes sparkle—"have dedicated their lives, their careers, their every ounce of energy and vigor and spiritual commitment to finding it. Yet none have."

I know that. I know that all too well. If there's anything the Consistory has impressed upon me—on all of us—it's how *long* this quest has been. How many generations have attempted it. How fruitless it's always been.

"What's your point?" I say, a bit tersely.

"My point," Emrys says, "is that perhaps you should take a leaf out of your classmate's book and *enjoy* some of this work once in a while."

My heart twists. "My classmate."

"Your partner in crime," he clarifies. "Your co-transcriptionist. My newest student. Gwenna."

Of course that's who he means.

"She's a lively one, isn't she?" he says. "Quick mind and a quick study."

"I suppose she is," I agree. "I hadn't really noticed."

"Hadn't noticed?" he cries. "My dear boy, you've been spending hours with her in the library, in class. You've been working through some of the thorniest and most hair-pulling manuscript texts in the Western world. Surely you've had occasion to notice her talents, her attitudes."

I swallow hard. "With all due respect, Professor, I'm trained not to notice more about someone like that than I absolutely have to."

"Ah." He lifts his head slightly, drums his fingers against his lips. "And therein lies the problem, methinks," he murmurs.

I swear to God, if this man weren't so well-connected, weren't the conduit to getting us every codex and folio and manuscript we needed, I'd have resigned from his class a long time ago. It's like he both understands and completely misinterprets the nature of everything we're trying to do.

"Do you know the book of Tobit, from the Apocrypha?" He leans back, studies the ceiling. "Chapter twelve, verse seven. *It is good to guard the secret of a king, but glorious to reveal the works of God.*"

I shake my head—because no, I *don't* know it, and no, I have no idea what that's supposed to mean.

"We have rules," I say, my voice hoarser than I want it to be. "Vows. A tradition—"

"And I am well aware," Emrys says. "I'll be the first to say that self-abnegation is beyond a noble cause, but the point of all this" —he spreads his hands wide over the sheaf of papers we've turned in, a few assignments from before then—"is to question the premise. Is it not? See the rules from a new angle. Understand that what goes on in here"—he presses his index finger to his breastbone—"affects what's in here." He taps his temple. "What's that saying again? As above, so below?"

I grit my teeth. "I don't know what you're getting at," I bite out.

That I'm supposed to, what, grab her by the shoulders and plant a kiss on her?

Ruin everything I've worked for, everything I stand for, just because of one infuriatingly brilliant girl I can't get out of my mind?

"I'm not getting at anything," Dr. Emrys says mildly. "That, I'm afraid, is entirely your job. And *I*"—he glances at his wristwatch—"I'm afraid, am due to catch an airplane to the Bibliothèque Nationale de France. A few days' visit—productive, hopefully."

He rises, puts his hands in his jacket pockets, and surveys me down the tip of his nose. "All I'm saying is, Mr. Pendragon, is that that is no ordinary young woman you're dealing with. But...what do I know? I'm just a silly old man." He pushes a sheaf of papers into my chest. "Transliterated by Monday, if you please."

THIRTY-ONE

GWENNA

AFTER LEAVING EMRYS'S CLASSROOM, my walk back to Camlann House is more like a trudge.

I don't know what I expected.

I don't know why I thought that Kingston would be anything different than the way he always is in class: aloof, distant, businesslike, uncompromising. And then he needs to kick me out so that he can do some golden boy power play with the professor.

I sigh and wrap my arms further around myself, buried in another cashmere sweater—bought and paid for by Kingston's father, no less.

How did my life get so confusing? I think.

At least the campus is pretty today. The leaves are all but gone, but that only serves to highlight the castle-like architecture, with only a few black spidery branches to block them. I pass Caliburn Memorial Chapel and look up at the front archway, thinking of how different things were when I burst through those doors my first day on campus. How he had been there too—Kingston—and just about as warm and fuzzy as he is now after knowing him for weeks.

I know he has this vow, knows that fencing is his life, and

school a very close second, but can he not have friends outside of the team?

Maybe not if they're girls, I think.

Or maybe just not if they're me.

A buzz against my leg snaps me back to reality. I fumble in my pocket and pull out my phone, only for my heart to plunge into my stomach when I see who's calling.

Mom.

Who else? I think. *Who else even cares enough to be in contact?*

I chew my lip and slow my steps. I think about hitting the reject call button, about how I could tell her I was in class, or studying—deep on the B level where there's no cell reception—but that would only be a temporary reprieve.

And if she's concerned enough to call in the middle of her workday, it's probably something I don't want to let linger.

I suck in a breath, swipe the screen, and lift the phone to my ear.

"Hello?"

"Why did the housing office say you no longer live in your dorm? And you missed your last two sessions with Dr. Riggs? What on earth is going on, Gwenna?"

My pulse spikes. Panic, bright and sharp as broken glass, cuts into me, but I resist. Instead, I clamp my mouth shut and try to marshal some words, unsure of where to start.

"Mom, hang on, slow down," I say. "It's fine, everything's fine."

"Is it?" she says, her voice quick and pointed as a poison dart. "I saw that your room and board payments were paused, so I called campus. And they informed me that there was *smoke damage* in your room?"

Shit, I think. *They had to be that specific about it.*

"I don't like this, Gwenna," she says. "I don't like it at all."

"I...Mom. Mom! I'm fine." It's all I can think to repeat. I

scramble for an explanation. "It was just...it was my stupid roommate. She loves these scented candles and knocked one over. It caught on one of her scarves and the whole thing..."

I trail off, my breath baited, hoping that my semi-reasonable, semi-finished explanation will be enough to satisfy her.

There's a long pause on the other end of the line. I stop walking completely.

"Mom," I say softly, "are you there?"

"I'm here," she says, sounding irritated. Then, after another long moment. "You should have asked for a single."

I roll my eyes to the sky. Well, if that's all she has to say about it.

"Where are you living now?" she bores on. "Shouldn't I be paying for something?"

"I..." Fuck. I didn't think this far into my lie. Maybe there's some version of the truth that will work.

"I'm rooming with the fencing team," I say. "As their equipment manager." Where that came from, I have no idea—so far as I know, the team *has* no manager. "They have an extra room so that I can stay nearby and keep on top of things, and I got really into the sport, so..."

"The *fencing team*?"

Her tone is utterly incredulous. And I can't say I blame her: a tipped-over candle is one thing. A sport I'd barely even heard of before coming to Caliburn is another. The skepticism is merited.

"I know, it's really random," I say, switching my phone to my other ear so I can shift my bag and walk faster. "But my roommate's stepbrother is on the squad, and—"

"Your roommate?" my mom echoes. "The same one who almost burned down your dorm?"

I wince. "She's...nice," I hedge, "just a little scatterbrained."

Sorry, Morgan, I think silently, *for throwing you under the bus. Not like my mom would have liked you anyway.* "It's all been a little hectic, so..."

"So you missed your appointments," my mom finishes for me.

I don't say anything. Let her fill the silence. The one interrogation technique I picked up from having two lawyers for parents.

At last, she sighs.

"I'm glad you found something that interests you," she says, almost mechanically.

And I hear the subtext loud and clear. *Something that isn't a dead language or religion adjacent.*

Something normal.

Ironic, isn't it, that my life is maybe the least normal it's ever been.

"When's the next fencing match?"

I'm not stupid. She's testing me. She wants to make sure that my story is airtight.

"It's Friday," I say. "A big rivalry, actually. Should be exciting. I'll take pictures," I add, as a cherry on top.

"That's great," she says, with the flattest possible tone of voice for someone who thinks something is great. "I'll look forward to seeing them." In the background, an indistinct voice calls for her, and she calls back an answer, her palm audibly pressed over the phone. "I need to take this, Gwenna. Take care now."

The call disconnects, and I realize I'm breathing hard. My skin crawls as I slide the phone back into my pocket, too exposed. Too visible.

The twin sensations of guilt and terror coil around each other in my stomach. I hate how easily she can shake me, hate how easily she can zero in on everything I'm unsure about, or still figuring out, or simply okay with not knowing right now.

My steps quicken, and then I break into a near run, my boots echoing against the bricks and flagstones, not caring if anyone notices or stares. How much worse could they think of me now, anyway?

I pound up the steps to Camlann House, desperate for the calm and hush that I know is in there.

Heart still pounding, I get to the top of the step, throw on the front door, and rush into the foyer. There, I freeze, breathing hard, letting my thoughts and blood pressure catch up with me, when I hear it.

No—him.

At first, I think it's a groan of pain, like someone's hurt.

But then the sound comes again, and my body seems to realize what it is before my brain.

Because my skin prickles. My lips part. Heat floods my entire body.

"Unh."

Because it's not pain.

It's a...moan.

Low. Male.

Wanting.

I freeze, stock still, a fawn on a highway. Listening intently, whether I want to or not.

There's a...rustling sound. Like fabric, or clothing. And then another human one.

A growl. Deep and guttural.

Oh. Oh my God.

My pulse races even as my rational mind kicks in.

No, my brain chides me. *There's no way. It can't be...that.*

And there *is* no way, right? These guys have...a vow. A whole thing.

They don't...do that.

Right?

As I stand frozen, the growls turn to words. Thick and choked, breathing heavy.

"Yeah. *Yeah.* That's it..."

I shouldn't be listening. But I am. I can't help it. More heat is flooding my body, pooling in my belly and lower, deeper, and I'm powerless to stop my gaze from drifting to where I now realize it's coming from.

The left, to the living room.

And—oh God.

Two bodies. Pressed close, tangled together. Mouths fused, hands skimming, *kissing*, desperate and intense.

Lanz and Callahan.

Stunned, I step back, trying to get back, slip out as quietly as I came, when my bag hits the floor with a thud.

And then I'm exposed.

Lanz, on top, swivels to me first, his bright eyes blown wide.

"Oh," he says, "Gwenna."

He lifts back, his shirt half-buttoned, sweeping a hand through his hair, visibly frazzled, trying to stammer what must be an explanation, while Callahan sits up: his face blank, his jaw tight, his eyes anywhere but meeting mine.

A chill follows the heat under my skin as the full realization of what I've witnessed takes over me.

"I didn't...I'm sorry," I stammer. "I'm sorry. I—you—"

I don't know if I'm addressing Lanz or Callahan or both of them, but it's Lanz who speaks first.

"You're...back from class early." He looks at me, desperate, almost frantic, but then, more intently, at Callahan.

Like he's checking that he's okay.

"I'm..."

Lanz gulps in a breath, sits back on his heels a little, his posture awkward enough to make me realize *oh my God, he's hard..*

Jesus. Of course he is, Gwenna. They're...this is...

"They don't know."

Callahan. Simple, strong. Yet his eyes on me aren't angry.

Only…soft. Neutral, at worst.
Almost…pleading.
I lick my lips.
"I won't tell," I say quickly. "No way. Why would I tell?"
"No one's saying you would," Lanz says, equally quickly. "No one's accusing you of…"
Callahan pushes up a little more, and I can see now down his own collar, where a few rough red bruises pepper the strong column of his throat.
My mouth goes drier still, and a twist of…something stirs inside me.
"Well, um…" I scramble for a way to end the conversation elegantly. "I'm actually—I was just going to get some air. Actually."
I pick up my bag, wave at them *for some freaking reason*, and head right back out the door, face burning and mind's eye *blazing* with the memory of what I just saw.
Lanz's teeth on Callahan's neck…
Callahan's head tipped back, mouth open, eyes closed…
"Wait," comes Lanz's voice. "Gwenna—"
"Let her go."
I hit the walkway and immediately hang a right, walking away from the quads, away from campus, no idea *where* I'm going beyond the fact that I'm going there quickly.
And as I go, despite everything—the sheer awkwardness, the implications that are still clicking together in my mind like Lego pieces—the overriding takeaway for me is…
I liked that.
And that might be more confusing than anything.

THIRTY-TWO

KAI

WELP, I'm drunk and throwing rocks at a lake.

Because that's a productive way to deal with your shit.

"Come on out, Vivian!" I yell, just loud enough that someone might overhear and send a rock sailing into the water's glassy surface. "I'm right he-ere. Waiting. Don'tcha wanna come give *me* your little seal of approval?"

Nothing, of course.

Just the ripples spreading out on the surface of the water, reflecting the purple and pink of the early-afternoon sunset.

Growing up, I never believed in so much as the fucking Tooth Fairy. And now here I am, praying for forgiveness when I bash some poor bastard too hard in a bout, and crying to a magical dead girl in a lake when God won't give me my way.

Cowards make the fiercest converts, I guess. Any port in a fucking storm.

I shiver.

It's chilly and I'm not wearing a jacket because I'm a dipshit. Just came right out from the salle with my hair still wet in my T-shirt. Practice wasn't enough. Drilling wasn't enough. Lifting wasn't enough. A healthy swig from this bottle of Clase Azul wasn't enough, although it certainly took the edge off.

So instead I'm here, dealing with problems the way my genetic forebears would, yelling at them and causing property damage.

I suck my teeth as the ripples abate, palm out my pack of cigarettes, and jam one between my teeth.

I'm restless, that's the problem. Every muscle tense, even when I've tried to wear it to fatigue. Petulant and throwing rocks like I'm twelve years old again and trying to hit the Green Line as it chugged past 63rd Street.

"Kai?"

I almost jump out of my fucking skin at the voice—not just the sound of my own name, but coming from a familiar source.

Female. I flick my gaze up from where I've settled on the grass, and there she is, Gwenna, winding down the worn path, breathless, her cheeks pink from the cold. I cock my head.

"You get lost?" I ask. "Campus is that way." I nod in the other direction.

"No, I just..." She trails off, hugging herself.

I don't know who Kingston got to buy her an entirely new wardrobe, but they did a good job. Those sweaters might cover a lot of skin, but they still don't leave too much to the imagination.

At least, if it's an imagination like mine, anyway. I'm a very visual learner.

And I have memories, too.

Of her skin.

Of that scar.

"I just needed some air," she finishes.

I sweep a hand in front of me. "Well, you've come to the right place. Plenty out here." My eye catches the smoky trail of my cigarette, and I stub it into the ground. "Er, sorry." I fan it away hurriedly.

She laughs, and I'm surprised by how good it feels to hear that sound.

"I didn't mean to interrupt," she says. "I'll leave you alone."

"Nah, nah, it's fine," I say, before my brain can acknowledge what I'm doing. Drunk Kai is nothing if not sociable. "Come on over, the water's great."

She balks. "You're not swimming, are you?"

"Ha." I run a finger through my damp hair. "No, this is from good old-fashioned indoor plumbing." I jerk my head back at the walkout door to the salle. "Just got done practicing, and now I'm..."

What, berating a ghost girl to give me the right to leadership that she bestowed on my foster brother? I think. *Yeah, even for a drunk guy, that sounds a little far-fetched.*

Instead, I just shrug. "Drinking." I hold up the decanter of Clase Azul. "You want?"

It's half a joke, but she considers.

"You know what? Yes," Gwenna says definitively. She settles into place next to me and I obligingly hand her the mezcal, which she lifts and drinks.

Drinks...a lot.

"Easy," I say, snatching it away. "You trying to drink to forget or something? Because that's an Alzheimer's level dose."

She laughs. "No. Just to...um." She blinks. "Escape my mother."

I jump like I'm startled. Look behind me in a comical overreaction. "Escape? Is she here?"

Gwenna laughs again. God, that sound is like pure dopamine. Heroin. I could drown in it.

"No, thank God," she mutters. "But she might as well be. She's watching me like a hawk. Or—correction," she says, dipping her head in acknowledgement, "watching my student account, making sure I'm on top of everything and not..." she fiddles with the knee of her black jeans, "...you know, screwing up."

I lean back onto my hands, tipping my head up to the darkening sky. "I know that feeling. Got you by the purse strings."

"Yeah." She leans forward, her chin on her knees, and we sit like that a while in silence. "She called me up, gave me the third degree about where I was living on campus now since apparently my room and board charges are on pause."

I lift an eyebrow. "And?"

"I told her I was your new equipment manager." Gwenna grimaces. "I hope that's okay."

Equipment manager? Sure. Why not. "Only if your mom bought it."

She sucks her teeth. "Hard to say. I...promised her photo proof."

"Eh, that can be arranged." I wait a moment. "She's a hard ass, huh?"

It strikes me that I don't know much about Gwenna beyond the...obvious traumatic backstory that's made its way across campus.

Gwenna purses her lips. "She'd probably describe herself as type A, but she's...Yeah, that's basically it. She and my dad had an ugly divorce, and that..." Her voice fades. "That kinda set everything in motion."

"I see," I say.

So she jumped straight from mommy issues to setting a church on fire? I don't quite connect the dots, especially knowing that someone wanted to hurt her bad enough to leave a vicious cut on her body. There's something missing.

But, then again, it's not for me to say whether that's logical. My own life narrative doesn't make much more sense. Go from a hardscrabble kid on the South Side to a collegiate fencing star with a multi-millionaire foster father? I sound like Oliver fucking Twist.

"They call it...spiritual psychosis," Gwenna says. Her eyes are resolute and forward, fixed on the far shore of the lake, but her tone is even and steady, like she's deliberately doling out this information. "What happened...I just..." She shakes her head, sighing, just a little shakily.

I listen intently without changing my posture, riveted to her every word, even as my alcohol-infused blood is making everything just a little bit wavy.

"I think it was the divorce, I don't know. I got so obsessed with what I had done wrong, all this stuff about sinning and losing favor, and I was studying a lot—Catholic school, you know—and I started thinking...I started to think I could change things, that I was hearing things, seeing things. Only in church, though, which is the craziest fucking part. We didn't even go that much when I was growing up. And then I started going all the time once I went to Catholic school. Somehow I got this idea that, like, I was on this kind of divine quest. That I was gonna unlock the secrets of the universe by reading everything I could. All the geeky medieval shit that I came here to study."

She laughs, but there's no humor in it.

And my blood, alcohol or no, has gone cold.

"Like, what...kind of stuff?" I ask. Trying not to sound too curious. Too suspicious.

"Oh, you know. The secret to eternal life. A cure for all wounds." She makes a sound that might be a laugh or might be a sob. "I...I thought I was this sort of vessel for, I don't know, the redemption of the earth. Basically one step down from thinking I'm Jesus Christ reincarnated."

I sneak a glance at her, and there's a tear glimmering in the corner of her eye. It physically hurts to restrain myself from wiping it away.

"Fuck me," I whisper.

"You got that right," she says, laughing. And this time there's a little color to it, some humor, which makes me feel like I've won the lottery and punched Satan himself in the face. Then she looks at me, and the feeling quadruples. "God, what right do you have to be so nice and understanding, Kai?"

"Excuse me," I say, in mock offense. "I am the very model of a sensitive, empathetic, modern gentleman."

She blinks. "You've got three piercings, God knows how many tattoos, and mezcal on your breath," she says.

More than three, I think, *but I guess you only know about the visible ones.* I catch my lip ring in my teeth for effect and grin at her. "Don't you know it's what's on the inside that counts?"

She laughs. "Tell that to someone like my mother." She sighs, but it ends on another little laugh.

"What?" I prompt.

"Nothing. It's just...remember that night at Porter's? When you tried to jump into my selfie?"

I squint, feigning recollection. *Of course I remember. How could I fucking forget?*

"I seem to recall," I say.

"Imagine I took that picture." She lifts an imaginary phone, tips her head, and grins. "Look, Mom, this is my new boyfriend. He's tattooed, pierced, and smells like an ashtray. Don't you love it?"

I laugh. Laugh because it's funny. And laugh because...yeah, I don't know. I'd love to be the bad boyfriend that makes her mom angry. Show up for dinner, scare the living daylight out of her old lady, and then drive home and fuck her till she can't walk straight.

I chew my tongue to quell the need for another cigarette.

"It'd be a veritable laugh riot," I murmur.

Gwenna sighs as the last of the sunlight fades behind the trees.

"Here." I stand up, halfway crouch-walk over to where there's a pile of good stones. "Take this. Chuck it in the water. You'll feel better."

She raises an eyebrow up at me, skeptical. "Really?"

"Yeah," I say. "Come on." I offer her a hand, which she takes. The brush of her fingers is electric.

"Like so." I show her how to hook the rock in my index finger, snap my wrist back, and boom. It hits perfectly. Skips one, two, three across the surface. "You want a nice flat one," I say, "like this." I press it into her palm.

"All right." Her brow knit in concentration, she shifts her weight back, withdraws her arm, and flings it wildly. It sinks like, well, like a stone.

I wince. "Yeah, you're gonna need to practice. Gotta start somewhere."

She licks her lips. Looks over at me. Well, up at me. Because as tall as she is, I'm still taller.

"Thanks, Kai."

"Anytime," I say.

"Thanks for..." Se blows out a hard breath, rolls her eyes, and blinks like she might cry again. "Not judging me about...my whole delusions of grandeur incident. Unlocking the secrets of the universe and all that. Being favored by God." She laughs a shaky laugh. "I know that shit's not real, for what it's worth."

The coldness returns to my blood.

"Yeah, no," I say, not able to meet her eyes anymore. "You're certifiable, Wednesday." I flash her a grin, even though it pains me. "But that's par for the course at Camlann House."

She laughs again—soft, trusting.

Except now the sound hurts.

Makes me feel like a thief. Like a fucking liar.

Because that's what I am.

Because she doesn't know the truth.

THIRTY-THREE

GWENNA

OVER THE NEXT THIRTY-SIX HOURS, I get the crash course in fencing I never thought I'd need.

Kai's given me a drill down on all the different types of weapon: saber (his), epee (Callahan's), and foil (Kingston's).

Lanz has given me the rundown on the general shape of the meet—both what I already knew from watching one, and all the intricacies that happen offstage. And Callahan's showed me the armories of the safety gear they wear, the jackets with metal thread to record touches, the knee-length trousers—"technically, they're called knickers," he says, a smile pulling at his lips—and, of course, the masks, covered in mesh and colored to match the Caliburn red.

"You look like beekeepers," I say. "Besides, I thought you weren't trying to hurt people, anyway? What happens if you just don't wear the mask?"

Lanz and Callahan exchange a look.

"I'll tell you what," Kai says, grinning up at me from his crouch. "This." He claps a hand over one eye and squints. "Remind you of anyone?"

Lanz gives me a tight smile. "That...doesn't happen much

anymore. In terms of injuries, modern fencing comes behind golf and synchronized swimming."

Callahan lifts an eyebrow. "Really?"

"Not if you're doing it right," Kai grumbles.

In the late afternoon, it's a dark, blue-purple kind of atmosphere, and the gym is packed. I don't enter with the rest of the spectators this time, but with the team, sitting off to the side on one of the benches, as everyone around us buzzes with tense, excited energy.

When I'm not carrying in bags, surprisingly light for all the metal inside, I'm scanning the stands for Morgan. Finally, I see her, smack in the middle, wearing a bright red sweater with a heart-shaped windowpane right above her boobs.

"Let's go, Knights," she cheers, using her hand as a megaphone.

I bite back a laugh. It's funny to see her turn into a sudden sports enthusiast.

The only one I haven't talked to, of course, is Kingston.

Emrys has given us another assignment, but ever since Kingston dismissed me summarily from class on Monday, we haven't spoken more than two words to each other, which is impressive considering we live in the same house *and* share an intensive class together.

Maybe it's for focus, I tell myself, same as last time. He can't deal with anything schoolwork related until after we're done, and that would make sense because tonight the banners hanging above are for Caliburn and a school I know only by reputation, the St. Ignaty Seminary.

"They've been here for over a week," Callahan mutters. "Getting over the time change, or so they claim."

"What, you think they're spying on us?" Lanz says, smiling, as he buckles on his jacket.

"Yeah, like flying little Sputniks overhead or something?" Kai cracks his neck and traces an imaginary satellite path through the air. "Be for fucking real." He jump squats and rolls his shoulders out. "I'm gonna turn them into goulash."

"Goulash is Hungarian," Callahan says. "Not Russian."

Kai rolls his eyes. "What fucking ever."

Amid all the chaos and their joking banter, my eyes drift to the other end of the bench, where Kingston sits, alone, straight backed, focused. His eyes are shut, his palms flat on his knees. And not for the first time, I wonder what it takes to be that dedicated to this sport or to anything.

I'm a passionate person, sure, and can arguably go overboard when I care about something, but not with any kind of regularity. Not with any system, not with a kind of unyielding dedication that neither rain nor sleet nor dark of night can shake me from. I love a good Latin translation, but I also love sleeping in on Saturdays, and maybe even cutting class on a warm spring day.

Kingston, though...

My train of thought is cut off by the announcement of the officials. We stand again for the usual ceremonies, the acknowledgements, the opening prayer, and then it's the first round. Sabre.

I open up the case, but Kai beats me to it. He grins like a devil, rolling his lip ring between his teeth.

"Here we fucking go," he says, and slips on his mask.

He strides onto the piste like he owns it, blade loose in his hand, easy, until the official calls for them to go en garde, and he's all tense and taut, like a tiger waiting to pounce.

It's a bloodbath. From the jump, his movements are aggressive, cutting fast. He wins decisively in what feels like no time, and the crowd roars. It feels different from this side, more energizing, more like, even though I had nothing to do with it, something I earned.

And for all I've been trying to shrink out of view, to keep to the side and not have anyone look at me, let alone notice I'm there, I can't help but sit up a little straighter when Kai swaggers back to our side.

"Nicely done," Kingston says, the first words I've heard him utter all day.

He nods at Kai, who nods back, a rare show of brotherly détente.

"Thank you."

Kai's breathing heavy, but grinning like the cat that got the canary, and sits heavily at the end of the bench, swigging from a bottle of water.

"Give him hell out there, O'Brian."

Callahan, of course, says nothing but *thank you* as he pulls on his own mask and takes the piste.

This time, it's slower, more methodical. The St. Ignaty fencer is deft, with a good amount of flourish to his movements that seem to propel him rather than waste energy. And it takes Callahan a while to catch up.

They go touch for touch, until finally he finds his rhythm and racks them up three in a row, a little masterclass in control.

The second round of cheering is more invigorating than the first. I nudge to the edge of the bench and clap wildly, thrilled and proud for him as I was for Kai. Glowing when I see him slap Lanz's hand as he pulls off his mask, their eyes locking for just a fraction of a second longer than they might otherwise. A little bit of a secret only I might know about.

And a strange feeling comes over me. Not a bad one, just...one I don't know how to parse.

I'm proud of both of them. All of them.

I...like them.

All of them.

Not all in the same way—God, not even close—but it's there. Something. Affection, attraction, in different ways for the different men—pulling at me or cracking me open, lighting me up or calming me down.

And I don't know what to make of it.

Don't know if I should make anything of it.

But it's undeniable, at least on the inside. Sharp Kai, tender Lanz, stalwart Callahan, and...

In front of us, Kingston takes the piste.

He doesn't loom over his opponent like Callahan did, or size him up as a psych-out like Kai. He simply stands at attention, eerily still, and precise, and that in itself is a kind of mind game.

"Third bout," calls the official, "foil. Fencing for Caliburn, Pendragon. Fencing for St. Ignaty, Moroslav."

The opposing fencer walks out in his gray and gold lamé, and in the half second before he pulls his mask down, I catch a glimpse of his face.

"Him," I whisper.

"What?" Lanz, who's closest to my side, whispers back without taking his eyes off the piste.

"I know him," I say. "The guy Kingston's fencing. He bought me a cup of coffee in town the other day." It sounds so weird and improbable that I almost doubt myself as I say the words, but there's no mistaking him. "Alexei."

Now Lanz looks at me, his blue eyes round with surprise.

"Alexei Moroslav bought you a coffee?" He sucks in a breath. "I hope you didn't drink it."

"Actually, I didn't." I think back to Morgan's warning. Good advice in general, not to take beverages from strange men. But... "Who is this guy?"

"He's..." Lanz considers. "I don't know. The second best fencer in our league? After Kingston?"

"The Lex Luthor to his Superman," Kai mutters from Lanz's other side, cracking a piece of gum between his teeth. "Or the Kryptonite."

Jesus, Mary, and Joseph. I look back on the piste as Kingston and Moroslav take their places. "Has he ever beaten Kingston?"

"In an official match?" Lanz asks and shakes his head no. "But in exhibition—"

"Showtime," Kai interrupts, leaning forward with his elbows on his knees just as the official calls for them to take their places.

Then Kingston moves. He looks at us at the bench and, for a moment, I wonder if I was talking too loud, if I was distracting him from the piste, if I blew it and totally fucked up his focus.

But I didn't. At least it seems I didn't.

Because his eyes settle on me, that golden, unwavering gaze, and something absolutely shocking happens.

Kingston Pendragon smiles at me.

Suddenly, I don't care if anyone else can see me, can perceive my presence or even is flat-out staring at me.

All I know is that looking at me makes Kingston Pendragon happy, and that is a kind of lightness I never could have imagined.

He slips on his mask, and—

"Allez!"

It's vicious. Moroslav advances immediately, quick on his feet, with sneaky flicks of the blade and shoulder slams that seem to take Kingston by surprise. It's so hard to know. Hard because I don't fully understand the sport. Hard because both of their faces are shrouded from view. And hard because Kingston's about as easy to get through to as a lead blanket over a brick wall.

But I can still sense something.

That Moroslav is out for blood.

Suddenly, I'm very grateful for the masks. My eyes flick to the sidelines, where Luther Pendragon sits, watching. The only person more impassive than his stone-faced son. And in the split second it takes me to look back at the action, they've made it to the other side of the piste, and are coming back.

"Come on, King," Lanz is muttering next to me, his leg bouncing up and down with nervous energy. "Come on, find his tempo."

I chew my bottom lip, thinking the same thing, with only half a notion of what it means. *Find the tempo, Kingston.*

And he does. His feet settle in to a rhythm, not yielding space anymore, as his foil flicks like a silver slash of lightning. Parry, parry, riposte, parry. Every move driving Moroslav back. Aggressive, unrelenting, precise. He lunges. And the blade buries itself in Moroslav's chest guard with satisfying force.

Bzzzt.

"Touch left," says the official. "Point Caliburn."

This time the crowd doesn't wait for the end of the match. They roar with approval, stamping on the bleachers and clapping and hooting. I feel the energy inside me, like a heartbeat, like a pulse. But I'm too nervous to clap, clutching my arms to my chest, just intent on not missing a single blow of the action when it resumes.

"Swordsmen, to your places," says the official. "En garde. Ready—allez!"

Moroslav's angry. I can tell. Not the type to shrug off a loss of the first point. He doubles down, hard, fast, and a little wilder, the tip of his blade arcing everywhere that Kingston is, but just a microsecond too slowly to touch him.

Kingston's on the defensive, ducking, dodging. Bolting backwards, the crowd gasps—*oh!*—as Moroslav lunges, and Kingston launches himself backwards, curling his body to the back to avoid the touch, and landing in a crouch, blade up, like Spider-Man.

Moroslav glances at the scoring table.

"No touch," the officials report.

He makes some half-hearted expression of dismay when Kingston roars back. And, drives his blade forward, right into the stomach.

Bzzzt.

"Touch left."

The noise is deafening, pounding like it's coming from inside my skull. Loud as a fire alarm or a tornado siren.

You wouldn't know it looking at Kingston, though. He simply resumes his place, walking a small circle, shaking out his limbs. Somehow, *somehow*, he's kept the world at bay. Locked it all outside of his head until he can get the job done. He could have every eye in the world on him and never trip. He's trained for it. And that's incredible.

"Swordsman, take your places. En garde. Ready? Allez—"

Moroslav barely waits. He attacks. Attacks like he wants to hurt Kingston and cut him down more than just score a point.

"Waste of energy," Callahan says, on my left. "He's gonna spiral out."

"I don't know," Lanz murmurs. "Maybe it's a tactic. Some kind of berserker mode thing?"

Kingston keeps pace. Parry, riposte. But there's something different now. Like Moroslav is a machine. No strategy, simply forward motion. He slices inches from Kingston's head as he ducks, then brings the foil back around, uneven, his blade landing with awkward force as he thrusts. Kingston parries, hard, and—

Crack.

Something hits the ground. The tip of Kingston's foil, sheared off entirely.

"Halt," calls one of the referees. "Broken blade. Fencer will replace equipment."

Kingston freezes, hands at his side.

But Moroslav doesn't. He lunges, hard, and not at Kingston's chest guard—at his calf.

"Halt!" roars the official again.

Another gasp from the crowd, this one rippling with concern.

"Kingston!" I hear someone cry.

Me.

Two hands hold me down—Callahan's on my left, and Lanz on my right. I didn't even realize I was trying to stand.

On Lanz's other side, Kai gets to his feet.

"That conniving bastard," he says. "That dirty, cheating, vodka-swilling motherfucking fuck—"

The officials have pulled the two fencers apart. Kingston keeps his mask on, so I can't see anything. Can't discern whether he's hurt or not, but from the slow nods on the official's part, it seems like he's okay, like he'll continue fighting.

"It's a low blow," Lanz is explaining to me. "Literally. You don't strike at the legs in foil."

The official talking to Moroslav, meanwhile, has twin patches of red flaring on his cheeks, the sides of his neck corded with tension. Moroslav has taken off his mask, arguing back something in some rapid-fire stream of words that don't sound English, but I can't make out from here. At last, the official holds up a red card, and the crowd gasps again, like this is some kind of fireworks display.

"What's that mean?" I hiss to Callahan.

"Same as soccer," he says.

"Which is?" I ask.

"You're out of the game," Kai answers for him. "Bad boys don't fence."

"Swordsman will reset," the official announces. "St. Ignaty will provide an alternate or forfeit the bout."

Kingston strides off the piste to pick up his blade as the alternate for St. Ignaty, whoever he is, takes the strip, bouncing gently from foot to foot. Meanwhile, Moroslav, face still lit with anger, storms to the opposite bench.

Lanz looks at me. "Looks like you're up, equipment manager."

He smiles, but it doesn't do much to melt the worry in his eyes. I scramble into action, darting around for Kingston's equipment bag and producing a replacement foil as he jogs over to the bench. This time, though, he does take his mask off.

"Here," I hold out a hand, ready to take the broken weapon.

He cedes it to me, and our fingers brush over the hand grip.

"Thank you," he says, taking its replacement from my other hand.

His hair hangs over his forehead a little, dark with sweat, and the strange impulse to throw my arms around his neck surges through me, but thankfully is held in a chokehold by my sense of social propriety.

"Are you all right?" I can't resist asking in a low murmur.

"I'm fine," Kingston replies, his tone so neutral I can't tell if he's being honest or just being polite. Then he looks at me, fixes me with those eyes.

"Why do you ask?"

That tiny, tiny flicker of a smile again. But it's like someone turned on the sun for the first time in a dark, cold universe.

"I just...can't believe you do this for fun," I say.

"I don't," Kingston replies. Pauses. "But maybe I should."

With that, he slides his mask back on, gives the blade a flick in the air for balance, nods, and takes his leave for the piste.

This time, it's like watching a whole new sport. Kingston is still precise, still quick, but more fluid, relaxed. Almost like I'm watching Kai or Callahan up there. Someone who's less locked in his head and more flowing in his own body.

It's easy. Playful, almost. The way he bats away hits. Darts out of the way, only to advance.

Bzzzt.

Kingston's blade flexes against his opponent's shoulder.

"Touch left. Point Caliburn."

Cheers. They barely have time to die down before they take their place again, and this time Kingston doesn't wait. Two steps, a parry, and...

Bzzzt.

"Point Caliburn."

It's like everything's on double speed. The remaining points fly by. Kingston dancing across the piste and tapping out his points. One, two, three, until final point, the official calls.

"Caliburn wins, 3-0 in bouts."

The space explodes. Sound rings and bounces and careens from every surface, out of every source.

Morgan leaps to her feet, hands smack on both sides of her face, astonished. Kai gives a whoop of victory and hooks an elbow around Lanz's neck, ruffling his hair, while Callahan just beams a big, broad smile and folds his arms, satisfied like I've never seen him. And I am overcome, overwhelmed, thrilled, happy, normal.

It's so good to feel this good, I think.

And for a moment, there isn't a dark past or a dark secret or vows and rules and complications and Latin puzzles and accidental kisses. There's just them. These four boys, four men, in exquisite victory, having disposed of their rivals with talent and sureness.

Kingston is still on the piste, his mask off and under his arm, finally caving and waving to the crowd, which only gets louder and more boisterous in response. But he's soon overcome by the other three, jumping to his side, mussing his hair, throwing good-natured punches at his shoulders and stomach, and he laughs. He actually laughs.

And it seizes me all over again, how much I love being around them, all four of them.

"So it is you. Their little whore."

The voice is cold as poison and dark as an abyss. I almost jump out of my skin. He's right next to me.

Moroslav.

"You," I say. "What—"

"The famous little choir boys of Caliburn," he says, running a hand through his dark curls, cocking his head. "The prim and proper chosen ones, always so pure. So they claim. Because they have you helping them out, eh? They have—"

He doesn't get a chance to finish his sentence because Kai's fist plows into the side of his head.

"Hey!" Kingston yells, throwing an arm across Kai's chest, looking not at Moroslav sprawled on the ground but at me. "Watch it," he says to Kai. To me, he says, "Gwenna, are you okay? Did he—"

"I'm fine," I say quickly. "Totally fine. He just—"

My hands are shaking, I realize. I tuck them under my arms, step back once, twice, putting as much distance as I can between me and the fallen fighter. From the floor he glowers up at me, suddenly wreathed by the legs of his teammates who throw me equally dark glares.

"Bitch," I hear him mutter and he spits blood onto the floor.

Kingston snaps his gaze to Lanz.

"Get her out of here."

Lanz nods. "We'll see you at the house."

Something claws at the back of my throat—a cry, a sob, I'm not sure what, just pure unadulterated angst at having the perfect moment cut short, but when I catch Kingston's gaze, it's like he isn't having any of it.

Go, he mouths.

And I do.

THIRTY-FOUR

KINGSTON

BY SATURDAY NIGHT at 7 p.m., I've already been awake for 14 hours.

I couldn't sleep after the match. I could barely get myself to calm down, to lie down, to get the rest my body so desperately needed. And when I woke up before the sunrise, I couldn't go back to sleep.

It feels incredible, all of it. Reminded me of everything I love about the sport: Precision. Restraint. Grace. Joy. Like a dance, an art form—

—and one where I completely pulverized my opponent.

And ordinarily, that feeling would be enough for me to bask in all day.

But not today.

All day, from before sunrise until now, I've been acutely aware that she's around somewhere. Footsteps on the stairs, a glimpse of her coat as she leaves to get coffee with Morgan. The soft click of her door.

Meanwhile, I pace the floors of Camlann House like a caged tiger, wondering if I should speak to her, whether there's anything to say, or if I should just keep my distance.

I don't need to bother her.

She has other things to think about, to deal with. And so do I, for that matter—schoolwork, cool-downs, active rest.

My mind should be anywhere but on her.

And it is.

I force it to be.

Until 7 p.m.

When I run a comb through my hair, pull on a sweater and a long coat—it's gently snowing outside—and I almost run across campus, Emrys's papers tucked into my bag, to the library.

Except I don't even make it inside the building.

"It's locked," Gwenna says, nearly scaring me out of my skin at the entrance to the building as she slips out of the shadow of a lamp post.

"Locked?" I repeat. There's a frown between her eyes and a set to her jaw.

"The B2 level," she says. "Our usual...where we've been working." She nods at the broad wooden doors. "I went in there just now and couldn't get in from the stairwell." She glances back again, slower this time. "We could work in the main reading room, but..." She trails off, and I know exactly why. It'd be all eyes on us—on me, if I'm being honest. And especially after last night. Not conducive to focus. Not what I want.

"We could go back to Camlann House," Gwenna suggests, but her tone of voice matches my thoughts.

"No," I say, "too chaotic."

It's not precisely the truth, but the presence of the others won't be suited to studying. There's no good private place to do it, either. The living or dining rooms are right on the first floor, and a bedroom, well...

My heartbeat spikes.

That's not an option.

I hear a faint clicking sound, and I look at Gwenna. Her teeth.

"You're cold," I say. "You should get inside."

"I know that," she says, "but where? The dining hall is closed."

And suddenly an idea grabs me.

"I know where."

I feel in my coat pocket. The key is in there, for emergencies only. Who's to say if this qualifies? But...

"Come this way."

I gesture and she follows, down the path that crosses Grove Quad, past the Classics building, to the quieter side of campus, where Luther Pendragon, president of the Caliburn University board of trustees, has his office. Gwenna's a silent presence behind me as I swing open the front door, walk down the hallway and to the right and fit the tiny key into the lock. The door gives and I push it open.

"In here," I say.

The frown returns to her face.

"Where are we?"

I don't see the point in lying to her.

"My father's office. We won't be disturbed."

She steps in, and I follow, and the door shuts with a heavy click. We're both inside, before I've really thought it through.

"Wow."

She looks up and around, taking in the massive space, the windows gleaming with moonlight, the desk and its platform, the books, the sitting area.

"I know. Hardly showy at all." I move to the light switch, and then think better of it—with the lights on in here, it'll be bright as a supermarket, a dead giveaway from outside that someone's in here when they shouldn't be.

Instead, I gesture for her coat, which she slides off and hands over. I hang it on the rack, followed by mine, as she steps closer to a display case behind the armchairs and near the bar.

A trophy case.

She leans in a little closer, alights her fingertips on the top of one of the golden figures poised in a lunge, weapon out, on top of the cup.

"Yours or his?" she asks and darts a look back at me. I don't answer because, to be honest...

"I'm not sure," I say. She gives a light snort, turns back to the case. A photo of me, age 11 or so, mask under my arm, blade held up in a salute.

"Would you look at that," she says, tipping her head to the side.

"What?" I ask, genuinely curious. I step to her side, fold my arms, and follow her gaze.

"You don't see it?" she says. "You look serious even then."

I remember that photo. The junior tournament in La Crosse, Wisconsin. Punishingly long days. Throbbing feet. Aching muscles. Aching everything.

"I won," I say.

"I'm sure you did."

There's a frisson of something between us. Unspoken. Intense. Too much. I've forgotten why we were here. And I need to remember. Having this much energy inside me is doing things to my thinking.

"I have the facsimiles," I say. Turn away from her and pick up my bag to put it on the coffee table. "I haven't looked at them yet, but—"

"So you've really always been all business," Gwenna says, turning very slowly as she walks to the chair opposite me.

She doesn't sit in it, instead glides down to the floor, sits cross-legged with her back at the foot of the chair so she can reach for the papers as I produce them.

"Focused," I say, tidying the stack of papers against the edge of the table. "Yes."

"But you enjoyed it last night," she says. "Didn't you?" She shakes her head, eyes still intent on the manuscript facsimile. "Granted, I don't know anything about fencing, obviously, but it was like...like watching an entirely different sport all of a sudden."

My heartbeat raises again. Like I've just lunged forward.

"I may have gotten carried away," I admit.

She gives a short laugh.

"Well, as your equipment manager, I'm glad you did. Gave me something to do."

I spread out the sheets in front of us, the spidery lettering in uneven tilting rows written out by someone arthritic in the days before college-ruled notebook paper. Gwenna's green eyes go wide, and she leans forward, intrigue and excitement all over her face, her hair brushing her shoulders as she scans over them. She bounces a tiny bit in place on her knees, like she can't wait, like this is fun.

I smile, and forget to fight it.

I get down the floor too, sink to my knees, look at the facsimiles, then look at her face. She must notice because she looks up, too. At me.

"What?" she says quickly, all enthusiasm drained away in an instant.

"I'm sorry. I didn't mean to make you uncomfortable," I say. "It's just..."

I tense my mouth to the side, press my hands to the table, try to pin down the thought that's floating around in my mind.

"I think that's how I felt," I say at last. "Last night, when I was on the strip against Moroslav. The way you're looking at these. Like it wasn't work or something I had to do, but..."

"...something you get to do." She finishes for me and catches my eye.

I can only nod. "Yes."

"*Yes,*" she repeats, mocking my tone of voice. "Who talks like that? You can't say *yeah* or *sure*?"

I smile.

"Sure."

Gwenna rolls her eyes, blows out a breath, and even though the light in here is dim, I catch a hint of a blush across her cheeks.

It's nice. I wouldn't mind seeing it again.

"Here," I say.

I rise, go to the console and pick up two of the tapers there, a book of matches. I set them on the table and I'm about to strike when realization hits me.

"Never mind," I say, gathering the candlesticks. "That was rude of me. I shouldn't—"

A hand catches my wrist, stops me.

"It's fine," Gwenna says. "I'm not—I can handle it."

I look at her, intently, making sure she's telling the truth and not just trying to please me.

And yet. The very thought that she would do something just to please me is…

I swallow hard. The blood in my wrist beating against the pressure of her fingers.

"Really, Kingston." She gives a small nod, releases me. "Get some light in here so we can work."

I nod, place the candlesticks on either side of the table, and light the wicks.

In the soft light, she looks…beautiful.

Very beautiful.

And I realize too late that I've set this up.

Candlelight.

Seclusion.

A Saturday evening.

"I can't make heads or tails of it," she says, shuffling some of the papers around, "if I'm being honest. It's probably some weird riddle again, like a Sator square, or a palindrome, or—"

I can't see anything from where I am. I ease myself around the edge of the table so I'm sitting next to her, bumping her knee by accident, which she ignores, and so do I.

"Hmm," I say, looking down at the text, squinting, pretending to focus on anything that isn't the brief touch of our bodies. "Maybe I need reading glasses."

"It could be Carolingian minuscule," she says. "The way it's all slanted like this?"

She points at the sheet, tilts her head again, brows drawn. "But that wouldn't make any sense. That'd be French origin. Didn't he say something about all the new manuscripts coming in from Italy?"

"I..."

I've barely been listening to a word she's said. I'm looking at her profile, the faint gold glow around the edges, the turn of her lips.

I keep trying not to do it.

Trying not to think it.

But my resolve is wearing thin.

"Or maybe..." She trails off, looks at me. "What now?"

There's exasperation in her voice, but it feels forced. Just a hint playful, with the curve at the corners of her mouth.

"Are you gonna keep looming like that all night, or are we actually gonna get anything done? We only have until Monday, you know, and—"

"I owe you a thank you." The words burst out of me like buckshot. I lower my eyes, embarrassed. "I'm sorry, I interrupted. You were—"

"It's okay," she says, and gives a little laugh. "Look, I'm doing it too." She swallows. "Thank you for...what?"

"For..."

For doing all the work on these godforsaken projects.

For getting my foster brother to calm down and Lanz to relax and Callahan to say more than two words in a row once in a while.

For Friday night.

For *this* night. Now.

"For lots of things," I say out loud.

For everything.

And in that moment, I know. I know I'm going to do it. I know all is lost, and I don't care.

I lean forward and kiss Gwenna Vale.

I was prepared to hold back. To press myself just to the edge of the line, commit the forgivable offense, the momentary lapse.

But as soon as I taste her, I know I can't.

A soft, startled noise from her throat gives way to something low and liquid—a purr, a hum, *Jesus God*—and I surge forward, clasping the back of her head and pulling her into me, against me, clutching for her waist with my other hand. Our mouths break apart as I ease her down, just enough space for me to rasp the only word I can remember.

"Gwenna."

Her eyes fly open, her hair fanning behind her as her head comes to rest on the plush surface of my father's Persian carpet, and the juxtaposition, the sheer sight of her, *here,* like that, only spikes the frenzied feeling coursing through me.

"Kingston," she whispers. "You…we…" Her throat bobs. "Is this okay?"

I know what she means.

Know what she's asking.

But I won't answer that.

"If it's okay with you," I reply.

She nods, and it's all the signal I need. I sweep down and take her mouth again, hard.

She's sweet and warm and suddenly I want all of her. Now.

I press deeper, kiss her even harder, but my hands feel clumsy, confused. For all my deftness with a weapon, all the grip strength and finger drills, I'm stymied by this—where to touch her, how and when and how fast. I skim a palm down her side, almost timid, as I kiss her deeper, pulse pounding, and she turns into my touch, pressing her breast into my hand.

God.

A choked sound escapes me. I'm half-hard already.

Instinct takes over. I skim my thumb over the peak of her breast, suck in a breath as it stiffens even through her sweater, then drag my touch lower, to the waistband of her skirt. At that, she flinches, and I pull back instantly, but when my vision clears enough to see her she's shaking her head.

"Sorry," she murmurs. "You...surprised me." She presses her lips together. "Don't stop."

I nod, and do what I do best.

I obey.

Or I try to.

Because there's something. A thudding sound, pounding, a rhythm that isn't the deafening sound of my heart.

My fingertips find her skin.

The sound picks up.

I don't want to hear anything, don't want it to be anything.

But my instincts are too sharp. My training won't let me ignore it.

Unmistakable.

Footsteps.

I tense, only a little, and Gwenna pulls back, panic sketched all over her face.

She hears it too.

"Is that—" She glances at the door. "Your father?"

In a half second, I'm on my feet. Look left, right, point to the corner with the fold-out screen—souvenir from Istanbul, a fruitless trip to investigate Arabic manuscripts.

"Hide," I say to her.

She doesn't question, just nods and scrambles up and behind it, and not a second too soon.

Because the door blows open, the shattered lock spinning as it rams against the wall.

It's not my father.

It's Kai.

"There you are," he says, panting, sweeping his hair from his face. "I saw the light in the window and—"

"What's going on?" I say.

Kai grimaces.

"You better come with me," he says. "Something's happened."

THIRTY-FIVE

GWENNA

I DON'T KNOW how long I stay in that corner.
 I count to one hundred.
 Then two hundred.
 Then a thousand.
 And after that, finally, it feels like maybe I can move again. All of me feels stiff and alien, stunned with shock from what happened with me and Kingston, and worried, terrified, actually, about whatever Kai came in to get him for.
 Swallowing the burst of panic rising in my throat, I grab my coat, grab my bag, and before I leave, blow out the candles.
 Can't be too careful.

ALL THE LIGHTS are on at Camlann House.
 When I come close, a different direction, a circuitous route, just on the off chance anyone's watching where Kingston came from, and a pit forms in my stomach. I know this isn't good, but I don't know what kind of not good it is.
 As I make my way up the steps, I hear voices in the living

room. Male voices. Some sharp, some low and rumbling, mostly familiar, but some not.

At the door, I pause, smooth the front of my sweater, tuck my hair behind my ears. No matter what happens, I need to look composed. I push into the door, thinking I'll glide past everything, go upstairs, catch up later.

That is not what happens. Every eye turns on me when I enter. Kingston, Kai, Lanz, Callahan, but also Luther Pendragon, resplendent in his suit, a woman I recognize as a librarian, and the dean of the college.

"Miss Vale," the dean says. His voice, somber. "There you are."

"What's...what happened?" Any attempt to keep my voice from sounding flighty and nervous fails instantly. I look instinctively at Kingston first, but he is standing soldier straight, arms folded, eyes front, not looking at me or anyone else or anything in particular. And that just scares me more.

"There's been an accident, I'm afraid."

"An accident?" My mind races. My *heart* races. "Is someone—"

"No." The dean cuts in quickly. "Nobody was hurt. But..."

"The archives," the librarian interrupts. "The manuscripts. They're...They're gone."

"Gone?"

I blink, clutch the strap of my bag. Images of jewel heists, Indiana Jones, tarp-covered shipping crates float into my mind.

"Destroyed." That's Luther Pendragon's voice. "In a fire."

Oh. Oh no. No.

"But..." I start.

"That's the B level," the dean goes on, "where I've been given to understand you spent a lot of time."

Oh no. No. *No.*

"Yes," I say, "but—"

"And this is yours?" The librarian bows her head and produces something, which she hands to the dean.

My scarf. Or most of it. It's half as long, now, one end fringed in ashy burn marks.

"No!" I say out loud, "I mean—yes, that is mine, but I didn't—"

"Things went dark at around 6 p.m.," the dean goes on. "From then on—"

My chin is stuttering, big fat tears are flowing down my face, because I know where this is going. Know what they're saying to me.

And yet I can't bear to hear it.

"I didn't do it!" I say. "It wasn't me. It—"

"She couldn't have done it," someone else bursts out.

My heart leaps. It's Lanz, gesturing wildly. "She wouldn't do that. She's—"

"So you have an alibi for her, then?" Luther Pendragon snaps.

"I—" Lanz withdraws a little, doesn't meet his eyes. "No, but—"

"Had I known," Luther says, "of this girl's predilections, of the fact that she was to be placed in a class with my *son*"—he angles his eyes at Kingston—Kingston, who doesn't move, who doesn't speak, who maybe half an hour ago was kissing me incessantly on the floor of his father's office—"I never would have allowed her on this campus."

"No," I say. "Please."

Something warm and firm wraps my shoulders. I look up. It's Callahan. He says nothing, barely even looks at me, but squeezes hard.

I don't know where to look. My eyes flail around the room, land on Kai, who's sitting in an armchair, jittering a leg and chewing on the edge of his thumb, saying nothing, eyes flicking to me and then away again.

"That was," the dean says, "a priceless collection of manuscripts and books, one which Luther Pendragon had personally financed, worked for years to acquire."

"Gone," breathes the librarian.

The pain in her voice is so real, so recognizable, that my stomach gives a guilty heave and I *know* I didn't do anything wrong. "Impossible to be replaced. And—"

"*I didn't do it!*" The words burst out of me again, cut off by another sob.

My shoulders are shaking even too hard for Callahan's grip.

Because I'm not an idiot. I'm Laura Vale's daughter. I know what a preponderance of evidence is. Malice aforethought. *Mens rea, actus reus, corpus delicti.* All the Latin phrases.

"I want to believe you, Miss Vale," the dean says, and his voice sounds like almost, almost he really does. "I do, but I'm afraid it doesn't…look very good for you right now."

"I wasn't there." I try one more time. "I was—"

The sentence hangs in the air.

Everyone looks at me.

Lanz, Luther, the dean and librarian, Kai, even Callahan.

Not Kingston.

"Where were you, Gwenna?" the dean asks.

I shake my head.

Say something, I mentally scream at Kingston. *Say it. Tell them. Tell them I was with you.*

But he can't.

No, I think, he won't.

He could if he cared.

He could if he ever thought about anything but himself. About what he needs to do to get ahead. About his goals, his objectives.

His needs.

And that, I realize, like a razor to my heart, *is simply not who Kingston Pendragon is.*

"We have a…lot to sort out," the dean says. "Obviously, the

library is closed until further notice. And we'll be meeting with the fire marshal—"

"But is she under arrest or something?" Kai drops his hand from his mouth, lifts his chin.

"Kai," Luther says sternly.

"I'm just saying," Kai gets to his feet. "Is she?"

"No," the dean says. "Not presently, anyway."

Not presently? I want to cry. Instead, I just sniffle, blink more tears down my cheeks and chin.

"Then why don't you leave her alone?" Kai barks. "Leave all of us alone. Come back when there's something you need us to do."

The dean stares at him, and Kai stares right back. To my surprise, the dean blinks first.

"Very well," he says, and glances around to the four of them. "I trust that you'll..." He purses his lips, doesn't finish the sentence. "Good evening."

He takes his leave with the librarian trailing, and Luther goes last, casting a look at first his foster son, and then his natural one.

"Pitiful," he mutters under his breath.

The door slams behind them.

The sound does something to me, sends my muscles weak, and I have to lean against Callahan even more than I was before. I'm ugly crying now, snotty, frothy, hiccuping, almost hysterical.

What will I do? I think. What will I do? Mom will find out. She'll get me. She'll be furious. She'll force me to—

I don't even get a chance to finish my thought. Something, someone, wrenches me by the elbow, away from Callahan, into the middle of the hall.

I trip over my own feet, look up. It's Kai.

"What are you doing?" says a deep voice from behind us.

Kingston. At last, he speaks, and the change in tone, the chill that's come back, the formality puts a crack in my heart.

I am such a fool.

"I'm showing her what she needs to see," Kai says, and pulls me firmly in the other direction toward the dining room and the door to the fencing salle. "What she should have seen long ago."

Callahan sucks in a breath. Lanz lunges forward.

"Kai—"

"*No*," Kingston roars.

But it's too late. Kai has me, pulls me away, through a door I'd barely even noticed before, downstairs.

Into blackness.

THIRTY-SIX

GWENNA

I CAN'T SEE where I'm going, can't see *anything*, like I've fallen into abyss.

Until I do see it, and I'm speechless.

A massive circular room, with high arched walls, flowing banners, no windows. It's chilly, almost earthy smelling. We're underground.

"What…" I say, voice trembling. "What is this place?"

Crossed blades and shields decorate the curving walls. At one edge is a seat, a *throne*, wide and spacious and a pearly sort of white, with a red velvet rope draped across its seat. And in the middle…

My heart plunges to my stomach.

La Tavola.

The table.

It's huge, maybe twelve feet in diameter, wooden but dark, almost black, polished to a sheen, and with the crest of Caliburn inlaid in it.

None of it seems real. It's like I've stumbled somewhere imaginary, somewhere fantastical, a movie set, or a museum, a recreation of how kings and princes used to live done up in a castle somewhere for tour groups.

I spin around to Kai.

"What—"

I'm cut off by the arrival of the other three. Callahan bangs through the door, Lanz practically jumping past him, and Kingston following, his face taut, but his eyes sharp.

"Kai," he says, "don't."

"This is it, Gwenna," Kai says, spreading his arms wide and walking backwards like a showman. "This is the big old secret, the whole kit and caboodle. You thought we were weird and reclusive before? Just keeping those vows for fun?" He laughs. "You had no idea."

"How is this…" I'm blank. Unable to think. "What does this even—"

"Kai," Kingston says again, "*stop*."

"What, am I making it worse?" Kai says, cocking his head at Kingston. "What difference does it make if they're going to throw her in the slammer for property destruction or whatever?"

A choked sob escapes my throat, and Kai's glance immediately softens on me.

"She didn't do it," he mutters. "All of you know that, and none of you…"

"I tried," Lanz said. "I *tried*, but—"

"Get back upstairs," Kingston orders, pointing at the stairs.

But none of them move.

Not Callahan, not Lanz, not Kai.

The only sound is my pathetic sniffling, until I finally manage to get purchase on my breath.

"What is going *on?*" I say. "What is all of this?"

"We are real holy rollers, Gwenna," Kai says. "Knights charged by God, governed by the Consistory of the White Brothers of Saint Vincent, and bound on pain of death to its vows and chivalrous code." He drawls it, like he's a bored tour guide. "Here on a quest for the cure to all wounds. The vessel divine. The fount of all founts and the secret of all secrets."

A slow, *deathly* slow pulse of panic rolls through me. Head to stomach, stomach to toes, and over and over. My ears are ringing, like my whole body is trying to reject what I'm hearing.

"What are you telling me?" I say. My voice lower, the tears gone. "What are you saying?"

"It's all real," Kai says, cocks his head. "Magic. Miracles. The holy spirit. Whatever the fuck you want to call it. It's all real and it's all bound up in one mystical *thing* that we and we alone are supposed to find. A holy grail." He curls at smile with no humor at his brother. "Isn't that right, Kingston?"

Kingston doesn't answer, doesn't move.

Until he does. He springs forward, arms out, like he's ready to strike or claw at or throttle Kai, but Kai is faster. He leaps backward, a practiced retreat, and lands at the foot of the wall, arm up, and wrenches a blade down by the hand guard.

"Not so fast." He holds it out, the tip inches from Kingston's face. "I will cut that smug little face of yours if you come even a *millimeter* closer, you prick."

Kingston doesn't move. Kai whips the blade left, right.

"Either of you wanna chime in?" he says to Lanz and Callahan. Not giving them a chance. "No? Fine." He looks back at me, blade still raised, but gaze fierce.

"We're a whole fuckin' *secret society*. There's *rules*. We shit the bed and they send the Prior of Arms after us. Strip us of our blades and invalidate a whole-ass *generational claim*. How do you like that?" His eyes are glassy. "Doesn't even *sound* real. But it sure fuckin' is."

"I don't…" My brain is still caught on what he said seconds ago.

It's real.

It's real.

"It's real?" I manage. "Everything I..."

Everything I saw.

Everything I felt.

Everything I *did*.

The church.

The fire.

The vision in the lake.

I knew I wasn't crazy.

Knew I wasn't.

And they knew too.

They knew, and—

"That night at the lake," Kai goes on. "Once you told me what you saw, what you felt when you..." Kai swallows, sweeps his hair out of his eyes. "I knew. I knew I couldn't keep the truth from you anymore." He pivots to Kingston, and his voice goes from a rasp to a roar. "But what I *didn't* know, didn't even fucking *suspect*, is that you, of all people, *mighty* Kingston *Arcturus* Pendragon, were fucking around on your vows. Oh, I knew this idiot"—he points at Lanz with the sword—"had had his dumb little spin-the-bottle moment with her after the Sainte-Odile match, whatever. But *you*. In our father's fucking office."

He shakes his head slowly. Looks at the distant, distant ceiling. Breathes out.

"It just kills me," he says. "absolutely kills me, that *I*, of all people, am the best at keeping my fucking *word*."

Kingston's warm eyes are hard, flat, and a sob wrenches out of my throat, shameful.

So Kai did know.

And he still wouldn't speak up for me.

It's all too much.

I run for the door. Lanz moves, *Kai* moves, as if they're going to stop me, but they don't. Can't. I'm gone too fast, even for them, pounding up the stairs through the unseeing darkness until I burst out on the landing of the house, *this* house, this terrible, beautiful house I never want to see again.

I run through the hall, through the door, down the steps, run, run, run until my eyes are too blurry with tears and my breath is too tight in my chest.

And then I get out my phone.

My fingers shake as I swipe it unlocked, my teeth chattering in the cold again. It's getting late now, an emergency hour time to call. She'll pick up—

"Gwenna?"

And she does.

"Mom?" My voice is thin and scared as a little girl's, and I can't make any more words come out. Only a sob.

"Gwenna?" Her voice turns urgent. "What's wrong? What's going on?"

I clutch my phone, stare up at the sky, clench my eyes shut and wish, desperately, desperately, to disappear.

"I need to leave here," I say at last. "You're right. You were right. I need…help."

THIRTY-SEVEN

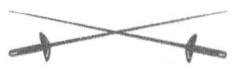

KINGSTON

"WELL."

When Emrys does speak, his voice is hoarse.

"Well, well, well."

We've been sitting in his office a long while.

Just him and me.

No other knights. They're at the house.

No Gwenna. She's…

She's…

I don't know.

Emrys takes a deep inhale. Steeples his fingers in front of his face.

"Well?"

It's all I can do not to snap it at him. But he looks…tired, for once. As old as he certainly must be.

"Well," he agrees. "'All shall be well, and all shall be well, and all manner of thing shall be well.' Julian of Norwich. Mystic, 14th century. A seeker like yourself. And the first woman ever to write a book in English."

I have no time for this.

"What do we do now?" I say.

"Do?" He says. "Now?"

"Now that it's all gone," I say, gritting my teeth.

Emrys sighs. "Have you not seen it yet, Kingston?"

"Seen *what*?"

I'm sure I haven't.

Because I haven't seen anything but Gwenna's face.

Awake, asleep.

For days.

Ever since she disappeared.

"The puzzles," he says. "The little word games. The assignments I put to you and your...friend."

The slight pause hits me right in the chest.

Friend.

If we were ever even that.

I'm losing patience.

"May I be honest, Dr. Emrys?" I ask. "Those *assignments* didn't need to be done."

"Maybe not," he says. "But *you* needed to do them." He pauses. "Both of you."

I don't follow. "What are you talking about?"

"You think I simply paired you two up by coincidence?"

"No. We—she—"

"Yes, yes, the little contest. She's brilliant, that girl. But you think *that* was coincidence?"

I frown.

"You needed to see what was plainly before you, and yet hidden. What is at once both above and below. Two-sided and yet the same."

"What," I grind out, "are you *talking* about?"

Emrys exhales hard.

"If things were less dire, I'd leave you to work it out. But I'm afraid we don't have the luxury of time." He fixes me with a stare. "The grail isn't a *what*, Mr. Pendragon. It's a *who*." He smiles. "And you've had her right at your side this whole time."

THIRTY-EIGHT

MORGAN

"CAN YOU FIND HER?"

I don't answer. The soft glow of the smooth marble basin of water shines up at me, the only source of light in the room, throwing shadows on the Black Table.

"*Can you find her?*"

My gaze flies up. "Jesus, Kingston. *Stop*. Stop." I brush the hair out of my eyes so I can get a good look at him, and—

"God, you look awful."

Kingston scowls. As if I'm not simply telling him the truth. Or, really, telling him what he needs to hear.

Bastard.

"Can. You. Find. Her," he repeats.

"I'm *trying*, Kingston." I sweep a hand over my basin. "Scrying isn't GPS, okay? And I'm new at this. You want her found instantly, you should've tied an AirTag around her neck." I set my jaw. "Or maybe not lied to her in the first place."

He doesn't answer that. Just leans back a little.

I almost want to roll my eyes. Love how he's willing to believe in magic when it suits him. Love how I'm sure that if the Consistory ever so much as breathes down his neck about this, he'd have me burned at the stake.

"Fine," he says, flat.

"*Thank* you," I say. "Now, as I was saying…"

I close my eyes again. Let my hands float gently back and forth over the surface. Back and forth, back and forth—

When I open my eyes, everything is brilliant white. Shimmering. I'm immersed in the vision, shapes coming into form.

But I see it. See her.

Gwenna.

I shiver, in spite of myself.

And then I'm back to normal.

"And?" Kingston presses, as soon as my eyes are open. "You found her?"

"What good is having a stepsister who's a witch if she doesn't use her powers for good once in a while?" I give him a bitchy little smile. "Yes, I found her."

"Where is she?" He pushes to the edge of his seat, like he's about ready to leap out of his chair and run whichever direction I points. "*Tell me.*"

I don't *have* to tell him. I know that. I told him that. Gwenna's my friend, first and foremost, and I simply want to know she's okay.

But Kingston…

Kingston's got it bad.

Got it *wrong*.

I can tell.

And maybe…

Maybe he needs one more chance.

"I will," I say slowly. "On one condition."

"Whatever you want," he says. And I can tell he means it. "Name it."

I lean in over the scrying basin, fixing my stepbrother with the most serious, most deadly look I can possibly give him.

"If you do get Gwenna back here, Kingston? You're going to grovel like *hell* for her forgiveness."

Made in the USA
Coppell, TX
31 January 2026